MW00712935

GENERATIONAL

"Perfect Imperfections"
Volume I
Presented by
Respect the Gender
Written by
Anica Walston

Respect the Gender Publishing

Dedication

To a woman who exemplified class, style, and grace. She was an elegant and sophisticated woman. Her life was fruitful and fulfilled. I will always be mindful of the lessons you taught and the support you provided to your entire family. For all you shared and legacy you left. I will remember you teaching me to, "take my burdens to the Lord, and leave them there." You will always be loved and remembered, my beloved grandmother.

Ruth Bell Ore

Walston

Contents

Preface...v
Introduction...vii

Part I
"Excuse the Reality"..3
Tracey...5

Part II
"Where was I?"..57
Diana..59

Part III
"Releasing a Good Man".....................................125
Veronica...127

Part IV
"Decadence and Divinity"....................................199
Bernice...201

Generational Dysfunctions Vol. II (Intro)......259
"Focused"..263
Zariah..265

About the Author..267
Acknowledgements...269

Walston

Preface

Generational Dysfunctions Volume I is a collection of stories highlighting four women who are connected by trials throughout their lives. The stories outline incidents, which are learning experiences for these individuals. There are choices, which have to be made. They encounter heartaches, heartbreaks, tragedy, and strife, but there are no assumed happy endings. Their circumstances are some women's reality. There is bliss, moments of triumphs, and their durability is tested in each situation. These stories do not outline their entire lives but are pivotal moments, which set a certain chain of events into action. You must read carefully to see their connections.

The truth is no one really knows what goes on in each other's minds. We do not always know why we make the decisions we do. Women sometimes put up facades because of shame, guilt, and insecurities. They hide secrets; cover up truths because they do not want the world judging them. In actuality, no one has any right to judge. When you start to examine these women's supposed exteriors of perfection, you find perfection is obsolete.

Generational Dysfunctions is a series of books that contain sixteen different stories of sixteen different women's plights. In each volume, you will find their connection through their environment, genetics, circumstance, or situation. This is the first volume in a series of four books.

Walston

Introduction

"Understanding the women of Generational Dysfunctions *Perfect Imperfections*"

Tracey

Tracey is a young woman who weds out of haste. She is a beautiful talented woman who allows others to dictate her existence. Her principal dictator is a young strapping man who all the women want and have probably have partaken in, at some point. These discrepancies never bothered Tracey. She is willing at all cost, to keep her man just to declare he is hers. As you read Tracey's story you find he has never been, or will ever be, completely hers. From the moment they marry, her life becomes chaotic. She is trapped in a mentally abusive relationship. Tracey wants to believe he is someone else. She maps out their lives together with the expectation they will weather through any storm.

Tracey has three children whom she loves dearly but tends to get distracted by the turmoil's which her husband has inflicted upon her. The mental abuse becomes toxic. Tracey finds herself allowing things in her life, which to most women see as insanity.

She has a supportive family. Her sister is loyal, but disgusted by Tracey's decisions. Tracey's mother assists her with her children because even in Tracey's decision-making she cannot allow her grandchildren to be subjected to the evil, which lurks in Tracey's home. Tracey does not openly discuss the private matters of her household. However, because her husband is not discrete with his actions, outsiders are more aware of his day-to-day activity than she is. She defends him because she believes in her vows.

No matter how hard she tries, it becomes apparent he does not wish to change. He has a woman who answers at his disposal, and appears to believe every lie he conveys. Is she naïve, or detached? This can be decided by you the reader, but not judged.

Tracey is like many young women who suffer through impossible relationships, due to lack of self-esteem and self-awareness. Should Tracey have to deal with such disrespectful actions? No, she should not. All of Tracey's decisions and actions are by choice. She wants to believe he loves her. As the story unfolds, she finds her husband has become her excuse. She is mentally broken down, and due to an audacious incident, Tracey must revaluate her decisions. Tracey is grieved with pain, which causes her to stop and reflect on her life, and how it reached such a damaging hiatus.

Tracey's character, as all the other characters, is introduced by a poem. *Excuse the Reality,* is Tracey's introduction. The poem outlines Tracey's emotional state, and present circumstances.

Diana

Diana is single mother. Her whole life is dedicated to her children. Diana sacrifices everything for the betterment of her children. Her story begins under very drab circumstances. She is attending a funeral. This funeral is devastating because she never believed this situation could ever happen to her. During a breakdown while attending the funeral, she begins to reflect on her yesterdays. She reflects on her life and the circumstances, which have led to the existing events.

Diana was born into a hard working family, which consisted of both parents. She was born in a time where black people were looked upon as inferior. Her father was a black businessman, which was not the norm during this time. Diana's father inherited land from his grandfather who was a slave.
He was an independent businessman who wanted the best for his family. Her mother struggled carrying her other unborn children to term. When Diana was born, her parents were extremely protective. Diana was a child of hope.

When her father dies, Diana is subject to straining circumstances. She becomes a single mother of four bastard children with no immediate help from their fathers. During her strife, her strength comes from her mother and another individual who pushes her to aim high for whatever she wants out of life.

Diana searches for comfort in her children. They fill the voids in her life and take the place of Diana every finding true love. The thought of being rejected by any man is frightening to Diana. Her only focus is to remain determined and provide a healthier life for her four children. She does not recognize her children are her crutch. Even though she is a supportive mother, she loses sight of her own personal needs.

Diana's story begins with a poem entitled, *Where was I?* This poem questions who she is as a mother and the trials of motherhood. Diana realizes, even in her commitment at some point her children will eventually make their own decisions. Even with her strong belief in God, she recognizes she cannot control the outcomes of their lives.

Veronica

Veronica is a heartbroken, bitter woman who is harsh to the world. She has closed off any possibilities of true love. She does not bounce back gracefully from her break-up. Her break-up hardens her heart. All men are the same, is Veronica's belief. Her only focus becomes herself. She is selfish and self-righteous and does not believe she has to compromise for any reason. She truly believes in her independence.

One day a man who adores the ground she walks on befriends her. Due to her internal issues, which she does not address, she continues to focus on self. Veronica hopes to reap the benefits of a good man, without having to reciprocate. When Veronica meets Kareem, she treats him poorly from the time he says hello. He deals with her brashness because he is aware she has had many disappointing relationships. He believes he has the ability to restore her wounds.

Veronica's story starts in her home where she is all alone. She realizes she has no one. She has her dream the house, car, and the career, but no one to share it with. She has shut out all possibilities of love.

Veronica's character is introduced by a poem entitled, *Releasing a good man*. Veronica's selfishness is unruly and intolerable. Her poem highlights her decisions and actions from not releasing the grudge of a prior faulty love.

Bernice

She is very dedicated to her role, and loves her security. She refuses to be spontaneous or take chances when it directly affects her stability.

She has given up the joys of life for surety. She has lived her life trying to accommodate everyone but herself. A co-worker questions her happiness one day while her husband is out of town. Bernice has time to reflect on the choices she has made. She questions everything she has embraced, and finds herself angry and disappointed in her decisions. She opens up feelings of regret, and she is angry at the façade she has created. Along comes a stranger who touches her spirit in an unbelievable manner. Her confusion causes anxiety, which leads her to make a decision; whether to stay secure or become the spontaneous women she never knew she could be.

Bernice's story begins in a doctor office where she believes she has run her body down and has contracted the flu. She begins to reflect on the secret she has held, which is constantly eating away at her conscious. She realizes if she reveals her secret, it could destroy everything in her perfectly structured life.

Bernice's story is introduced by a poem entitled, *Decadence and Divinity*. This is Bernice's defining moment in her life, which sets the stage for her to question who she is. The poem describes a secret that she can never share or lives will be destroyed.

PART I

Excuse the Reality

Tracey
"Detached?"

Excuse the Reality

He smiled because he appeared gentle
He promised, because words are free and unjustified by his actions

He smelled of cool water, which caused fire in her femininity
Unlike Jeremiah his soul was tainted
Spurned with a closed evil, which could only be recognized by the prey
he hadn't pounced

His grasp caused tension, which crippled the spine
His love came with the condition, due to his lack of morals

His body fit the crevices, of her once shapely form and those that were
his secret
His outburst created guilt in her, lest his own,
Buried in her unconscious causing fear

Though his power mesmerized the flesh for a moment in time,
She could not help but recognize,
The hole that was separating her heart from her sanctity
The birds bellowed songs of ruefulness
As detriment was a midst
The banter and chuckles of those who opposed her position
Ran wild through the ears of ugly, planting seeds of regret

She remembered the yesterdays of whimsical bliss
Yet she wondered, how and where was the creature God created
She had sold her soul to a devil
Which was unrecognized by her naked eye and opened heart

Not understanding why the retreat seemed so hard
She satisfied her disdain with the understanding; this may be the only
love she would embrace

And a least his presence was panoptic

Nevertheless, she veiled her battle scars, internal and external,
And proceeded to complete the task of settlement, for loving self was
but a mere remembrance.

Why not, he still appeared gentle
Smelled of cool water but a bit tainted
Satisfied her flesh by impregnating her with un-discerned spirits
His smile still illuminated, but a contradiction of truth
His words now rumbled with aches and were tarnished
With unlikely colorful metaphors
His actions now accepted under no duress
But he was her reality,
He was her excuse

Tracey

Tracy was tired. She stared at the floor wondering, trying to figure out what her next steps were. She closed her eyes as the tears welled. Her body was stricken with stress. She had no answers she just knew the mental dismantling had been more than enough for her to sustain any sanity. *All of this for love?* Not realizing his implication of love was false. She tried to retrace her steps and figure out what were the sequences of events that had led her to this very moment. Her mind was not clear; she could not even remember one kind word that had ever been whistled in her ear. As the tears left indentions in her cheeks, she heard footsteps coming closer to her bedroom door. The anticipation caused her heart to flutter for she could not embrace any more disgust. It was bad enough she had just seen the man who promised his life to her, till death do them part, in a compromising position.

The door creaked open and their stood the image. This image she fell in love with so many years ago. Now the man she thought she loved was a flagrant mystery. In embarrassment, and shame she refused to lift her head. She refused to observe the lie that was going to spew out of his mouth. She had heard his untruths so many times before but never accepted them as a part of her reality.

"Tracey babe," the very masculine tone fell from the lips of the perpetrator. "Tracey…"

Tracey did not know whether to answer him or just leap in anger. Tracey did not have the strength for either action so she sat still. He walked closer to the bed still calling her name, but still no answer. *In my house, she thought.* In her house while she and her children were asleep. She wondered how he proposed to get out of this obvious blunder. *He cannot, she thought.* There was nothing he could say. Something in Tracey's spirit stirred because her curiosity would get the best of her.

In a shallow tone, she answered, "Yes."

He opened his mouth and poured these audacious words. "Look I don't have time for all this crying tonight! Janine woke up because she pissed all over her bed, and I think you need to change her sheets. You know I do not know where nuthin is, so go on girl! She is in there crying just like you. I shouldn't be forced to listen to everyone whaling in this house! Now get!"

Tracey's jaw dropped. *What did he just say? What did he just murmur out of his mouth? Is he serious? Was I the only the one that was present at the ungodly sight I just witness?*

"Tracey dangit…," he bellowed. "Get the sheets changed, man I'm tired! I don't want to hear all this damn whining!"

Shocked with no refute, Tracey sighed and began to exit her room to remedy her child's mishaps. As she was leaving, he proceeded to remove his wife beater, and basketball shorts. Once he had removed his clothes, he climbed into the bed.

"Are you not going to shower?" she asked.

"Man nawww…, its late I will take one tomorrow."

He proceeded to put his soiled body between the sheets she carefully washed weekly. She was sickened but did not mum another word. Tracey closed the door behind her and went into her child's room.

"Mommy, Mommy!"

Tracey heard screeching through the hallways. She had fallen asleep on the floor of Janine's bedroom without notice. She was so tired from the trifles of the night before. She did not realize, once she repaired the boo-boo's, she had laid her head on the carpet and cried herself to sleep.

"Mommy, wake up!"

"What Janine?"

"Brystal is trying to cook in the kitchen and you said she couldn't turn on the stove, and she did."

Brystal had a nasty disposition and was extremely disrespectful. Janine was the baby of the house and felt she needed to tattle on everyone and everything. Tracey was tired and did not feel like listening to her whiny child or her disrespectful teenager.

"Mommy, mommy…!"

"What Janine!" Tracey said now agitated.

"Brystal is in the kitchen!"

"Okay, okay," said Tracy, trying to get up off the floor. It wasn't as easy as she thought. Tracey was more than voluptuous these days. Since her wedding day she had gained an additional fifty-five pounds plus, from her once curvy one hundred and fifty-five pound frame. Things were now placed in hidden spots, which moved around freely if they weren't taped or wrapped. Tracey began to pick herself off the floor when she heard her nine-year-old running through the hall. *What the…?*

"Jo-Jo…!"

"Yes ma," he answered.

Jo-Jo was nine years old and full of energy. Tracey made sure she never gave him sugar because apparently he was born high. High is how he acted until the very moment he fell to sleep, which Tracey prayed for often. His body never stopped, he kept running and running like an energizer bunny. He did not stay still long enough, or allow his food to settle in any place of his body. Tracey prayed to God for peace because she knew her children were going to drive her loony.

Boom, blub, blub! A terrifying sound came from the hall. It sounded like an earthquake tearing her home apart. Tracey could not deal with any more destruction to her once beautiful home.

"Jo-Jo…!"

"Yea," he said in a devilish tone.

"What on earth are you doing?"

"Skatin…," answered Jo-Jo.

Skating? Tracey knew Jo-Jo couldn't be skating because she had never purchased him a pair. She became concerned with her only son's activity. Tracey got a burst of energy to see what her child had destroyed. She walked to the door and wanted to let out a loud scream, but she couldn't; her mouth trembled when she witnessed the hideous sight before her eyes.

Jo-Jo decided he was going to make his own skates using the wheels from one of his many monster trucks, and super glued them to his brand new pair of Air Jordan's, she had just purchased not even a week ago. Trying to roller skate, he slid down the steps and grabbed the railing, which was not sturdy enough to hold the impact it endured. A loud scream came from the bedroom.

He yelled, "What are you doing!"

Just then, the bedroom door open and this well of fire dispersed from Satan's mouth. The colorful metaphors spewed out of his opening, sounding like an unedited rap song, by Fifty Cent.

"Get your dumb ass up! What in the hell are you doing you stupid mother…!"

"But, dad," Jo-Jo wailed.

He screeched, "Shut up! You dumb SOB!"

Jo-Jo began to cry and ran to his room. Tracey stared in amazement because she never used such harsh words ever in her life, let alone directed them at her children. Tracey stared at the evil figure as he rolled his eyes and returning to the bedroom slamming the door.

Brystal was in the kitchen, cooking breakfast without permission. She was 14 years old. She had a body like a sixteen year old. Brystal was developing in areas, which were in comparison to women seen in music videos. She possessed a sharp tongue and a nonchalant attitude toward authority. Brystal had no respect for Tracey because she witnessed the monstrosity of her mother's lack, daily. Even if the ugliness was from father, she believed her mother was weak and could not fathom ever-falling prey to such deceit, lying, and cheating. To Brystal, her mother wasn't a mother she was just a shell of a woman who lacked a soul.

Brystal was a mediocre student, who was more concerned with her looks. People always echoed and praised her beauty. She believed she didn't have to work hard. She assumed her beauty would send her on journeys of the impossible. Brystal lived in a fantasy world with big pipe dreams with no true rational.

She was 5'6 coco colored skin weighing about 134 pounds. She had a Coke bottle shape. A shape her mother possessed before she lost sight of keeping up with her appearance. Perfection is what she hummed daily because she believed she was perfect. Brystal had the ability to be very articulate because her mother stressed the importance of speaking clearly, so others would comprehend her dialect. Brystal however chose a different route somewhere around the age of thirteen, right after she and Mother Nature went to war.

"Come on mane! What up with dis," Brystal screamed! "This snitch is crae-ezy...! Jo-Jo I hope you break your freakin neck. I am sick of all this got dern noise!"

She could hear the train wreck on the second floor. She knew Jo-Jo was the conductor. She heard her father correct the tyrant and began to laugh, after Jo-Jo was silenced. As she continued to cook, she could hear someone coming into the kitchen.

"Hey baby," she heard a soft voice say while she proceeded to cook.

"Hey daddy," she grinned.

Despite the way her father treated her mother she held no ill will towards him because he favored her. He allowed her to do anything she wished. This was one of the reasons Brystal found all of the hypocrisy in the house to be, her mother's fault. He kissed her on the cheek.

"Whatcha cooking baby girl?"

"Sum eggs, sum hash browns, and grits," she said grinning.

She knew her dad was not going to complain about her using the stove as her mother often did. Brystal had caused a kitchen fire while cooking and her mother banned her from using the stove. Brystal was only allowed to use the microwave. She deliberately ignored her mother's commands because she knew her father did not oppose.

"You want sum daddy?"

"Sure baby girl," as he stared at her, with a non-paternal look.

His eyes pawed over her body as she danced promiscuously while flipping the eggs. She was only fourteen, but there was something familiar about the way she moved. She looked like a younger version of Tracey. The version he had set to conquer, and did.

Tracey was always eye candy for the boys in school. She wasn't aware of the attention and talk and didn't really care. She had her sight set on one person. Although he was a grade ahead of her, she couldn't help but desire that their paths would cross at some point. He was a smooth talker and pretended to have his eye only on her. From the moment, he slithered into her path Tracey was never the same.

"Here you go daddy."

Brystal handed her father a large plate of scrambled eggs with cheese, side of corn beef hash, toast, and a bowl of grits. She handed him some utensils, and a paper napkin. She loved the attention she received from her father because she knew her other siblings were not as adored as she was.

"Thank you baby, that's daddy's girl. You gonna make sum one real happy one day. Just be careful with all this rich food you cookin, or you gonna end up like yo momma. Sloppy and fat, you see how she don't do sh…"

Just then, Tracey walked in with a hurtful stair. She had overheard the comments he was about to share with their daughter. Instead of directing her anger towards him, she looked directly at Brystal with fire in her eyes.

"What are you doing Brystal?"

"What it look like," Brystal replied sarcastically.

"I thought I told you…"

"She doin more than you ever do around this house and the food taste better! Leave da girl alone! You should stand over there and take sum lessons. Maybe she can teach you sumthin, your lazy behind never learned. Leave her alone and go make yourself useful! Starting with that faggoty boy you got upstairs you can't control. He tearin up errythang in dis damn house and you don't say nuthin to him. That's why I had to cuss his dumb ass out this morning."

He continued to rant and rave at Tracey not even caring that Brystal was present. Brystal just stared with a sly grin on her face because she knew her father was about to put her mother in her place. Brystal didn't care about the impetuous words because he was taking her side.

"And where is Miss Pissy? Let me guess, she somewhere crying? I don't know what happened to those two porch monkeys, they must get their traits from yo side da family," he snarled.

Tracey was stunned; she was just checked in front of her fourteen year old. Her heart became heavy and instead of responding, she stood silent. Tracey walked over to the sink and began to clean up the mess Brystal created from her so-called breakfast. Brystal and her father began to taunt the weak woman.

"Ain't that right baby," he said to Brystal.

"You kno it iz. Ma since you cleanin, imma get ready for school. Oh yea, I made the wonder brats breakfast too, but I am sure you can't mum a thank you. Maybe you should ast permission first."

Brystal giggled as she began to walk out of the kitchen. Before she left the room, she stopped and kissed her daddy on the cheek. Tracey refused to turn around and look either of them in the eyes. She was ashamed of the belittling she just endured.

"See ya daddy, I'm on my way to da bus stop."

"Hol'on Brystal, Ka-jon is bout to be here, we can run you to school."

Run her to school? Tracey thought. Tracey was trying to figure out why Ka-jon was coming over so early. Neither he nor Ka-jon had a job. Tracey knew she had to get to work, and her two younger children had to be dropped off at the bus stop. If she waited for both of them to get on the bus, she knew she would be late to work. Tracey did not have any other options but she refused to voice her concerns. To avoid any arguments Tracey said nothing and continued to clean the kitchen.

"Sure daddy, no problem, let me get my stuff." Brystal said as she ran up the steps.

He exited the kitchen at the sound of the doorbell. He said nothing to Tracey and acted as if she were not present. This was Tracey's household. This is what she had become accustomed to day in and day out. After last night, she wondered how she had gotten to this place in her life. What was Tracey's excuse for allowing this to happen?

When Brystal and her father left the house, Tracey began to ponder. She could not believe what had just happened. Her fourteen-year-old daughter had just spoken to her as if she were trash in the street. Her husband had berated her and placed her in another compromising position.

Tracey could not believe this was her life. However, she knew she was only fooling herself; this had always been her life. She began to wonder if she was still asleep on Janine's floor trying to balance out the other montage of issues, which had taken place in her home. Tracey knew she couldn't fool herself because this activity always took place in her home. This chaos had gone on since the day she had married him. Since the day she said, "*I do.*"

Tracey was ignorant to the man she married. She didn't budge at any of the signs. From his slick talking, numerous girlfriends, and despicable rumors, Tracey had ignored everything that was dangled right in front of her eyes. Tracey ignored the red flags because she desired this man. Other women were jealous of her and treated her cruelly. Tracey never stood up for herself and when he approached her with an offer, she immediately grabbed it. Tracey felt she deserved to be with him. She knew it would anger others because they would want what she had. She wanted to make a point to the people who taunted her daily. Tracey was determined to show them how wrong they were about her. She had the "guy" every girl wanted. What Tracey did not know was most of the jealous woman had already stumbled upon his deviance.

When Tracey and he started dating, they appeared to be so happy. He was her first love and first encounter. He loved her naiveté, and knew he could take advantage, at any given time. They were inseparable in the beginning. From that, moment on Tracey knew she would make it her life's work to make him her husband. She was willing to do whatever was needed to keep her dream alive. She refused to argue even if he was wrong. Tracey did not want any confusion to cause a wedge in her relationship. He knew she would remain under his control for as long as he desired. Tracey believed most women made the mistake of not letting a man be a man. Tracey was going to handle her relationship differently so she could keep him happy. She refused to nag, question, or bother him about issues, which seemed trivial. Her concern was that he came home to her. Somewhere in her warped sense of thinking, she believed if other women lived by the same principals then they would be able to keep a man.

She could not appreciate when women would scream about what they would or would not tolerate. Tracey's understanding of companionship was if you want to be in love, and want it to work, you would have to tolerate something. Running out at the first sign of any obstacles was not an option. It was going to work. She didn't care what her mother, daddy, or friends thought. She and he were going to weather the storm and prove all of the naysayer's, wrong.

Tracey sat down at the kitchen table trying to remember the way it was. She now found her decisions to wreak total oblivion. She remembered the smiles and could not help but wonder if she could have done anything differently. She closed her eyes to meditate.

****

Tracey and he were married, on June 30, two weeks after their high school graduation. He had left school for a brief period. Rumors had circulated about him having trouble with the law, but nothing was ever documented. When he returned he found himself in the same graduating class as Tracey. She helped him complete all of his credits so he could walk with her.

Tracey found out later that she was pregnant with their first child. Her parents thought it would be appropriate for Tracey to be married. They did not want her to be a single mother because of the appearance it would have created. They were not happy with the idea of her marrying him; however, they were strict Christians and did not believe a child should be born into this world without both of their biological parents. *Tracey had no idea she came into this world under a false pretense, because her father was not her biological father.*

Nevertheless, she and he were married in her grandmother's huge backyard under a white gazebo. There were not many guests. Tracey's sister and best friend Cynthia stood beside her in their JC Penney's pink flowery dresses. Tracey wore an off-white suit. Tracey didn't think spending a lot of money was necessary.

He was looking for a job and they were going to live in Section 8 housing. Tracey's Aunt Barbara got a hook up from one her friends who worked for Social Services. Since she was pregnant, she qualified for all of the benefits. She just needed to make sure they didn't find out about their marriage. Therefore, they didn't change anything legally until four years later, but the ceremony was necessary for her parents. They took vows under God, which was enough for her and her parents.

Now she was married and didn't have a care in the world. She had one of the finest men at her side daily. She was getting herself prepared to go to college because she had promised her mother she would not sit at home and become a welfare mom.

"The system is a temporary means of assistance." Her mom would say.

She knew an education was necessary because she had always dreamed of becoming a Social Worker. Her pride would not allow her to ask her family even though she knew their financial stability could assist her in her time of need. Tracey wanted to do things her own way.

Everything in Tracey's life appeared to be moving fast. She spent two years at community college and changed her major to Business Administration. Somewhere in between classes and all the issues other people had keeping their households together, no longer interested her. She too had enough issues at home. Tracey miscarried in her first trimester. She tried and tried to get pregnant right after but things just did not seem to be going right.

He supposedly was working long hours. He didn't talk to her, or even notice she was present. He seemed to have a chip on his shoulder since the day they said, *I do*. When they went to sign their official marriage license, he was two hours late arriving at City Hall. He claimed he was working on something and lost track of time. Tracey had never seen or been to a job of his, she just assumed, he was preoccupied. Tracey believed there was no need to bother him. It was ok for him to help when he could. He had been hired and fired so many times before; the pressure of her nagging was not going to help the issue. It didn't matter to her at first; she was getting money from her financial aid. Rent was only fifty dollars; they had a nice house, and never went without anything. Section 8 was fantastic; they didn't question anything going on in her house because she always kept things up to par. They were not going to increase rent because she was receiving assistance from the state. Tracey knew if she really got in a bind, she could swallow her pride and ask her family for help. In Tracey's mind, this would be her last resort. Therefore, she and her husband lived in a four bedroom home, with two baths, living room, den, and a porch, for only fifty dollars a month. She was pursuing her education and had success on her mind.

****

Cynthia and Tracey were out making plans for graduation later on in the spring. They were so excited to finally graduate.

The program Tracey had entered allowed her to add extra credits to her already strenuous schedule. She doubled up on her classes and pushed herself to finish school. She believed the added stress of school might have caused some of the issues in her house. With her being out of school, she felt she could try to spend more time with her husband if he allowed her to. She assumed her plan was going to work out perfectly.

Tracey never got a chance to enjoy college life because she was bound to her home. He did not want her going out to parties and interacting with others.

Cynthia thought her friend was foolish. She never liked him from the time Tracey had expressed her feelings for him in high school. Cynthia was aware of the rumors, which circulated around his reputation. Once Tracey fell in love with him, there was no talking to her. Cynthia decided she would stand beside her friend regardless of her decisions.

They had been driving around all day trying to figure out how they were going to celebrate when they received their diploma. Tracey became hungry and wanted Cynthia to stop so they could grab a bite to eat. Cynthia wanted to continue to shop and plan for their big day, but Tracey insisted.

"Girl I am craving hot dogs and French fries," said Tracey.

"Hot dogs and French fries Tracey? We can eat in my momma's kitchen girl."

"No Cynnie, I want Andrew's Grill," pleaded Tracy.

"Andrew's Grill, really, are you crazy? Girl they are nasty and their hotdogs are not that big."

Cynthia laughed because she made a joke with sexual undertones. Cynthia had a dirty mind. She was always making dirty jokes and talking about her sex life. Cynthia was single and living life to the fullest. Tracey always insisted she try to settle down.

"You are out of your mind. Andrew's has the best hot dogs I have ever eaten in my life."

Cynthia laughed again.

"I am just craving them for some reason."

"Girl you have been craving anything that won't bite you back. You better slow down before graduation gets here; we are going to have to put you in a tent all by yourself."

Tracey knew she had put on a few pounds but she was not aware if they were actually noticeable. She thought it could be the stresses of her home but she would never admit it to anyone let alone her best friend. Cynthia went ahead and verified her suspicions of her weight gain.

"Girl you're becoming a fatty," said Cynthia. "When is the last time you saw your woman's works?"

"Huh…," Tracey said.

"Key lo-lo, down low…" Cynthia said while pointing her hand to her femininity below her belt.

"I see it all the time," said Tracey as she rolled her eyes.

"Uh, huh, in the mirror as you admire your naked body," Cynthia burst out into laughter again.

"Don't start Cynthia I have been under a little stress and sometimes I eat for comfort."

"Sure, it does. So I guess I should ask you what you don't eat, cuz you have eaten everything you have come in contact with for the last month. Except the dog that was going to fight you, after you sniffed his bowl."

"Girl shut up! Look lets go get my hot dogs."

While Cynthia was turning into the parking lot of Andrew's Grill she noticed, a green Honda Civic parked with a couple who appeared to be in a heated conversation in the corner near the garbage cans. The windows were cracked because it was cold outside. Their faces were a blur but anyone could see they were arguing. Tracey and Cynthia could make out some of the words they were saying but not the entire conversation. Just then, the young man, in full throttle punched the young woman in her face. She began to scream and belt profanities at him.

The man said, "You stupid bitch! I told you there is nothing I can do!"

She returned the blow hitting him with some object she must have grabbed. Cynthia and Tracey became concerned and wondered if they should interfere. Tracey looked to see whom she could signal for help.

"Girl stay out of folk business," said Cynthia. "They are going to fuss and make up. Trust me the police will get hear and then she will be sorry they were called."

They watched the couple go back and forth for a few more seconds just to make sure there was no immediate danger. It appeared she was throwing just as many blows as he was. The debacle was a sight for sore eyes. The women decided not to stay to watch the rest of the action. Cynthia drove off never to even enter the store.

"Girl what did we come out here for?"

"I don't know, but at least we didn't have to go home to watch the Jerry Springer show. Ha, ha," laughed Tracey.

"Folk is crazy," said Cynthia.

"But she a good one, I would have tried to kill his ass, if he hit me like that," Tracey said rolling her eyes.

"Does it really matter the type of abuse whether it be physical or mental?" Cynthia retorted.

Tracey ignored Cynthia's question. Cynthia could not believe Tracey's rational of abuse. She knew Tracey was detached but not this far-gone from reality. Tracey did not believe her situation was as devastating as the fight she just witnessed. She thought to herself. *As long as that nigga do not get crazy, and act like he wanna fight, we will be all right.*

That afternoon, Tracey prepared a feast for her man because she thought she needed to make more of an effort. He appeared to be stressed. She didn't know what to do for him. His imaginary job was keeping him out at all times of the night and he was hardly ever at home. They didn't even have enough time to make love. The last time they made love, he appeared very angry and distracted. Once he was finished he hopped up and left the house. This was about four weeks prior. Tracey was determined she was going to get some affection that night.

Nine, nine thirty, ten, ten thirty, eleven, eleven thirty, twelve…
Oh God where is he, she pondered? Just then, her phone rang.

"Hello," Tracey answered.

A recording came on, *"You have a collect call from the City Jail, from…"* Tracey froze and began to become anxious. *What is going on God what has happened?*

"Yes I accept," she said in a panic.

'Tracey," he said. "Baby I need you to come and get me."

He seemed so disheveled over the phone. Tracey did not give him time to explain. She heard her husband's voice on the other end and all she could do was grab her bags and run to his rescue.

Tracey waited outside with the bail bondsmen who had agreed to meet Tracey at the jail and get him released. Tracy did not even bother to ask what was going on, she only knew she needed to be there for her husband now, and ask questions later.

The steel doors opened to the jail and out came her husband appearing as if he had been battered. He had a slight head trauma with dried blood to the upper left part of his eye. His lip was swollen and face was scratched up.

"Baby what happened to you!" Tracey screamed. "Who did this to you?"

Feeling ashamed, he held his head down. He did not want to explain any of the happenings of the evening. He knew Tracey was not going to pressure him. He was just happy to be out of jail.

"I am okay baby. Thank you for coming to get me."

The bail bondsmen shook his head in astonishment of Tracey's response to her husband. She automatically assumed he was the victim even though he was the person who was locked up. The bails bondsman was aware of the charges and did not a mum a word to Tracey. When he realized the bail, bondsman did not go over his charges he decided he did not need to explain himself. He never said exactly what happened, and told Tracey, he would take care of it.

Tracey was so worried and scared. She believed someone was after her husband. He took the time out to explain how he was attacked but because he was drunk in public. He claimed that was why the police arrested him. Not once did Tracey figure out he should have been at work. She did not even question when he had time to get a drink. He did not smell like alcohol, he smelled like cheap perfume. *Wild Irish Rose, she thought.*

"Baby you can't be drinking that stuff, it will kill you. Come on upstairs let me give you a bath."

That night he made love to Tracey, as he had never done before. Tracey was happy and believed every word her husband had uttered.

****

Seven and a half months later Brystal Renee Collins was born. Tracey was already portly before and after graduation and the level of stress she was going through during her husband's legal activity did not help. Tracey developed blood clots in her legs, and at one point, the doctors were not sure if she or the baby would survive. Luckily, she was already on bed rest at the time Brystal was delivered prematurely. Brystal was small and beautiful. Her father thought the world of her.

"She is perfect," he said. "She is going to make my life so much better. You watch baby, she is our good luck charm."

He had been supportive since he spent his time in jail. Tracey was not able to attend his court hearings because of the issues she was having during her pregnancy. He knew she was going to support him even if she was not aware of all the details. He was relieved she was not aware of all the despicable particulars.

"Baby, why do they keep continuing this court case?" Tracey asked.

"Baby don't worry bout it, the lawyer said he is working on sumthin, because the guy is saying it was self-defense. You know a bunch of technical terms, I don't even care bout."

He could not get his lie straight so he pretended to be focus on the baby. He did not want Tracey asking any more questions. He was trying not to be insensitive but he knew if he provided any elements of the case, then Tracey might ask more questions.

"I just know we are all better now, since baby girl is here."

When she looked at his face and saw how happy he was, she thought it would be a shame to steal his joy. She stopped asking him questions because, in the end, it really did not matter. She had her family and this was all she wanted.

"I know we are baby. We are going to be just fine."

He followed Brystal around the house. He would not let other people talk to her or touch her. He kept Brystal on a pedestal and most of the time he didn't even want Tracey to interfere with anything that they were doing.

I will take her here, I will do this, and I will do that.

He paid more attention to Brystal than he did Tracey. Tracey was upset by this at first, but she found an excuse for his behavior. She convinced herself she had never seen a man love his child the way he did. *If people know like I know they had better not ever bother her because her daddy would kill them.* She considered his actions territorial because Brystal was his first-born.

****

Tracey began getting Brystal ready for daycare because she had to recertify her paperwork for Section 8. She could have kept Brystal at home but she believed she needed to interact with children her age. She wanted to go back to school, so she could have a chance of getting better employment opportunities. The money she was bringing in paid the bills but she still had to depend on assistance to cover his part. She knew she would only have to use the government services just a little while longer with him going through his court issues.

He told her he had been fired from his job because he had been locked up. There was only one car in the household, and Tracey needed to get around daily. Not to mention it was her car that she had purchased. Every morning he left bright and early to make it to the city bus so he could complete his daily tasks. Well at least that is what he told Tracey.

Tracey walked into the Department of Social Services realizing how much she hated coming to the office. Tracey felt her circumstances were different from the other women present; she was only receiving partial assistance. She could not believe most of the women survived from day to day, off one check that was issued monthly. She refused to live under those conditions. Tracey knew she was not going to have to wait long because she still dealt with her aunt's friend who had handled all of her affairs for years.

Sitting diagonally from Tracey, was a woman who stared at her as if she knew her. Tracey was positive she had never met the woman a day in her life. Tracey thought. *She had better look the other way before I drop this 190 on her frail ass.*

The woman was about 5'6 brown skin, and her hair was pulled back into a ponytail. She was not skinny but she definitely was not Tracey's stature and clearly did not want to get stomped after Tracey gave her the look of death. The woman had a child with her who appeared mentally retarded. Tracey gathered her thoughts and immediately felt bad when the woman picked her son up and moved her chair to the other side of the room. He could not have been more than 3 years old.

Tracey thought to herself. *Lord I thank you for taking care of Brystal during our time of need. It could be the other way. But we are so, so blessed to have our baby girl. Her daddy adores her and I love her dearly.* A tear almost fell from her eye but she noticed the young woman had left some papers in the next chair. When Tracey went to pick them up and hand them to her, the woman immediately snatched the paper work right out of her hands.

She shouted, "This is mine!"

Tracey stood back and realized something was not right with this young woman. She did not want to cause a seen so she cracked a fake smile. Tracey tried not to over react but the woman was starting to get under her skin.

"Ma'am I know that," stated Tracey. "I saw that you had left them on the chair, and I was actually bringing them to you."

"Look I don't need nuthin from you. I will get what I need. Trust me... me and my son are fine!"

Tracey looked puzzled. She had no idea what the woman was talking about. She looked at her son and her heart became heavy again. She knew arguing in front of the child was not the appropriate thing to do. Tracey stepped back from the agitated woman.

"I don't know what your problem is but you have a good day," said Tracey.

"Tracey? Tracey?"

The woman behind the counter called her name. She saw the confusion, which was glaring up in the waiting room. She didn't have time to intercede so she called Tracey's name repeatedly to get her attention.

"Mrs. Cunningham will see you now."

Tracey had fallen into a daze trying to figure out what just had transpired. The woman continued to stare at her with abhorrence. She looked as if she wanted to pounce on Tracey for no apparent reason. Tracey turned from the woman. She walked over to the counter and asked the receptionist where she needed to go. Tracey tried to take her mind off the mysterious woman. Tracey had other pressing issues in which she was more concerned.

"Mrs. Cunningham, thank you for always seeing me in such a timely fashion."

"Not a problem Tracey, I needed to talk to you because some changes had to be made on your rent."

"Changes?" questioned Tracey.

"Yes ma'am you have been paying fifty dollars for rent for the last six years. Times are changing so we have to update your paper work with your information. Do not worry, I have not added anything about you being married. Since he is not working, right now you would not have any issues in the first place. Now I received your paycheck stubs about a week ago. You seem to be doing okay with the income you are getting. Therefore, there will be an adjustment of $250 to your current rent payments. Now this will not take affect for another three months. This should be enough time for you and your husband to resolve some of the issues you are having. These payments should be manageable."

"Please, this is still a blessing there are some people that are probably paying double that. I have no complaints ma'am."

Tracey gathered up her paper work and proceeded to leave. When she went back in the waiting room, she realized the young woman she previously had a confrontation with was no longer present. Tracey did not think much of the incident and returned home.

****

Two years later, Tracey received a letter from the Department of Social Services notifying her that her Section 8 was going to be terminated if she did not provide paper work of all her income for her household.

The letter stated:

Mrs. Collins,

This letter is to inform you that you may be due for an increase in rent. If your marital status or income has changed, you will need to update our records immediately. If we do not hear from you by 9/10/2000, your rent will increase to $875. This is the original renting price. This is not including benefits from Section 8. Please note this information will not be backdated. However, this information must be updated before the following date above.

If you have any questions or concerns, please speak with your new caseworker. My information has been provided below. Thank you for your immediate attention with regard to the matters listed above.

Sincerely,
Ms. Bello
(434) -554-2145 Cell
(434) -535-2117 Office
Hours of Operation
Mon-Fri 8am-5pm

What the heck is this? Tracey thought. *Where is Mrs. Cunningham?* Tracey went to grab the phone and down the steps ran Brystal.
"Mommy, Mommy where is daddy!"

"I am not sure honey but mommy has to take care of something right quick so give me a second," Tracey said agitated.

"But mommy, I want daddy!

"Brystal," Tracey said firmly. "He is not here. I will take care of whatever you need in just a few minutes."

"I hate you," Brystal screamed! She began to stomp away from her mother.

Tracey was shocked, at the words of her 4 year old. She could not believe a child knew such a strong word as hate. Where did she learn this from, her mother pondered?

"You hate me?"

Tracey immediately dropped the phone and went to snatch the soon to be five year old. Right when she grabbed the little girl, the phone rang. She looked at Brystal and wanted to throw her across the room. Tracey knew she needed to channel her anger before she hurt her child.

"I don't know where you got that from but I will smack the piss out of your mouth, if I ever here it again."

Brystal was shocked her mother had grabbed her in such a manner. She was rarely disciplined and thought she could get away with murder.

Her father always stepped in during her time of need. She was a very keen child. Even as bold as she knew she could be around her father, she did not feel the need to take any chances with her mother today.

Brystal got herself in order, wiped her nose saying, "I sorry mommy", and ran up the steps.

What had gotten into that child, Tracey thought? Tracey needed to focus on the matters at hand. She remembered the phone had rung. She ran over to the caller ID and she did not recognize the number. It was the *Clerk's Office*, at the courthouse.

"Hello," said Tracey. "I just received a call from this number."

"Yes, is this Mrs. Collins?"

"Yes."

"I was asked to give you a call by a Lawyer named, Mr. C. J. Jenkins. He stated he needs you to come to the courthouse tomorrow at 9 am."

"9 am, what is this about?"

"This is about a legal matter ma'am. He will answer all of your questions when you meet. If you have any additional questions, you will need to contact Mr. Jenkins at the following number 434-665-8986. Thank you Mrs. Collins, have a good day."

Tracey was puzzled. She did not know any Mr. Jenkins, and she had no legal issues that she was aware of. *What the hell? What is going on today? First Section 8… Oh, my God Section 8.* Tracey almost had fallen over the phone cord. Everything around her seemed to be going at a fast pace. She needed answers about the letter she had received. She needed to call Mrs. Cunningham immediately.

Tracey picked up the phone and dialed her number. It rang several times until the answering machine picked up. Tracey was infuriated.

"You have reached…."

Tracey immediately hung up and called her aunt. She knew she would have an answer because all she did was gossip and keep up with the latest news. Besides, Mrs. Cunningham was one of Barbara's best friends. Aunt Barbara answered the phone.

"Aunt Barbara what is going on? Where is Mrs. Cunningham?"

Tracey did not announce herself so that her aunt would know who was on the phone. Barbara had caller ID but was too lazy to look at the phone. Barbara finally recognized the other voice on the phone. It was her niece.

"Tracey?" questioned Barbara. "What are you talking about?"

"I am trying to call Mrs. Cunningham and I can't reach her."

Aunt Barbara sighed, "Baby…Cunningham done got herself fired. All of her files have been turned over to new case workers."

"What?"

"Before you start it is not because of paper work. Apparently, Cunningham has been living in Section 8 housing, and receiving benefits for over twenty-five years under an alias. I can't even tell you about the mess she in. I am too stressed."

Tracey wanted to scream about what her aunt was telling her. She couldn't believe Mrs. Cunningham could be so underhanded. She soon forgot what Mrs. Cunningham was doing for her was illegal. She had known this woman since she could speak. Tracey didn't want to hear anything else but her aunt continued to talk and Tracey could not interrupt her.

"You know she has always done my paperwork for my house. That is why your uncle and I have been here for so long. If they start reinvestigating her claims, we could end up owing every penny we hadn't paid in the last thirty years. You know we can't afford that. I just don't know why she would do that."

Tracey knew her aunt was a bit delusional. She had no reason to be broke. She had lost her birthright when she decided not to further her education. Instead of waiting to become financially stable, she hastily had gotten married. Barbara had a chance but decided to take the low road. She blamed everyone else around her anytime a trial appeared in her life.

"Girl, look, at least you went to school, got you a job, and you got an able bodied man in that house who can work. Your uncle and me is diabeticle, and got the gout. Your momma offered us to stay with her if this didn't pan out, but you know how yo momma is. I refuse to ask your grandma for anything. And we ain't staying in her house either!"

Tracey didn't have time to listen to the troubles of her aunt. Barbara was the example her mother used when insisting Tracey complete her education. Tracey's mother could not stomach her older sister. She believed she wasted all of her potential due to laziness and complacency. She had no dreams; she did not aspire to do anything with her life. Tracey's aunt fell in love with her husband and a few of the world's trinkets. Her aunt loved her Section 8, food stamps, lottery tickets, southern comfort, and especially her disability check, which paid for it all.

Tracey finally got the nerve to interrupt her aunt's victim cries. She did not want to worry about Mrs. Cunningham or the outcome of her Section 8. She was still working and her bills were manageable. Tracey had saved throughout the years so there was some cushion. She knew her husband was doing the best he could and expected he would bring in some income soon enough. *Oh well. It lasted long enough.* Tracey expected everything to be fine.

Tracey began to wonder where her husband was. He had been in and out of the house, for the last few days. He had received a call two days ago, and claimed it was very important. Tracey assumed it was a job because he had to go to the Social Security office and Vital Records to get copies of his Birth Certificate and Social Security Card. She knew her husband was making every effort to be supportive and play the role of a loving husband. She understood people fell on hard times and she was not about to let this incident put her in a negative mind frame. *We will manage, with God on our side, we always do.*

Tracey had almost forgotten to call the Lawyer. She was still trying to figure out why she needed to go to court. Tracey was about to pick up the phone and there came a knock at the door.

"Arrgh!!!," Tracey bellowed aloud. "What is it today? God did you open up the flood gates!"

Tracey opened the door and it was Ka-jon, his friend. She didn't have time to talk. She had to make some phone calls and try to figure out everything that was transpiring. Ka-jon annoyed her. She didn't see that he ever held any purpose. She believed he just hung around her husband because he was a follower. Ka-Jon didn't say much when he came to Tracey's house and when he did, she was disgusted by his slang.

"Hey what up…."

Tracey wanted to slap the taste out of his ignorant mouth. She didn't have time to be irritated by Ka-Jon. Tracey decided she would run him off without having to answer to any questions.

"Look, he is not here, and I don't know where he is..." Before Tracey could finish her sentence, he interrupted.

"Yo, dude is in jail and gonna be there for a while."

"Huh, what?" questioned Tracey.

"Look he ain't have no way to call you. But when I left him today he told me to run by through the spot, and let you know what be up. I'm out," Ka-jon turned around and proceeded to walk to his car.

"Ka-jon!" Tracey screamed. "What the hell happened?"

"Yo ma, you need to holla at dude when you can, he will straighten it. Peace..."

Now Tracey really wanted to smack the taste out of his mouth. The way he dragged his speech and sounded so nonchalant left Tracey vexed. She couldn't believe her husband would even associate with someone of his caliber. While she was mulling over her disgust for Ka-Jon the phone rang.

"HELLO!" Tracey screamed.

"Mrs. Collins, this is Mr. Jankins I work in the district attorney's office. I have been waiting for you to respond to several letters I have sent to your home. You are to be in court at 9 am tomorrow morning. If you do not show up for court you may be held in contempt." The district attorney exaggerated. He needed Tracey to help make his case.

"Sir what is this for?" interrupted Tracey.

"The malicious wounding and attempted murder of Ms. Justine Peebles," Mr. Jankins stated. "I will see you in the morning ma'am."

"What, who, what, when?"

"Your husband," snarled the district attorney.

Tracey dropped the phone and stood in silence.

It was Thursday morning and Tracey was on her way to the courthouse. She had no idea what was going on, and she had no clue what was happening to her family. She just knew her husband had not been home since yesterday morning. When she walked in the courtroom the officer asked her name and directed her to where should would need to be seated. Tracey felt her spirit weighing heavy as a man in a navy blue suit approached.

"Mrs. Collins?"

"Yes," she responded.

"I am the district attorney who is trying your husband's case. I have tried to reach you on several occasions even at your brother's home. I understand that you are having and have had several issues, but when there are matters of the court, we can't have people think they can just ignore requests."

Tracey had no idea what he was talking about but she refused to say anything until she found out more about what was going on. Just then, another man in a navy blue suit walked up.

"You can't talk to her! Mrs. Collins do not say another word my name is Mr. Jenkins. My secretary called you yesterday."

"I know," Tracey said. "I spoke to you on the phone."

He laughed rolling his eyes at the district attorney.

"Ma'am you didn't speak to me on the phone. You spoke with Mr. Jankins the district attorney. He is Mr. Jankins with an "a." I am Mr. Jenkins your husband's attorney."

Now Tracey was confused. Mr. Jenkins told Tracey he had his secretary call her when her husband stated she was back in town. Tracey was trying to figure out when she had left, and in fact, where did she go? Probably with the same brother, she had not met.

"Mrs. Collins, please come with me. I need to go over some information with you."

Tracey was already lost but she could not afford showing instability while being in the courtroom. She wanted someone to explain to her without assuming she already knew. More important than the explanation she wanted to know what all of this had to do with her husband.

"Yes sir," she stated.

As Tracey walked out, she noticed a young woman walking toward the district attorney. The woman cut her eyes at Tracey as if Tracey had committed a crime. *Where do I know her from?* Tracey thought.

Mr. Jenkins guided Tracey to an undisclosed room. He had a large folder in his hand, which looked significant. The lawyer closed the door and asked Tracey to sit down.

"Mrs. Collins, I understand this has been hard for you and I truly sympathize with you. I wanted you to be here showing support for your husband."

Tracey knew she had always supported her husband. The way the attorney was speaking to her felt as if this were an issue. Tracey continued to be silent and allowed him to continue.

"He is facing 5-10 years in prison for this charge, and on top of that, he owes about fifteen-thousand dollars in child support which could carry another twelve months."

"Hold up Mr. Jenkins, what is going on? Why would I ever file child support against my own husband?"

Mr. Jenkins stared at Tracey's and realized at that moment she had absolutely no idea what was about to take place. He became concerned with his clients discrepancies and did not want to divulge any information his wife was not privy to. Mr. Jenkins tried to minimize the situation.

"Maybe we should wait for your husband to be transported in."

Tracey looked at the lawyer and was becoming irritated. She was not going to let him stop with sharing the details after she had been humiliated in the courtroom by the district attorney. It also bothered her that some strange woman was present and she had no idea what she had to do with the case.

"Hell no! Dammit, you are going to tell me what is going on right now! I have a right! You people called my house, disrupted my home, and then put my husband in jail for God knows what. Mr. whatever his name is said something about murder? Are you crazy! What is going on!

The lawyer tried to calm Tracey down. He was trying to figure out exactly what Tracey knew. He did not want to alarm her but he was aware that all of his dirty secrets were about to be aired in the courtroom. He felt sorry for Tracey because she had been totally detached from this court case. He questioned Tracey about the information her husband had shared with her.

"The only thing I know about is that a few years back before my daughter was born, he was in a dispute with some people, and got beaten to death. He told me he was drunk in public and the police arrested him. So sir, you tell me what is going on or I will assume you have the wrong Mrs. Collins."

"Ok, Mrs. Collins we have about an hour before your husband's case is called. Let me tell you what has transpired."

Mr. Jenkins gave Tracey an overview of the case. While he was sharing the details, Tracey became uncomfortable. Tracey had the urge to vomit, cry, scream, and call her mother all at once.

"Oh God, no…! What is going on this cannot be. When did all of this happen?"

"A few years back your husband was in a physical altercation with a woman named Justine Peebles…."

After Mr. Jenkins explained the story to Tracey, he escorted her back into the courtroom. In walked her husband in shackles with his face down. She looked over at the woman sitting behind the district attorney. The woman still had an eerie look when she stared at Tracey. Finally, it hit her… *Social Services!*

Tracey watched in the courtroom as her husband's lawyer tore Mrs. Peebles' integrity to pieces. Justine was a prostitute who had a crack habit. She was one of her husband's supposed customers. She would turn tricks and had other indiscretions, which assisted her in financing her habit. Once Justine did everything, he had asked they started having an illicit affair. Justine and Tracey's husband allegedly carried on for months when she found out that she was pregnant with his first child. She demanded he leave his current situation but he did not want to be tied down by another woman.

All Tracey heard in court was Justine say he would not leave his family. At this moment, she was convinced this woman had tricked her husband. She had never known her husband to sell drugs; he had never been arrested for any criminal activity. Tracey assumed this woman fabricated the entire story. Tracey ignored the testimony of how he battered her in the parking lot of Andrew's Grill while she was pregnant, and made her go into premature labor. The child and Justine lost a large amount of blood and lacked oxygen going to his brain, which caused the baby to be delivered with a birth defect. The doctors could not tell if it this was due to the crack habit, or the premature labor. They could not decide if the crack put her in premature labor. The defense claimed Justine had inflicted this on herself due to her promiscuous behavior.

When it was time for her husband to testify the story was very different. He claimed he was trying to calm Justine down and she just went into a rage. He stated she always went into a rage when she did not have access to the drug. He told the court, he never sold drugs or was ever caught selling them either. He claimed he met Justine through a mutual friend. Supposedly, their relationship was just sexual. He had not realized she was pregnant but promised to take care of the child when it was born.

Justine's testimony refuted his statement. She claimed he wanted her to have an abortion because he hated children. Tracey knew at that Justine was lying because of how much he loved Brystal.

He stated, Mrs. Peebles began hitting him and he was trying to defend himself. He said he had never hit a woman in his life. "You can ask my wife." He looked directly into Tracey's eyes.

The judge and jury stared at Tracey even though she was not on trial. She felt sorry for her husband. She knew he would never do anything intentionally to ruin their marriage. She began to think where she went wrong and how she could have been more of a supportive wife. Then maybe he would not have resorted to such activities.

"It was all happening so fast," he pleaded.

The next thing he knew they were in the hospital and Justine was in labor. He had panicked he did not want anything to ever hurt Justine or the baby. He claimed he was not able to think clearly, because Justine was having so much pain.

Justine could not believe the story he was feeding to the jury. She remembered vividly the details of the incident and they were not the same as his. Justine had cried out for help when her water had broken. This was after she received a blow to the face. She could hear the conversation play repeatedly in her head. *"What the hell you want me to do; I didn't want the little bastard in the first place."*

He was about to jump out the car but he recognized Cynthia's car. He saw Tracey with her and waited a few minutes to see when they would leave. When they pulled out of the parking lot, he moved Justine to the back seat and drove her to the hospital. The child stayed in intensive care for six months. He refused to acknowledge that the baby or Justine existed.

He never said a word of about the vivid details; instead, he continued to lie to the jury. He stated he would have been there if the police hadn't picked him up after speaking to Justine about why she had bruises all over her face. He explained to the jury that he had created a story that would throw Tracey off just enough for her not to question him, when he was released from jail. He admitted he did not want his wife to worry. He told the jury, they had been trying to have a baby since her first miscarriage and it was stressful and causing tension in his home.

"How could I go in my house and tell my wife another woman was pregnant with my seed. It would kill her, your honor. I love my wife. She has always been there for me and I couldn't let her down again." He began to cry and sobbed. "Tracey I love you…I am so sorry."

Tracey began to cry as she watched her husband be torn apart. She could not believe this Justine character was trying to cause so much confusion. She knew how hard her husband was working. She remembered the tension in her household after she had lost the first baby. Tracey did not realize it had been so stressful for him and wanted to run to his aid.

"Stop it!" Tracey stood up and screamed in the courtroom. "Stop harassing him. Can't you see she is trying to kill him! You crazy bitch you can't have my husband he doesn't want you!"

The judge shouted, "Order, Order in this courtroom!"

Justine was disgusted, crack head or not, she knew everything she stated on the stand, under oath was the absolute truth. Everything he uttered was a lie. At that point, Justine did not care because she knew she was not the fool who was going to deal with him now. She received money each month to support her habit. He knew Tracey was loyal and was not going to bother with other technicalities.

No matter how Tracey viewed this woman, one thing was for certain, the baby was his. He had a list of receipts he had kept which covered all of Justine's expenses. The judge reduced the charges to assault and battery. Apparently, Justine had pulled a knife on him on several occasions, but he did receive an assault charge. The judge condensed the amount of the receipts from the back owed child support which left Justine with an allotment of $478.62. Tracey did not even question where or how he had the money to pay almost fifteen thousand dollars within the last few years. He received a misdemeanor, and not allowed within one-hundred feet of Justine or their son. Tracey believed this was a perfect arrangement. *Let the bitch be gone.*

After his court issues ended, Tracey knew she was going to be in his good graces because she stood beside her man. Now it was more like standing behind her man. He did not get better he got worst. He began to go and come as he pleased just as he did before, but now he would disappear for days. Tracey did not mum a word. She realized after court she was pregnant with their second child, and she needed to concentrate on how they were going to survive. Brystal was older. The rent was increased to $875. He was not working nor was he trying to find a job. Her lively hood depended on what she was doing and how much she would work. The little money he did receive went to Justine and the baby. He made sure to stay away from the any court issues. She never asked how he was able to manage that. Tracey was still ignorant to his personal affairs. As long as he did not have to spend any time with either of them, he was free to do what he pleased. Tracey was not receiving a dime. Clearly, it was all on her shoulders because now he was free from all issues and ready to do his own thing. His own thing was exactly what he did while he disregarded his family.

****

Jo-Jo was Tracey's heart. She loved him so much. She remembered the day he was born. It was Thursday February 18, and it was raining. She was in the kitchen pacing the kitchen floor trying to figure out where he was. He had left earlier that morning claiming to follow up on a lead he had for some employment. She had waited all day at home, forty-one weeks pregnant, and in agony. She had uneasy back pains the night before and was not able to keep down any food.

She told him she wasn't feeling well but he ignored her, as he usually did. Tracey felt helpless because there was nothing she could really do or say. She was pregnant and about to pop. The doctor had for warned her of her hypertension prior to her first trimester because of her rapid weight gain. Tracey was also diagnosed as a diabetic while she was pregnant with Jo-Jo, and had to remain on bed rest for several weeks until her condition improved. She was at his mercy day and night.

Tracey's mother covered all of the household bills while she was out of work. Her sister Veronica came over frequently to help with Brystal from time to time. Veronica made sure Brystal got on the school bus daily. She attempted to prepare meals when it was needed. Veronica wasn't the best of cooks but she saw her sisters current situation and vowed to be their when she was needed or asked.

However, Veronica could not stand the sight of him. She didn't understand why Tracey dealt with this fiend, since first parade of incidents that had taken place in their relationship. Most of their conversations were disagreements concerning him.

"What is wrong with you Tracey? Are you a fool? I know momma taught you better than this. You don't have to take this abuse from any one."

"Shut up Veronica! You don't even know what is going on."

"I don't have to know what is going on; every time I come by he is not home. When I call you, you sound as if you have been crying. No, I don't see scars or bruises but they exist internally. You are being mentally battered and you just sit there and take it. What is wrong with you? What happened to you Tracey? Why are you not fighting back? Why do you let this man treat you this way?"

Veronica's questions were valid but not embraced by Tracey. Tracey felt she was doing what she was supposed to do as a loyal, loving, and devoted wife. She felt that she was doing right by her husband. Tracey would ignore her sister, and fight back the tears that were welling in the pits of her eyes.

That evening, Tracey paced the kitchen floor while Brystal was quietly asleep in her room. Suddenly, she felt a sharp pain starting from her back and ran directly into her pelvic area. She looked on the floor as she watched the water drizzle between her legs.

"Oh my God," said Tracey as she began to panic. Her water had just broken. *What am I going to do?* She picked up the phone to dial his cell for the seventieth time. Knowing he was not going to answer, she immediately called Veronica.

Ring, ring...

"Hello?"

"Roney!! Roney!! My water has broken can you come get me, Brystal is asleep, and he is not here."

Veronica looked at the clock and rolled her eyes. "Yea sis, I am on my way."

Tracey tried to make it up the steps to get Brystal together. Veronica showed up to Tracey's house within twenty minutes. Veronica ran in the house grabbed Brystal, and placed her in the back seat of the car. Tracey was stepping carefully because it was cold, and wet outside. All she could put on her feet were bedroom slippers.

"Come on missy before you catch a cold," said Veronica. She helped Tracey in the car and sped off to the hospital.

"You have to call him Veronica so he will know we are going to the hospital." Tracey cried in pain while Veronica was driving.

"Girl did you not call him before you called me?"

"Yes," Tracey cried.

"Then he doesn't care where you are going. Look, I don't mean to be cruel but my only concern is my niece who I had to drag out in this cold weather, and my unborn nephew. Now concentrate girl and don't have that baby on my leather seats."

Tracey wanted to laugh because she knew Veronica was dead serious about her leather seats, in her 2003 Acura. Veronica sped into the driveway of the emergency room and jumped out of the car to get the assistance of a nurse.

Out of the revolving doors came a male nurse.

"Ma'am I understand you are in labor. I need to get you in to our maternity ward." He appeared so gentle; she had not heard a man be that gentle in a long time.

"Ok," said Tracey, and climbed into the chair with the help of Veronica and the nurse. He wheeled her to maternity.

"I will take Brystal to Moms house and I will be right back."

"Call him Roney; let him know I am here."

Veronica smacked her lips and said in a condescending tone, "Of course I will Tracey."

Veronica did not intend to call him for any reason. As she drove to her mother's house, she thought about her sister's request. She picked up the phone and dialed his number. It went directly to voice mail. Therefore, she left him a message.

"Hey this is Veronica. I just took Tracey to the hospital, her water broke, and she is in labor. She is probably going to have the baby any minute and she is looking for you. Is it possible to grace us with you presence before he turns six months? Oh yea, by the way I am taking Brystal to momma's house and then I am going back to the hospital. Hopefully, we will see you there. Hopefully...!" She pushed the end button and shook her head. *My sister must be out of her mind!*

Back at the hospital Tracey, the nurse began checking how far she had dilated.

"Two centimeters, ma'am did you want medicine for the pain."

Tracey looked at the woman agitated, and said, "Do you want some medicine?"

"Ma'am there is no need to be nasty. I am just trying to help you get a little comfort."

Tracey knew this woman was not the cause of her pain. It was this eight-pound bundle of joy pressing on her pelvic area, trying to see the light of day. She could also not help but wonder where he was, and why was he not there.

"Ma'am someone is here to see you."

Tracey's heart jumped because she just knew Veronica had followed her orders, found him, and brought him back to the hospital. The door opened, in walked Veronica with the bag. Covered in disappointment Tracey dropped her head. Veronica noticed the dismay on her face and knew exactly what the look was.

"Hey girl you ain't popped that big head boy out yet. Ummm... he must be waiting on his favorite auntie." She tried to cheer up Tracey.

"His only auntie," laughed Tracey.

"Awe…is that a smile. They must be giving you some good drugs." They both laughed.

In walked the doctor to examine Tracey. He pressed his fingers on her pelvis. "Oh my little guy is ready to come. Are you ready ma'am?"

Tracey shook her head. "Yes I am."

The nurse was checking her blood pressure and showed the doctor the results.

"Ma'am your blood pressure is 140/139. Your body is in duress and you have dilated 3 centimeters. We are going to try to get your pressure down and once we do, we are going to have to perform and emergency C-section."

C-Section? "Why can't he be born the normal way?" Tracey started to panic.

"Ma'am I am going to need you not to worry, this happens often. Is your husband in the waiting room?" Tracey's head dropped.

"No he is not. He is working but he is trying to get here as soon as possible."

"I am here Doc what do you need me to do," interjected Veronica?

"I just need some paper work filled out, just a few consent forms. She is going to need a person in the room just to hold her hand. Looks like it is going to have to be you since you are here. The nurse will give you the forms and get her prepped for surgery. You are going to need to change into a sterile uniform, and the nurse will bring you to the operating room."

"Sis I am here right by your side, you, and my nephew are going to be just fine," said Veronica. Veronica kissed Tracey on the head and followed the nurse out of the room. Veronica immediately followed the doctor's orders, and after stood beside her sister, as she had promised.

3 hours later, Tracey was the proud mother of a nine pound and one ounce baby boy.

"He is absolutely adorable," said Veronica.

Jo-Jo was a busy body and ate as if it was his last meal.

"Sis, he looks just like you, he is an angel. The nurse said she would bring him to the room after she cleaned him up. You rest."

Before Tracey closed her eyes she mumbled, "Is he here."

"No baby he didn't come or call."

Tears filled Tracey eyes and she closed them in disgust. Her husband had disappointed her again.

Tracey was concerned with his appetite because she did not know whether she could produce enough milk to feed her hungry little bundle of joy. Most children nursed every two hours. Not Jo-Jo, if he could get it every hour he would cry for it. Every time she turned around, he was attacking one of her breasts.

"Girl... you better put some rice in that boy's milk."

"Veronica you are crazy," said Tracey. "He is only two weeks old."

"Honey please, he eats like he is two years old. Look at how fat he is. Look at aunties little fat Rasta...boogie, boogie..."

Veronica played with Jo-Jo. She was a proud auntie. Veronica loved Brystal and Jo-Jo. Jo-Jo just laughed and tried to eat her fingers.

"Girl, give that boy some cereal before he eats your nipple," Veronica laughed as she removed her fingers away from his mouth.

"Maybe your right," said Tracey.

Tracey had not been able to sleep through the night since Jo-Jo came home, not because he was a bad baby, but because he was a hungry baby. She was not use to his appetite. Brystal was premature and ate like a bird. Boy, how times have changed Tracey thought. Jo-Jo was loving, and loved by Tracey. Brystal had catered to her father since the day she was born. It was not that she hated Tracey, she was Daddy's little girl, his perfect angel.

"Veronica, go to the store and use my WIC checks. You should be able to get a few boxes of Gerber Rice."

"Now you are talking with some sense Tracey."

Just as Veronica was about to leave out of the house he was pulling up in the driveway. Veronica was still disgusted with him because he showed up to the hospital the day Tracey was being released. Four days he was gone and not to be heard from. When Tracey confronted him about his whereabouts he ignored her and said, "Where is my boy?"

Veronica wanted to slap the taste right off of his tongue. *This fool is out of his mind,* Veronica thought to herself. *Let me keep the peace my nephew needs to be fed and I am going to the store to take care of his needs. Forget grape ape with his fake, Imma grown ass man crap.* He passed Veronica and didn't mum a word.

"Hello to you too," Veronica said sarcastically.

"Why is she here?" He groaned at Tracey.

Why? Because she is my sister and she is helping me with our son. She wanted to say aloud, but was not in the mood for any confrontation.

"She is here because I asked her to be here. She is on her way to the store to get the baby some rice."

"I thought he had all he needed with them big ole saggy titties of yours." Tracey's mouth wanted to drop but she knew she was not going to have any emotions that would seep into her young baby boy.

"Ha, ha" he just laughed and grabbed a container from the refrigerator and proceeded to place it close to his mouth. He had picked up the wrong container and did not realize it until he tasted the watery substance. Tracey tried to stop him but he ignored her and continued to drink.

"Hey!" She screamed, as he spat out the liquid substance.

"Ugh what da...?"

"It is breast milk did you even bother to look at the container. That is the milk I pumped for Jo-Jo!"

"Yo...!! You need to keep this shit out the refrigerator that is nasty!"

"It is not for you! It is not for you to drink! Are you retarded? That is a day's worth of milk! Now I got to pump some more!"

He and Tracey began to go back and forth in an intense argument. Tracey did not usually argue with her husband but was territorial when it came to Jo-Jo and his needs.

"Who are you talking to you stupid….."

"I am talking to you, you lousy nigga."

"What?"

He went to throw up his hand; Tracey put the baby in the carrier, and grabbed the knife on the sink.

"Nigga…!! I wish you would lay one hand on me. I will cut you up into little pieces and spread you over a bed of pasta. You had better get out of here before you see red and I don't mean the color. I mean your blood!"

He looked at her and saw hell in her eyes. He was not about to start with a post-partum chick who could snap out at any given moment. He grabbed the keys and was about to walk out the door.

"Where do you think you are going?"

"Out, he screamed!"

"Nigga...! You do not have a car and if you get in mine, you will be calling your mammy for bond money. Try me today. Today is good day, go head and gamble. Just ask yourself, do you feel lucky!"

Oh, she done went Clint Eastwood up in this piece!

Tracey was defensive when it came to Jo-Jo and just to see the milk she pumped for the nourishment of her baby wasted, stirred a fire in her. He dropped the keys on the counter.

"You raggedy, bitch, I don't need you! Imma call my boys. I am about to bounce!"

Tracey said, "Well bounce nigga!"

She appeared to be more serious than she had ever been in her life. He walked out of the door and slammed it behind him. She placed the knife back on the counter, picked up her baby Jo-Jo, and began to sing him one of her favorite lullabies. She felt a release for the first time in a long time. She really didn't care where he went because she had all she needed.

Just then, Brystal walked down the steps. She was wiping her eyes and had woken up early from her nap. She saw her mother, and her baby brother, but she thought she had heard her father's voice.

"Mamma, where is daddy going?"

"Brystal…! Go back upstairs. I don't know where he is going and right now, I don't even care."

He stayed away for eight days and dragged himself back to the house reeking of alcohol and perfume. He had misplaced his keys, and so he began banging on the door.

"Tracey, Tracey, open the door I am sick."

She tried to ignore him but she knew he was going to wake up the neighborhood with the ruckus. She wasn't in any mood to deal with him tonight. She would have preferred that he stayed gone.

"Tracey, Tracey girl stop playing. Open the door."

Tracey got out of the bed to go answer the door before he woke up the baby and Brystal. She refused to let him in and made him talk through the door.

"What do you want?"

"I am trying to get in the house. I am sick and I don't feel well." Tracey had heard that lie so many times, she was well aware there was nothing sick about him. He was so desperate for her to in; he would have said anything to get Tracey to give into his request.

"Go to the hospital," she said sarcastically.

"Tracy please open the door, please baby please. Tracey I am sorry. You know how it is. I promise."

Tracey tried to ignore his cries and whimpering. She wanted him to go away. She was tired of her situation and wanted God to give her the strength to let him go. He had caused so much confusion and had been so disrespectful to her.

"Tracey don't do this to us, what about our family?"

Just then, Tracey felt helpless. *What about our family? He is my husband and I have to stick by him for better or for worse. He gets out of hand sometimes but he has so much to deal with.*

"Tracey, you know I love you."

At that moment, Tracey opened the door and let in the soiled man who reeked of alcohol and the streets. God only knows where he had been and what he had been doing. Did it really matter he was home now.

****

Four years had passed and Tracey had reached her highest weight, two hundred and twenty-five pounds. She had endured trials and tribulations she wouldn't have wished on her enemy. Her marriage was getting worse, but not bad enough for her to give up. She believed in her vows for better for worse and she carried the worse with her 24/7. He stayed in the streets when he wanted. During the day, he had different people in and out of Tracey's house. Ka-jon and all types of characters would lounge on the couch day in and day out.

Tracy walked in the house after pulling a twelve-hour shift. She prepared herself for her part-time job. She had become a medical transcriber. The convenience of this job was that she was able to work from home.

He and his friends had devoured all of the groceries Tracey had purchased the day before. All of the kid's snacks, potato chips, little Debbie cakes, peanuts, the microwave popcorn and the Rice Krispy treats were gone. Tracey was furious she wanted to snap but didn't have the energy. She did not have hot dogs or corn dogs to make the kids dinner. She was going to have to defrost a meat and cook them a meal.

"Hey Tracey, get your fat ass in here and bring me and my boys a couple of beers."

He was yelling at her from the living room. Tracey wanted to cry but she couldn't. This is what her life had come to. She heard giggles and taunts from her living room. Just then, Brystal walked down the steps in just a T-shirt. Tracey was walking in the living room while Brystal was parading around. The men were laughing and giggling while they watched the young girl sashay in front of them. Her father didn't say a word. Tracey could not believe her eyes. She knew she had never neglected to teach her children manners and discretion.

"Brystal, do you not see your dad's friends are here! Go upstairs and put some pants on, now!"

"I don't want to Tracey, you put some pants on!"

The men continued to laugh. He just looked at Tracey and giggled. He couldn't believe Tracey couldn't handle her own child. He refused to correct Brystal because she was his baby girl.

"What are you worried about ain't nobody looking at her. I thought I told you to get us some beers."

Tracey did not respond and went in the kitchen refrigerator and grabbed four beers. She placed them on the table and snatched Brystal up on the way out.

Brystal screamed, "Daddy!"

Tracey turned around and slapped Brystal in the face. "Shut up! Shut up! Shut up right now!" Tracey screamed in Brystal's face. She wanted to scream at her husband and his low life friends.

The house was dead silent. He was about to stand up, but was so shocked he didn't make a move. Brystal held her face and was about to cry. By that time, Tracey had scooted her up the steps, and back to her room.

"If you come out of this room I will break your neck!" Tracey forgot about the chicken she pulled out to defrost, went into her room, and slammed the door. She sat on the edge of her bed and cried until she had fallen asleep.

The next day Tracey felt horrible and called her mother to come pick up Jo-Jo and Brystal. She needed to go to the emergency room. Tracey was extremely nauseated, and had been vomiting all night. She was light headed, and just wanted to die. She could not afford to have the flu. Having the flu would surely put her out of work, which she could not afford. She was not on salary and had no sick days left.

"Well Mrs. Collins you do have the flu. However, it will last for about nine months… you're pregnant."

The doctor had made a joke. Tracey didn't find any humor in what he had just stated. She was not thrilled about being pregnant as she was with her other pregnancies.

"What?" Tracey wanted to scream. I cannot be pregnant. I don't want to be pregnant!"

In an instant, Tracey drifted off into the land of the unknown. Tracey was transported to the fifth floor of the hospital where she stayed for three weeks. The doctor said she was on the verge of having a nervous breakdown. She was also suffering from dehydration and exhaustion. The doctor and her mother agreed that Tracey would need to get some rest before she became a danger to herself and possibly her children.

Tracey was dopey for the first week until her body became use to the medication. She stayed in the hospital while they monitored her and the baby. The doctor prescribed small dosages since she was in the first trimester. Veronica and her mother both took turns getting the kids. Her husband did not assist her family or her. He was not available to care for their children. It was as if it didn't even matter that Tracey was in the hospital.

He lived life to the fullest, he had access to her car, and he spent every dime that she had hidden in secret spots, in their home. He drank daily, and had different women in and out of the house. He nursed both of his habits; cocaine and alcohol, and didn't have a care in the world. He was disgusted to hear that Tracey was pregnant again.

He hated the sight of children and didn't particularly care if Tracey carried this baby to term. He had vivid dreams she would miscarry just as she did when they lost their first baby. He was hoping he could knock her down a flight of steps just as he did before. This time he wanted her to know it was him, and not think she had slipped and fell by accident.

Tracey returned home on Wednesday afternoon to find her home destroyed. She had taken the city bus because she refused to call anyone to pick her up. The carpet had stains, and there were beer bottles everywhere. The house reeked of death. The paint was chipping and there was hole in the living room wall. *What had happened to my house?* Tracey was only in the hospital for three weeks and now her home resembled a broke down brothel and crack house. Tracey stopped in her tracks and broke down on the floor.

"Why God?" asked Tracey as she cried, Why?"

There was a knock at the door. Tracey answered the knock. It was Ka-jon. She did not want to see him or any of her husband's friends. Ka-jon looked at Tracey. He noticed she seemed a bit distant but didn't want to bother her.

"Yo, Tracey is he here?"

She did not know because she was still stuck in the living room in shock. Ka-jon noticed she had been crying and began to become sympathetic.

"Yo ma, don't cry."

"Why not, it doesn't even matter. Look at what he has done. No better yet, look at what I have done. Look at my house, this is the thing I said I would never let happen. I was not going to destroy the home I worked so hard for."

For years, Tracey was very critical about people that moved into Section 8 homes and ruined them. Tracey would say, *black people never took care of anything and that is why they couldn't be successful.* Now she was eating her own words. It did not matter that she was no longer on

Section 8 it was still here home. Ka-jon felt extremely guilty because he was a part of the fiascos, which took place in her home.

"Look you gotta do whacha gotta do. If a nigga ain't treatin you right then you gotta do whats good for you and yours." Just then, his cell phone rang.

"Yo…"

Ka-jon moved to a different area of the house and took the phone call. Tracey knew whom he was talking too immediately. Ka-jon got off the phone.

"Yo ma, I am bout to bounce."

"Ka-jon…?"

"Yea ma," he answered.

"Where is he?"

Ka-jon sighed, "He at da spot. Look ain't trying to get in your business but maybe you need to see for yourself." Ka-jon gave Tracey the address to where her husband was. Ka-jon had three sisters and he could not fathom any of them putting up with what Tracey endured. He knew he would kill a man that treated his sister the way his homeboy did.

"How am I going to get there, he has my car."

"Take my ride."

Tracey hopped in the car and went to the address where Ka-jon said he was. When she pulled up to the house, she could not believe her eyes. It was a rundown shack. *Who the heck, would come here?* She got out of the car and went to the door. She hesitated, but she knocked any way. He answered the door in shock. He was standing there in his boxers. The door was opened wide enough for her to notice a very thin white girl in the middle of about five black dudes, propped on her knees. Tracey was stunned. She knew the sight before her eyes was a complete abomination.

"Whacha you doin here?"

"I am here, looking for you. I want to know why you are here."

"Look I am trickin this girl out to my boys for a couple of dollars. We need money in the house and since you decided to take a vacation we ain't got a damn thing to eat in there. Yo, mom's got the kids cuz she know I am trying to do the best I can do with what I got to work with. So go on home I will be there in a little while. The house is a mess you need to start cleaning it up. I will holla at you later."

Tracey was appalled at his story. She knew he was telling a bold face lie. He hadn't seen the kids since she was admitted to the hospital. He had business to attend to and didn't have time for Tracey's antics. He looked her square in the eye and brushed her off. Tracey stood in silence while he went back into the house and closed the door in her face.

Tracey went home and cleaned the house as her husband had told her to. She was at the end of her first trimester and she knew this was going to be another long pregnancy. *When I have this baby, I am going to burn my tubes.*

****

Six months later, little Janine arrived. She was a fussy baby. Tracey assumed Janine did not cooperate because this was the most stressful pregnancy she had ever experienced. This time he told her he was not coming to the hospital to watch another baby come into the world. He stated he had enough with the kids.

"Make sure you burn those mother f***in tubes before you come back home."

That is exactly what Tracey did. She had her tubes burned. *Before he impregnates me, again it had better be an act of God.*

Janine cried day in and day out. Tracey did not know what to do with her. The child was so fussy and Tracey felt helpless. Her mother and sister did the best they could by helping her out, but Janine just was not compromising. During Tracey's first post-partum check-up, she explained to the doctor she was losing her patience with Janine, and felt as if she could hurt her child. Luckily, her mother decided she would take Janine for a while just until Tracey adjusted.

Janine became attached to her grandmother. She was closer to her grandmother than she was to anyone else. Tracey's mother was able to be soothing to Janine. When Janine had to stay with her parents, she became nervous and shaky. This lasted for years until it turned into bed-wetting. Janine had an accident every day after she was potty trained at the age of three. Tracey refused to keep her in diapers because she was embarrassed. Tracey's mother tried to explain to her, that in order to correct the problem she would need to recognize first, that it was a problem. Tracey did not want to hear anything her mother had to say about how to raise her children.

"Ma look I got this. Janine is going to be fine. Let me just deal with it."

Her mother refused to argue about the matters of how she was living her life. Her mother knew the only way for her daughter to change her circumstances was to surrender all of her earthly hell to God. She just knew she would have to do it in her own time.

Tracey embraced her earthly hell and decided that she was going to make the best of what God gave her. The children became a stress but the only reason she would live.

His women were no longer a secret, but friends who came to her house and laughed in her face. She loved her husband and she decided she would stand by him no matter what the cost.

"He is mine, I am his, and that's all to be said."

****

Tracey's reality hit, it was Monday morning, and she had to be at work by 9 am. She had no baby sitter for Janine and she had to put Jo-Jo on the bus with-in the next thirty minutes. *What am I going to do?*

Tracey pondered. She had just mentally relived the horrors of her reality. When she stopped reminiscing, she realized she still had to move forward. At this moment, there was nothing Tracey was willing to do.

I gotta to go to work today. I called in twice already this past month for some uncontrollable nonsense. Brystal had already left with her daddy and Kajon so she had no other options. Tracey mulled over her options and could not think of any resolution. Calling into work could have ramifications she was not willing to be accountable for, at this moment. Tracey had just called into work two weeks ago because he had taken her car while she was sleep and had not returned for two days. Luckily, her neighbor was willing to drop her off and get Jo-Jo to his destination. She also kept Janine while Tracey went to work. Janine was having fits and could not be taken to daycare. Her neighbor didn't ask her what the circumstances were she just agreed to help her in her time of need. The other incident included memories she just assumed she blocked out. She just remembered standing in front of the Super 8 befuddled after she had received a call from her friend Gina who worked at the front desk. Tracey knew she had to get to work, someway, somehow.

After last night catching him having sex in the living room with his so called home girl while they were all asleep, she knew there was nothing she could do. She knew she had accepted this mental torture. She knew this was the only man who would every love her. She believed she was now used goods. Therefore, Tracey realized she could no longer focus on the horrors of yesterday she could only pray for small moments of peace. Tracey thought; *when it is good, it is good; when it is bad, it is good.* Therefore, she called the only person she knew who could help her out on a short notice. She was dreading the call. What else was she going to do? She picked up the phone to dial the familiar numbers.

The phone rang twice and she heard the voice on the other end.
"Hello…"
"Momma…?"

"Yes," the voice on the other end replied.

It was Tracey's mother. The only support she had. Her mother was her resolution. Tracey hesitated for a second before she went into her request.

"Um Mom, is it possible…"

"Yes Tracey, bring them over." Tracey's mother had bailed her out of the unnecessary drama that polluted her life time, and time again. She was always going to help Tracey when she called her in her time of need. Her mother felt a bit responsible for Tracey's self-destruction, but could not share her deep dark secrets because they would probably tear her apart even more. These were her grandchildren and no matter what Tracey allowed in her life, she did not believe her grandchildren should endure the ugly of their mother's mishaps. Besides, he was Tracey's excuse, not her childrens.

PART II

Where was I?

Diana
"Isolated?"

Where was I?

Where was I when the sun beamed on your face for the very first time?
I was holding you in my arms

Where was I when your cry was as recognizable as my favorite song?
I was standing over you massaging your belly hoping your pain would
subside

Where was I when your first word began with a, M?
I was embracing your childhood with a sense of pride

Where was I when you wanted to comprehend the abstracts of this world?
I was holding the bible teaching you Gods principles

Where was I when your cares were pieces of a new imagination that you
were about to disperse in the universe?
I was their trying to make sure your dreams came true

Where was I when you got in trouble?
I was there disciplining you, and explaining the rights and wrongs

See I was there, I was there
And in the midst of knowing

In the midst of trying to keep the world safe for you
I overlooked a hurt that a mother should never imagine

In the midst of trying to keep the world safe for you
I let the troubles of my day blind my vision

In the midst of trying to keep the world safe for you
I let unnecessary mental duress wear me thin

Walston

In the midst of trying to keep the world safe for you
I let you down

And in the midst of trying to keep you safe in this world
I need you to know that I am sorry

It is my duty and honor to keep principles and morals sustained in our life
And if it had not been for the grace and mercy of God

I would never be able to express without shame

That we as parents are not living in the life of perfection

But we should be in the mind state of protecting the lives that create

We should be aware and be able to let our children know
That in all of our storms God will be present

Cry every tear that has cause inadequacies in your life

But hold onto God
Because we as parents sometimes fail

But when we give our children back
to the living God
that has given them life

Then it is God
who will guide us in our journey of parenting

Diana

Diana was a mother. She did what she needed to do with what she had. She thought working hard, and staying focused would lead her children on the paths where they could become more successful than she would. This was not a day of joy, this was a moment filled with sorrow. She never imagined she would ever have to witness this unimaginable sight. Yes, she was disappointed often in her life, but never had a disappointment, which caused her to crumble into a mere nothing.

"What can I do Lord?" Diana said. "What can I do to remove this nightmare? I have never asked for much and I have accepted everything you have laid in my path, but God I cannot do this. I will not do this."

Something in her spirit would not allow her to scream or spew out bitter hatred. Something in her spirit seemed distinctly calm. Diana had not realized God had interceded on her moment of break. People gathered around her waiting for her to lose her sanity. There were even hands on her shoulders telling her how she should feel.

"Diana, it will be ok."

She wanted to tell them where they could go but her tongue was numb. A young man in a black suit moved through the crowd. He grabbed her hand.

"Sister I am sorry but it is time."

At that moment, the realization hit Diana and the tears set still in the wells of her eyes. She became overwhelmed with sorrow. She did not want to move or accept the trial she was enduring.

"Sister, we have to go."

Diana's feet would not move. Moments of her life began to flash before her eyes. She stared at the woman wanting, longing to kiss her. She wanted to hear her voice. The woman made no movement and couldn't say a word. She had a look of peace, but this did not settle Diana's soul. Diana wanted an explanation. She wanted to understand why. *It cannot end like this.*

As the people began to exit, Diana's refusal to leave alarmed Barbara, Bernard, and Bernice. Her children were always present when she needed them. She depended on them as they had depended on her throughout the years. She knew each of them had their own lives now, but this was the moment she needed them the most.

"Mom, it is time to go," they said in unison.

"Momma...?"

Diana began to turn around and her knees buckled. Before she hit the floor Bernard ran to her rescue and caught her in mid-fall. Bernard was her only son. He was the only man in her life she could depend on. Even though he lived out of state Diana found comfort in him just being with her now.

Bernard said, "Yawl, get a chair."

Diana's eyes were closed and her face began to get puffy and swell. Her lips began to tremble, and the tears began to bulge under closed eyes waiting to be released. Diana would not let the tears fall. Her body began to ache in agony. She wanted to close her eyes and wake up to a new veracity. The pain of this reality had been so brutal; she wanted to curse its very existence.

"Momma what do you want us to do?"

The man in the black suit motioned the children from around the torn woman. Her children did not want to leave her side but knew she needed some space. Their mother was devastated. They could not bear her hurt but hoped they could to ease some of her pain.

"Give her some space. Sister, maybe you need a little more time. I will give you a few more moments."

He understood it was unthinkable. She could not move and just forget everything in her life. She began to ponder on the yesterdays. She closed her eyes anticipating that her tears would dissipate. She thought back to the beginning of her childhood which was non-existent after her fifteenth birthday......

****

"Girl you done gone and got yourself knocked up! What were you thinking! We ain't got no more room in this house to feed another child. What are we going to do? I tell you what. I am going to call Ms. Percy."

The woman was not happy about her child's situation. She wanted to find a quick fix to her daughter's problem. Ms. Percy was the voodoo doctor of the neighborhood who knew how to fix young girls who got themselves in bad predicaments. The woman talked to herself as she paced the floor in a panic. She knew that her daughter being pregnant may have caused shame to her family. Having a fifteen year old who was pregnant would have caused unnecessary talk in her community.

"Ok, ok, I will wash a few more loads for Mrs. Landers and that should be enough for a down payment. I could just ask her for an advance. No, No then she would find out. Lord have mercy!"

"Momma, please," Diana said. "Momma I am keeping my baby."

The woman ignored the Diana and continued to talk to herself. She was not focusing on her daughter's at all. She wanted to do what she thought was best for her daughter and her household.

"Ms. Percy will take care of this."

"Momma…!! I am keeping this baby. Ms. Percy ain't chopping me up on some table in her living room."

Diana knew Ms. Percy's craft lacked safety. She had heard the horror stories of young women who visited Ms. Percy because of their mishaps. Once a woman visited Ms. Percy they may never be able to bare children again, and Diana was not willing to take that chance.

"I will get a job; I just won't go to school. I will get my learning on my own. I will take care of this baby, and you won't have to do anything. If I can't stay here, I will fend for me and dis baby. But you can't make me momma. I won't kill my baby!"

The woman looked at her daughter and realized at that moment there was nothing else to say. Her daughter had made up her mind and was not going to change it for any reason. Diana didn't expect any handouts from her mother or anyone else. She knew her situation and was willing to endure any strife that came. Her mother did not agree with her decision. She knew trying to force her to take an alternative route may cause worse ramifications. She loved her daughter and respected her choice.

"If you feel that way, then you will take care of this baby."

Her mother had made up in her mind that she was going to let her daughter bear all the grief that came with her unborn child. She knew her daughter was going to experience some heartache. She never wanted her child to go through such a painful experience but she was willing to allow her to decide her own fate.

"I ain't no baby sitter. You will feed dis child yourself. You will work with me at Mrs. Lander's house until you get too big to work. But I ain't, taking care of no baby. You got yourself in this mess and you are going to do what needs to be done, since it is you that has this problem. I will do what I can".

Diana did exactly what her mother said. She worked at Mrs. Lander's house until she was too big to move. She began to do odd jobs such as sowing, and ironing, for the remainder of her pregnancy. She was able to bring home two dollars a week. She knew this would at least bring food in the house for her and the baby. In spite of her mother's personal feelings, she knew she was going to do whatever she needed to help her daughter. She added additional duties to her already stressful workload.

Diana's father built the house she and her mother lived in. The white folk in the neighborhood thought he was an uppity nigga cause he had more than the average black man did during those times. He had migrated down south where he had met Diana's mother. He had made a little money while he served in the military. Once he finished his duties, he moved down south and took over a piece of land his great-grandfather had inherited from his slave owner. It was unusual for blacks to have any status in those times but Diana's father was smart. He knew how to talk to the white folks to keep them focused on matters, which didn't concern him. He utilized the resources he had on the land he occupied. He grew collard greens and tobacco. His farm was not as large as other farms but just enough to generate income in their home. He didn't feel the need to be in competition with other farmers because he knew at some point it could cause a conflict. His goal was just to supply the needs of his family. So they were conservative. They didn't speak much or interfere with matters which didn't concern them. This didn't mean white folks didn't try to cause confusion. Her father just would not buy into the confusion. He remained meek and humble. He encouraged his vocal wife to do the same.

He would say, "Honey we don't need any attention drawn to us so sometimes it is ok to keep quiet."

Diana's mother was from the south and was always bitter because of how white folks treated black people. However, because her husband was modest, she listened to him. She didn't have issues with all white people just those who tried to belittle her. She had support in her husband and some of the people around her. She didn't have any family because they had all migrated up north. They didn't visit or return to the south once they had left. Watching her husband and his sacrifices for his family, she learned some valuable lessons when dealing with people.

They were a Christian family who believed in God. They went to church every Sunday and attended church events throughout the week. God was their foundation and they trusted in his word. Diana's father was a noble man. He helped those in his community whether they were black or white. When he migrated south, he worked with the Landers family who welcomed him with open arms. He did odd jobs for Mr. Landers. Mr. Landers taught him his business, and how to manage his own affairs. Mr. & Mrs. Landers always held him in high regard. They never treated him as if he were beneath them. They respected him and loved his family. They loved him because he treated them fairly and was always willing to assist them in whatever they did.

He worked diligently until fell sick with pneumonia. Times had gotten difficult and Diana's mother became the sole provider. The house was already paid for, the land belonged to him, and the bills were very manageable. The Landers helped her as much as she would allow. Diana's mother was careful not to take to many handouts because of her pride. That winter Diana's father died, and her mother shut out the world. He was the love of her life.

Diana was the only child she was able to conceive and carry to full term. She had been pregnant at least five times and each time for whatever reason, she miscarried. Diana's mothers gave birth to her the summer of 1926. Due to her labor being problematic she nearly died. Diana's father was not willing to see his wife suffer again. She loved her husband because he always held her in high regard. He was sweet, gentle, and treated her in a manner in which a woman should be treated. He was the only man Diana's mother knew. No other man could or would ever get her attention.

****

"Momma…!" Diana screamed.

"Push girl. Stop all that screaming. This baby can't come into this world with all that wailing."

Diana bit her lip until it began to bleed. She felt as if she had been constipated and just needed to release. The birthing experience seemed unbearable. Diana had never felt so much pain in her life.

"Push gal, push."

Miss Johnson was a mid-wife and was assisting Diana with her delivery. She had delivered most of the babies in the small town. Diana's mother trusted her with her daughter. Diana's mother was holding her hand during the entire delivery. She knew her child was frightened and she was determined to see her through.

"Yep I see da head. Come on child two more pushes."

"AAARRRGGGHHH!!!!"

Diana pushed for the last time and out came a beautiful baby girl. Diana's mother was proud of her. Diana was relieved that the pain was over. The baby was beautiful. Her features were intriguing. She weighed nine pounds; was fair skinned, had a head full of hair, and her eyes were grey.

"You did it child, you did it. What you going to call her, child?"

"I am going to call her Barbara-Jean. I will call her Barbara for short."

Diana was ecstatic and proud she had survived the delivery of her first-born. Diana's momma was also happy. Barbara-Jean was happy baby. She didn't cry or fuss. She ate, when it was time to eat. She slept, when it was time to sleep. She played, when it was time to play. Barbara was delightful and a joy to the household.

Diana was able to go back to school in the fall just so she could take her reading and math classes. She was uninterested in school. She just wanted to be home with her baby. She loved being a mother, even if she was sixteen. She didn't have brothers or sisters and at times the house was lonely when it was just her and her mother. Her mother didn't talk to her much about anything but she stayed focused on Barbara. Barbara was spoiled rotten. It was as if her mother had taken over the responsibilities. *I ain't gonna be nobody's baby sitter.* Her mother had contradicted herself. Diana no longer felt like Barbara belonged to her. She felt like she had to share. She had a bit of resentment for her mother because she treated Barbara and Diana as if they were sisters.

****

It was almost summer and Barbara was about to turn sixteen months. Diana had just found out she had passed all of her classes with satisfactory grades. While she was walking home from school, she felt a sharp pain in her pelvic area. A pain she had never experienced. *I just got to make it home, and just lay down.* She could see the glimpse of her house from the street. Before Diana could take another step, she closed eyes.

When Diana came to, a strange man was standing over her. She didn't know where she was or how she had gotten there. She figured she was in a hospital room because of the décor and smell.

"Diana?"

Diana's eyes fluttered as she regained consciousness. She saw her mother in her peripheral. She smiled and thought of her baby girl.

"Where am I?"

"Ms. Green you're in a hospital. The neighbor found you on the street, passed out, and called the ambulance."

"What happened?" Diana said. "Where is Barbara-Jean?"

"She is at Ms. Johnson house. You just lay back child and listen to the doctor," her mother interjected.

"What's wrong with me?"

"Well, Ms. Green you are severally dehydrated and you are slightly anemic and…" the doctor paused.

"And what sir," Diana asked?

"Well Ms. Green you are pregnant, about sixteen weeks." Diana did not budge.

"Ok Doctor, what do I need to do to get better?"

The doctor was amazed that her, nor her mother seemed to have any issues with the current diagnoses. He thought it was odd that the young woman did not become frantic about her diagnosis.

"Ms. Green, my chart indicates that you are sixteen years old."

Her mother interjected. "Why does that matter? What does she need to do? We can't have her passing out, it may hurt the baby."

"Yes doctor, what do I need to do to keep my baby healthy?" Diana smiled.

Bernice was born December 31st, right after the Christmas holiday. Bernard was born November 2nd, of the next year. Beatrice was born a year and a half later after Bernard. By the time, Diana turned twenty-one she had four children, a high-school diploma, and had started taking some classes at the local university. She was happy, satisfied with her children, and the outcome of her life.

****

Diana's mother began working as Mrs. Lander's nurse. Mrs. Lander's husband had died and left her with a wonderful inheritance. All of Mrs. Lander's children moved away and went abroad. She had grandchildren who she only saw during the holidays. Mrs. Green had grandchildren and a daughter she could go home to daily. Mrs. Landers envied Mrs. Green. She yearned to have the love she felt daily from a family. It was all but a mere memory. Nevertheless, she felt joy every time Mrs. Green showed up.

Mrs. Landers made sure she helped Mrs. Green and her family as much as she could. Mrs. Green never worried about food or clothes for her grandbabies because Mrs. Landers made sure they had everything they needed.

"How are those grandbabies of yours?" Mrs. Landers asked.

"Oh they are just fine and they getting big too. Diana is doing well she done got her a nice ole job at the university. She is a secretary. You know she was able to take some college courses and learn how to do some typing and filing. She and the children are doing just fine. You know... for her to be a single mother."

Mrs. Landers sighed, "That is real good. You must be so proud she is with you and taking care of her children. Imma old woman in this great big house and I am all by myself. You got a daughter and four grandbabies. I know it is getting cramped over there at your place.

"We manage," said Mrs. Green. "God has just been so good to us we have never wanted for nothing. You should know that. You have been an angel to my family and me. I thank God you are in our life."

"Please, it is the least I can do. But yes, he has been good, and I am more than happy to do the little I do."

Mrs. Landers knew how loyal Diana's mother was to her family. She had vowed to her husband to make sure the Greens had everything they needed. Mrs. Landers wanted to do more, but she did not want to overstep her boundaries.

"Well you know at some point Diana is going to need a place when she is ready? You know, to move closer to town so she can get to and fro work a little easier. The kids will start school soon."

"Yea you probably right. I am not ready for them to leave yet. Barbara done started school already and Bernice isn't far behind."

"Barbara, that girl is as smart as a whip. Them children is sumthin else."

She says grandma, have you ever noticed when it rains and the sun comes out, you can see all the colors beaming in the sky?

"I tell em chile dats a rainbow you see. That's God letting us know he has stopped crying and is smiling again."

She says, grandma why God crying?

"I say, cause he washing all the ugly and hate out of this world"

She says, grandma his eyes going to dry out cause he gonna have to cry every day.

"I laugh cause she is telling the truth. I tell her there are some hateful things in this world but as long as there is a God above, we will be fine. She just sits with a puzzled look on her face."

Ok Granma. But shouldn't we at least get God some tissues cuz there is going to be too much water. If it don't dry up it will be all in the streets and grass.

"She is something else. They all are."

Mrs. Landers and Mrs. Green laughed.

Mrs. Landers loved Mrs. Green and her family. Mrs. Green and Diana helped with her family businesses and never complained. They interacted often and made Mrs. Landers comfortable so she would never have to feel lonely. They were her family, the only family she had close to her.

****

That winter Mrs. Landers was growing tired, weaker, and needed more assistance from Mrs. Green and her family. Mrs. Lander's took ill and then a turn for the worse. Diana's momma was with Mrs. Landers day and night. Finally, Mrs. Landers decided it was no need to fight with God anymore. She decided it was her time to go home and be with the Lord. Go home, she did.

Mrs. Landers died in the comfort of her best friends arms. She was tired and her last wish was to see the faces of her grandchildren. Her children were so preoccupied with their big polished lives they did not make an attempt. Mrs. Green, Diana, and the kids were there with her so Mrs. Green was able to honor a portion of her dying wish.

On the day of funeral, Mrs. Lander's children decided they would make an appearance. Her death appeared to be an inconvenience. They were too focused on their lives to even care that their mother, the woman who had given birth to them, would no longer have a physical presence. They were more concerned with the assets she had left behind. Before she was warm in the ground the children began to argue about the property, their father and mother owned. Mrs. Green interrupted abruptly. It was still not the time for a black woman to be outspoken, but Mrs. Green was Mrs. Lander's friend. Her only friend and she would not allow them to disrespect their mother or her home going service. Mrs. Green knew Mrs. Landers' children were ungrateful and unruly. She had been around them and cared for them when they were young. She really did not care if she was their mother because she was Mrs. Landers' best friend, her only true friend.

"I will be dog gone if I allow you heathens to speak about a woman who is not even warm in the ground. Now you hush up and show some respect you ingrates."

The children paused and could not believe the hired help was speaking out of turn. They did not hold the same regard for Mrs. Green as their mother and father had. They saw her as colored woman who was employed by their parents.

Mrs. Landers' oldest son was a racist. He did not learn his prejudices from his parents. His arrogance was always intolerable for Mrs. Landers. She could never understand why Larry was so cold and calculating. His fathers never stood for his ugly acts, and would discipline him often for his mistreatment of people. Especially his behavior when he was around the Greens. He had always detested the Greens. He did not like the way his parents treated them as family. He believed colored people had a place and were not to be befriended by anyone but their own kind.

Larry Jr. replied, "I can't believe you all are going to let this nigger woman speak to us like this."

The guests were in shock at Larry's outburst. He did not care if he was a making a spectacle of himself. Mrs. Green was about to correct Larry for his brash remarks, but Diana had heard his comment, and interjected before her mother could speak.

"Call her whatever you want but she is right. You had no respect for your mother dead or alive. I will not let you stand here and disrespect mine. You have lost your mind."

The crowd was now focused on the commotion. The pastor walked over to see what the issues were. He knew Larry was belligerent and was not going to stand for his outlandish behavior during Mrs. Landers' funeral.

"Now, now, I need some order."

The pastor knew how important Mrs. Green was to Mrs. Landers. He was aware that she would have forbid Larry to conduct himself in this manner. The pastor refused to let Larry speak so harshly to Mrs. Green.

"This was your mothers best friend and we don't carry on like this in the house of the Lord. So take your seat boy before a quick sound of lightning comes through and knocks you on your hind parts."

Diana chuckled. With a look of disdain, Mrs. Lander's kids found themselves at a disadvantage. People who actually cared for Mrs. Landers outnumbered them. People who stood by Mrs. Landers side, until she closed her eyes. That number included Mrs. Green, Diana, and Diana's children.

The Monday after the funeral, Mrs. Green received a call from Mrs. Lander's attorney, Mr. Turner. He explained she and Diana needed to be present for the reading of Mrs. Landers', Will. Mrs. Green was in complete shock because she knew she had been faithful to Mrs. Landers for years but she never thought twice about Mr. & Mrs. Lander's estate.

When Diana and her mother arrived at Mrs. Landers house, her children were already present. Mr. Turner instructed all parties to meet in the family room. Larry Jr. was in shock.

"What the, uh ….Why are they here!"

Diana and her mother did not make a sound. Larry remained standing demanding an answer. Larry's reaction did not disturb anyone present in the room. Mr. Turner interjected.

"Can we please come to order? By the way Larry, your father and mother wanted them here for your information."

Larry seemed shocked and fidgety. His face had turned beet red and he wanted to scream out obscenities. He was disgusted to see Diana was also present. Mrs. Lander's other two children refused to make any statements. Even though they did not visit their mother often, they were not as disrespectful as Larry. They were embarrassed by their brother's actions. The lawyer ignored Larry's discomfort and proceeded to explain the reason for the gathering.

"We are here for the reading of the late Mrs. Landers, Will. I will begin by reading this information aloud. After I am done, I will answer any and all questions."

I Elizabeth Landers of sound mind and body do disperse my estate as follows:

- *To my oldest son Larry Jr., I leave you, your father's 1940 Convertible, and the sum of fifteen thousand dollars.*

- *To my son Alfred, I leave my collection of books, which you so loved to read when you were a young lad, along with the sum of fifteen thousand dollars.*

- *To my daughter Katherine I leave my entire collection of custom-made hats, dress collection, and the sum of fifteen thousand dollars.*

- *To my grandchildren Timothy, Beth-Ann, Laura Elizabeth, William, and Joanne, trusts have been made in each of your names not to be dispersed until you have satisfied all of the terms outlined in this Will.*

Mrs. Landers' children looked puzzled. Mr. Turner had only explained a third of their mother's estate.

"Ok this must be a joke, what did the old lady do, leave the rest of our fathers inheritance, to some nonprofit mumble jumble," said Larry.

Mr. Turner said, "Please be quiet I have not finished the rest of the terms."

- *To the First Baptist Bethany Church I leave a sum of Five thousand dollars.*
- *Ten thousand dollars will be given to the Homeless & Keep us Safe Shelter*

Finally, for the rest of my estate:

- *To my very dear and only friend, Mrs. Green, I leave the sum of fifty thousand dollars.*
- *I leave my home and all the preserved land to Ms. Diana Green. Diana will also receive a sum of fifty thousand dollars. Ms. Diana Green and her children are also the sole owners of our bakery and fabric store.*

Ms. Green and Diana are both responsible for making sure each of the grandchildren, (Barbara, Bernice, Bernard and Beatrice) receives an equal share in the equity of the businesses to assist them with their college tuition and other financial obligations. Each child will receive a sum of ten-thousand dollars.
Conditions of the terms:
Ms. Diana's will receive fifty thousand dollars after the completion of her college education that will be paid and distributed by my attorney.
Mr. Turner, Diana must complete a four-year degree in order to receive all gifts outlined in this Will. In order for her children to receive any equity in the property, or monetary gifts they must first complete their college education at a four-year University.

All final monies will be used to pay any outstanding debt obligations, (lawyer's fee, contracts, etc…) after my passing.

My husband and I have a burial plot, which has been preserved, for my family. My children have access to the family plot in the event of their timely passing.

I hereby signed this document in sound mind and body

Mrs. Elizabeth K. Landers

Diana and Mrs. Green's and jaws dropped. They both knew that the Landers were extremely wealthy but to be millionaires in those times were unheard of. *What just happened? Did he really say that?* Diana and her mother were dead silent. A loud scream broke the silence.

"What the hell! This will never stand. We will fight this to the end," said Larry Jr. "This will never stick. The old woman was out of her mind! She cannot squander our inheritance on these peasants. These niggers cleaned her house and she thought she was in obligated to them! They must have tricked her!"

Diana had heard the word nigger one to many times out of the mouth of the ingrate. She knew firsthand what an insensitive bastard

Larry could be. Diana had enough of Larry, and his biased remarks. She stood in front of Larry Jr., drew back her hand and smacked him across his face.

"That may not be the last time you call me a nigger but it will be the last time you call me a nigger to my face in my house. Now get out!"

Mr. Turner did not blink. He was shocked but thrilled with how Diana handled Larry. He was more than happy to cosign Diana's statement because what she stated was correct. This was now her house and there was nothing Larry or his other siblings could do.

"She is right. I suggest you leave Ms. Green's home immediately before I am forced to call the authorities."

The other children continued to sit still. They were mortified with the terms of the will. They knew they were not as loyal as the Greens had been over the years. They never visited their mother when she requested to see them or their children. They saw her as a burden. Mrs. Landers was never given the attention she needed in her last days by her children.

Mrs. Green had not moved since Mr. Turner had completed the reading. She finally stood up. She looked around the room she had kept tidy throughout the years. Everything that surrounded her now belonged to her daughter. She felt blessed and overwhelmed at the same time.

"Thank you Mr. Turner I am on my way back home I really need to lay down."

Mr. Turner looked at Mrs. Green who appeared flustered. He knew it was so much to digest. Mr. Turner knew why Mrs. Landers felt the way she did about the Greens. Mrs. Green truly loved Mrs. Landers and always stood by her side. He knew Mrs. Green would have rather had her friend, rather than everything outlined in the Will. She was a humble woman and all that mattered to her was her family and friends.

"Are you ok?"

"Yes a little overwhelmed but I am ok."

"Before you go we need to go over some paper work."

Mrs. Landers wanted to make sure Mrs. Green and Diana understood the terms of the Will. She wanted Mrs. Green to have a Will in place at the time of her passing. Mrs. Landers believed things should be completed in an orderly fashion. She wanted Mr. Turner to assist Mrs. Green with whatever she needed. He was only going to be in town for a few days and wanted to take care of her affairs immediately.

Mrs. Green and Diana agreed to stay and review the technicalities of the Will. When they had completed the terms, Mr. Turner pulled a long manila envelope out of his briefcase and handed it to Mrs. Green. He had been given orders by Mrs. Landers to deliver the letter once they had completed the terms and conditions. Mrs. Green was not sure what was in the envelope but she decided to open it when she returned home.

****

"Mommy, Mommy!"

Barbara was running through the house. Barbara was as excited as were the other children about their new home. They had spent time in Mrs. Lander's house but never had they dreamed of living there. Children were able to have their own room. Diana had so many plans for her new home. She did not want to do much decorating because the house was full of exquisite antiques.

"Diana!"

Mrs. Green shouted coming thru the front door. Diana's mother was so excited for Diana. However, she missed her daughter and grandchildren in her own home. She knew this was such a blessing God had granted her child.

"Momma you look tired."

"Chile I will be alright. These old bones are not as strong as they use to be but they work just fine."

"Momma please, you are not old. You have more energy when you are running around with these children."

"Ha, I know that is right."

"Momma what's wrong?"

"I don't know child. I told you I am alright."

"Did something happen?"

"No nothing happened, really."

"Momma what is it?"

"You know, some folks just are never happy about any good fortune of a colored person."

"Momma, don't talk like that. We have been coming around these parts for years and ain't ever had an issue."

"Well it ain't just the white folks. You know it is other people too. They think we stole this from Mrs. Landers. There is talk around town."

"So what if there is talk around town," said Diana. "People talk mamma they always do."

"I know, I know but..."

"Momma what happened?"'

"Well when I was asleep last night someone through a brick through my window and it had a message attached. Look here."

Diana picked the note and it read, *NIGGA THIEF YOU GONE GET IT*. Diana looked at the note and was puzzled.

"Who would do such a thing? Momma this is crazy all these folks know us round these parts it would have to be an outsider. Did you call the police?"

"Call them for what they is white folk too. They ain't fittin to do nothing. Hmm... they probably feel the same way."

Diana looked at her mother square in the face. She knew this couldn't have bothered her mother that much. Diana's mother was feisty and never let anyone walk over her. Diana knew this note couldn't be the issue.

"Look here now, not many people are blessed with what we have been given. People always gonna want what you got if they think it is worth something. But momma like you always tell me you gotta trust in God cause he is the author and the finisher of our destiny."

Mrs. Green smirked. Deep down inside she knew she did not really care what people thought. She missed her family being around. She loved Diana and the kids, and she did not want to be alone.

"You is so smart. Just like yo daddy. I miss him so much," she sighed.

"Is that what it is momma. Are you lonely?"

"I am, a little."

"Then momma just come stay here with us. You can have your own room. The kids would love for you to be here with us."

"What about the house Diana?"

"Momma we can rent it out. Have some extra money coming in. The house paid off we can use that money as the upkeep. We can help other folk who need the opportunity. Momma we have money saved and money in the bank. We need to use this blessing and help others. It will never hurt us to be smart and invest. We have to think about the future of our generations. We have to think about the kids."

Mrs. Green wanted instantly say yes. She wanted to be with Diana and the children. Nevertheless, she knew Diana was an adult and needed her space. She believed Diana would want to get married one day and she did not want to be in the way.

"But you are a young girl. You still have time to meet a man and perhaps get married one day."

"Momma please what man is gonna marry me. I have four mouths to feed."

"But baby don't you want somebody in your life."

"Momma I don't even think about it, at all."

"Diana you don't think about it? What is wrong with you girl?"

"I love my children and that is all I have ever wanted."

Mrs. Green had a question that stirred in her heart for years. She did not know if this was the time to bring it up. Diana was not prepared for what her mother was about to ask.

"Diana," Mrs. Green said in a very cautious voice. "Where are those children's fathers?"

Diana was so shocked. Her mother had never asked her once about the children's fathers. The topic never seemed important. Her mother never seemed to mind each time Diana had mysteriously showed up pregnant. Since she never asked, Diana never told. She loved each of her children. She never regretted conceiving her children. However, due to the circumstances she did not want to disappoint her mother. She had kept their fathers secret for so long. The children never asked, and so she never felt the need to discuss them. She did find it strange that her mother wanted to know after all of these years. Diana could not understand why she was being questioned now. She knew at some point this question would arise she just never thought this would be the day. Diana dropped her head in shame.

"Why momma, why do you want to know now? Why does it even matter? They don't care mamma, why do you?"

"They...?" Mrs. Green looked astonished.

"Yes momma, they..."

Diana began to tell her mother her story:

"When I was younger you would take me to Mrs. Landers' house quite often."

"Yes girl, I remember."

Diana proceeded to tell her mother about the day she was playing with Mrs. Landers dolls in the back room. On this particular day, Katherine was at a recital or out doing some activity. Diana told her mother how Larry Jr. was always watching her and making snide remarks. Larry Jr. always made Diana feel quite uncomfortable. While she was playing, he came in the room and shut the door.

Mrs. Landers and Mrs. Green were in the kitchen and would have never suspected, because the house was so massive. When Larry closed the door he told Diana, *You little nigga girls is good for something.* He had a wicked look on his face and Diana became scared. When she tried to walk out of the room he proceeded to push her down and began dragging her over to the couch. He forced her down and lifted up her skirt placing all of his weight on her. Diana was struggling to get him off her. He began slapping her in the face repeatedly and told her not to scream. Diana's face had turned red but there were no scars or scratches. Larry began removing her panties to the side and stuck his fingers in her private area. Diana remembered it felt like he was stabbing her. She remembered how uncomfortable and painful it felt. She trembled while remembering his brutal force. He kept her skirt heisted and began to unzip his pants.

Diana's face began to swell. She did not want to relive this moment. She could feel Larry's breath smothering her, as she wanted to call out for help. She paused because the memories were becoming too vivid. Mrs. Green held her daughter's hand. She could see the pain in her face. She too wanted to cry but she knew she needed to focus on Diana.

"Go on baby I am listening."

Diana finished her story. Larry then forced himself inside of Diana. Diana felt like he was ripping her apart. She did not realize how much it was going to hurt. Diana had never been with a man and thought she would be a virgin for a long time. At least until she was married. By the time he completed his treacherous act, Diana had become numb. He looked at her at with disdain and began laughing as if her were proud of what he had done. He zipped his pants up, wiped the sweat from his face, and went on his merry way.

Diana could not cry or speak. When Diana stood up, blood began to run down her legs. She hurried herself to the bathroom. Mrs. Landers just so happened to come down the hall and noticed drops of blood in the hall. Mrs. Landers became scared and followed the trail of blood to the bathroom. When Mrs. Landers walked in the bathroom, Diana had a frightened look on her face. She was stunned. She wanted to know what had happened. Mrs. Landers thought Diana had fallen down, and cut herself. She then caught a glimpse of where the blood was coming from and immediately became nervous.

Mrs. Landers was about to get Diana's mother as Larry Jr. walked by with a smile on her face. She remembered she had just sent Mrs. Green to the store to pick up some supplies. She turned to get some towels and a change of clothes from Katherine's closet. She was so upset she did not know what she was going to do.

Mrs. Landers saw the evil in her son's eye and knew he was responsible. Mrs. Landers began to panic. She knew Mrs. Green would not understand and she did not want any confusion. Diana was a little black girl. She would never have gotten the justice she deserved. Mrs. Landers knew deep down inside no one would care except her mother.

Mrs. Landers tried to comfort Diana as she cried. She put Diana in the bathtub so she could clean herself. Mrs. Landers still did not know what to do. Luckily, Diana did not want Mrs. Landers to tell her mother because she was too embarrassed. Deep down inside Diana thought it was her fault. The Landers were always good to her, and her parents, so she believed it had to be something she had done.

Mrs. Landers retrieved a change of clothes for Diana and allowed her some time to pull herself together. She walked into the hall and found her son who was acting as if nothing had transpired. She snatched him up and demanded him tell her what had happened. Larry was such a pompous. He continued to smile. As he smiled, he told his mother, *whatever that nigger said she is a lying.* Mrs. Landers could not believe how cold her son was being.

Mrs. Landers could not focus on her son's indiscretions so she scurried him away. She went back in the bathroom to check on Diana. She told Diana she would take care of her. She told her she would never have to worry about anyone else hurting her. Mrs. Landers did as she had promised. She cleaned Diana up and put her back together. Mrs. Landers told Diana, that Larry did not mean to. She made the excuse that boys think with only one part of their bodies. Mrs. Landers felt there was no need to alarm Mrs. Green. She promised Diana she would take care of Larry, herself. When Diana's mother returned, they both pretended as if Diana had an accident in her clothes and Mrs. Landers had come to her rescue.

Diana said to her mother, "I don't know what happened to Larry but he never tried to hurt me again until later after his father died. That is when Bernard came. Bernice and Beatrice's fathers are different. When you latched onto Barbara, I wanted to have a baby who felt like she was my own. So when the summer came I kind of went out and found myself a friend who was nice to me at school. I didn't know him that well but I figured if we did it a couple times then maybe I would get pregnant. I know it sounds foolish and yes, I was being careless. I asked God for Bernice. Larry saw that I had two children and said that I was spoiled goods anyway so he proceeded to have his way again, when I was doing odd jobs for Mrs. Landers. I confided in Mrs. Landers so she knew about this incident as well."

Mrs. Green was flabbergasted. She hadn't realized all that her daughter had endured. What was even worse her best friend knew more about her daughter than she did. She wanted Diana to finish her story but deep down inside she felt she had failed her daughter. She never questioned or asked for her own selfish reasons. She wanted to have more than one child and she couldn't. So Mrs. Green began to live vicariously through her child without fully understanding the circumstances.

"Now Beatrice was a different story," Diana said. "His name was Robert Jones. I met him when I was working. He was so, so handsome momma. I think he came into town on a white horse just looking for me. He had hazel eyes and was a fair skinned boy."

Robert was not from the same town. His family was stationed at Ft. Bailey. It was a military base right outside of town. He had an accent that sounded like he was from a foreign country. He would always compliment Diana on how beautiful she was. She instantly became smitten. She never wanted to bring him home because she did not want him to know how many children she had. As the weeks passed, he began talking about getting married. Diana knew she was going to have to tell him eventually. They had already been intimate when he asked about her parents. Diana told Robert her father had passed away. Diana did tell him how wonderful her mother was and that he would definitely love her if he had gotten the chance to meet her. Robert asked over and over again to meet Mrs. Green, so Diana had no choice but to tell him about the children.

Robert was not pleased. It was almost if Diana had stolen something from him. He had a look of disgust but acted as if it did not bother him. He appeared very interested in the children. Robert wanted the names of Diana's children and their fathers. Diana conjured up a lie. It didn't matter because soon after he found out Robert disappeared.

Soon after, Diana found out she was pregnant with Beatrice. When she gave birth to Beatrice, she told God; as long as she had her children, he never had to send her another man. Diana meant everything she had said.

Diana looked at her mother and said, "I never had to have any other love than you and my children."

Mrs. Green did not say a word. She just looked at her daughter filled with sorrow. She felt pain in the pit of her stomach because she did not realize how much her child had suffered. After listening to Diana's story, she realized how selfish she had been. She was so wrapped up in the fact there was laughter in her house she forgot to ask how the laughter was created.

****

Diana loved her children and she catered to their every need as time passed on through the years. Barbara was now 15, Bernice 14, Bernard 13, and Beatrice was 11.

Diana was the happiest she had ever been. Mrs. Green had moved in and was renting out her house bringing in additional revenue. Diana was extremely smart. She created jobs for people in the community with the businesses Mrs. Landers had entrusted to her. She handled all the accounting and the books to ensure everything stayed in order. She also was working diligently on completing her degree. She wanted to ensure that her children would never want for anything.

Diana was preparing the children for church. She noticed her mother had not come out of her room for her morning coffee. Diana went up to her mother's room only to find Mrs. Green has not gotten out of the bed.

"Momma...?"

"Yes Diana."

"Are you getting up today?"

"My legs hurt."

"What? Your legs hurt. Let me call Dr. Bell."

"No child don't do all that, yawl go on to church. I am just going to lay and rest today."

"No Momma," Diana said. "We can stay home."

"Girl if you don't take them chirren to church you going to have a time on your hand later on in life. Chirrens do not need to miss one Sunday. There is a lesson to be learned each Sunday. Pastor Wright gives the word of God and we need to receive it."

Mrs. Green believed that children had to have a strong foundation. God had always been a part of their lives. She had taken Diana to church since she was a little girl. Diana had followed her mother's lead.

"Well if that is the case momma, then you need to get dressed because God has a word for you too."

"You right. Let me see what these old bones can do to get ready for her blessings today."

Diana helped her mother to the bathroom and helped her prepare for the good word from God. Mrs. Green was happy Diana had insisted she spend the day with her family in the house of the Lord.

Pastor Wright preached up a storm. Diana and her mother listened attentively as he gave the Lord's word.

Pastor Wright spoke:

"Family, please listen and understand, what he said. The word of God says he leads me beside still waters. He takes us to a place of peace, away from harm. He keeps us patient. He preparest a table before me in the presence of thine enemy. Doesn't matter who is trying to cause issues in your life God has the ability to have your enemies submit. He covers you with the blood. Thou annointest thine head with oil... He makes sure that you are covered so that no one can touch or harm you for any reason even if there is an apparent strife in your life. Do you know why family? Because saints, surely goodness and mercy shall follow you all the days of your life; if you dwell, in the house of the Lord! The lord lives in you, and as long as he dwells in you, surely goodness and mercy shall follow you."

"Hallelujah, Hallelujah!" Mrs. Green shouted. "Thank you almighty father I praise you!"

Diana looked at her mother. She had never seen complete peace in her until that day. Tears welled in her eyes. Mrs. Green began to cry and pray. Diana did not understand. She just knew her mother had the spirit of the Lord all over her.

"Whew, momma that was some service."

"Yes baby it was."

The children made noise as expected from a bunch of rowdy teenagers. They were laughing and screaming in the back seat as they were riding on their way home.

"These children are something else," said Mrs. Green. "You have to keep them focused Diana. Keep them focused and keep them in the house of the Lord. That is where they will be able to run to when we are not here."

Diana looked at her mother. "Momma, where are we going?"

"Right now, Diana, we ain't going anywhere. You just need to remember, one day we will not be here, and we have to leave our family with the word, which holds balance in their lives. You ain't promised tomorrow and baby I ain't promised. Just promise me this is the foundation you will lay."

84

Mrs. Green told Diana to pray with them daily and tell them about God. She wanted Diana to remember to tell her children how much she loved them as often as she could. She told Diana she needed to pray without ceasing for the covering of her children. She had been praying for Diana since the day she came into this world. She had watched Diana make mistakes, and right her wrongs.

Mrs. Green said, "I have watched you love your children. I have watched you as you honor and respect me daily. You are a wonderful daughter and it is my pleasure for me to be able to call you my own."

Diana looked at her mother. She was serious but had a loving look in her eyes while she talked to Diana. A tear fell from Mrs. Green's eyes.

"Momma you ok?"

"Yes baby I am just so grateful and thankful God has allowed me to be in you and my grandchildren's life. The loneliness has left my spirit and it is at rest."

"Momma you are not lonely."

"No baby I am not anymore. It is just today I feel so overwhelmed with joy and I do not know why. So I just will go on praising his name."

"Momma when I get home I am going to fix a big Sunday dinner. We are having fried chicken, dumplings, greens, cornbread, cabbage, and chocolate cake." The kids started to scream.

"Yawl hush," Diana said.

"Girl you don't need to cook all that."

"Yes I do momma because I am honored and feel privileged to do something for you."

Diana did just as she promised. She cooked up a feast. The children set the table as they always did but Mrs. Green insisted that they use the best china. She wanted to eat on Mrs. Landers antique dishes. Mrs. Green had cleaned those dishes so many times she found it to be quite ironic, years later she was eating on the very same plates.

She no longer had to wash the dishes because her grandchildren were old enough to tackle that chore.

They ate like kings and queens. There was nothing left on the serving dishes. After dinner, Mrs. Green called her grandchildren to the living room and had them gather around her.

"Tonight I am going to show you your grandfather."

"But grandma, grandpa is dead."

"I know he is dead. But I have some photos that I would like to share with each of you."

Diana was stunned she had not seen a photo of her father since he had passed. Her mother did not leave his photos out to be viewed because it brought so many memories. Mrs. Green began to pass around the photographs.

"Here is your grandfather…"

The children were in awe looking at pictures of their grandfather. Diana could barely look at the pictures. She remembered her father but it had been so long since she had seen him. She was speechless. She remembered how soft spoken he was. She remembered sitting on his lap and he would share stories of how he traveled. He told her how special she was. That she was the only baby he had and he loved her more than anything in this world. Diana never loved another man as she loved her father until she met Beatrice's father. Diana felt the need to cry but she fought back the tears as she watched her four children with their grandmother. Diana began to walk into the kitchen.

"Diana, where are you going?" asked Mrs. Green.

"Momma I am just going to straighten up."

"Leave it child this is our time."

Diana looked at her mother's face and smiled. Mrs. Green held her box of memories tight as she passed one picture out at a time for the children to look at. They stayed up all night laughing and talking about memories until the children fell to sleep. Diana woke each child up and escorted them to their room. She began to wake up her mother. Her mother opened her eyes and smiled at her.

"I love you Diana."

Diana looked her mother in the eyes and said, "I love you to momma. Let's go get into bed."

"Diana," said Mrs. Green. "Lay in the bed with me?"

Diana never refuted her mother's request. "Sure momma, I will lay with you."

Diana woke up early that morning. When she got out of the bed, she noticed her mother still had the box of memoirs folded in her arms. Diana let her sleep. She knew they had stayed up half the night and was extremely tired. *Lord let me get these kids up and ready for school. Ah ha that is right the kids don't have school today. It is the summer time.*

Diana smirked and went into the kitchen. The house was still quiet as she put on a pot of coffee. She knew her mother would be requesting her cup of special blend soon. In the kitchen walked Bernice.

"Momma, what are you doing?"

"Girl I am making your grandma's coffee. Get in that bathroom and wash your face."

"But ma..."

"Don't sass me. Get movin. Wake up your sisters and brother. Bernice, don't wake your grandma."

Diana watched as her pre-teen shuffled up the steps to follow her orders. Diana's troops swarmed in the kitchen one by one. They hadn't washed their faces and still looked sleepy. They rubbed their eyes and began to listen to their mother's command.

"Okay now let's get ready to get this house clean. I think we need to plan a big exciting day with you and your grandmother. We need to do something special for her since she took the time to do something special for us. But first we need to clean this house."

"Awe, momma do we have to?"

"Yes you have to. Everyone pick a room and let's get to it."

The children began to clean their designated areas; they were all disgruntled because they would have preferred to stay in the bed. Diana noticed that her mother had not gotten up yet. *I don't know what has gotten into Mrs. Green this morning but she sure is taking sleeping to another level. I will just wake her up after we finished cleaning.* Diana chuckled to herself.

The children were dressed, the house was clean but Mrs. Green had not left her bedroom. Diana knew it was not normal for her mother to stay in bed all day. She just assumed she was exhausted from the day before.

"Barbara go wake up grandma."

"Ok momma."

Barbara went upstairs. She tried to wake her grandmother but she did not move. Barbara felt her face and it felt cold. She did not know what to do. She called her grandmother and did not receive a response. Barbara stepped away from her grandmother's body and stood. She heard her mother calling from downstairs. Before she exited the room, she kissed her grandmother and went to tell her mother. Barbara walked in the kitchen. Her eyes seemed a bit shallow.

"Barbara, Barbara," Diana called her but she received no response. "Barbara!" screamed Diana. "You hear me talking to you?"

"Momma…momma, grandma is not moving."

Diana's heart began to beat rapidly. Diana dropped the cup and ran up the steps. Mrs. Green lay still in the bed still with the box of memoirs in her arm. Diana removed the box ever so gently.

"Momma, Momma!" Diana shook her mother but did not receive a response. "Momma!! Momma!! Wake up momma!! Please, Wake Up! Momma, please don't leave me! Not today momma, not today, because the kids are ready to go. We were going to drive today momma. Wake up momma wake up!!!"

Mrs. Green did not respond. She had died peacefully in her sleep while she lay beside Diana. Diana was distraught she couldn't believe her mother was dead. She continued to cry out as tears fell from her eyes. All of the children ran upstairs. They stood in the doorway and watched their mother as she held their grandmother in her arms crying. Barbara called 911. She preceded to tell them that her grandmother was not responding. When the ambulance arrived they tried to resuscitate Mrs. Green. After pronouncing her dead the ambulance removed Mrs. Green's body from the house. The children cried in unison and Diana was shaking. She could not think straight.

"I just talked to her. I just kissed her. What happened?" Diana bent over and screamed again.

The children went to hold their mother. They could not stop crying either. They all loved their grandmother so much and could not believe what had just taken place.

"She is gone, my momma is gone," said Diana as she trembled.

The children were at their mother's side. The house was eerie, and all anyone could feel was death as it exited through the front door. They held onto their mother as she released her heaviness.

Mrs. Green's casket was cream, her dress white, outlined with lace. She was absolutely beautiful. The whole town attended her funeral. She was well respected in the community because of her community service. She always kept a smile on her face in spite of circumstances, just as her husband had done.

The guest brought flowers, cards, food and monetary gifts. The Repast was held at Diana's house because Diana wanted to be surrounded by friends. Since her mother had no immediate family, Diana depended on the people who had surrounded her for years.

That night Diana could not cry another tear. Her eyes were swollen and dry. She missed her mother and could not believe she was gone. Bernice came into the living room where her mother was sitting.

"Momma we can clean up," said Bernice. "Don't worry about anything we will take care of it."

Diana did not say a word and proceeded to make her way up the steps. She went into the room her mother had occupied and laid in her bed. She felt the urge to cry but couldn't. Diana noticed the box on the dresser and she picked it up. She pulled out the pictures, looked at her mother and father, who were now gone to their destinies together.

"She went home to be with you daddy," Diana said to the picture. As she continued to go through the box, she found a white envelope. *What is this? It is probably a love letter from daddy. She opened up the letter and proceeded to read:*

Dear Betty,

If you are reading this then I am home with my maker. However, because you are my best friend and have been for most of my life I just wanted to talk to you one last time. We have shared so much through the years. I want you to know there is a piece of me who has always been envious of you. You have always had a wonderful center in your husband and your daughter. I know you knew how much your Barry loved you. He was an admirable man. He was honest and the two things in this world he loved more than collard greens were you and Diana. When you worked, he was not happy. He didn't want you to work for some old white woman. Yes, I am laughing because he would never call me that or mean any harm if he thought it. He wanted you and Diana to be taken care of regardless. I know you had loss the love of your life when he died.

When Larry Sr. died, I lost a piece of me. The kids left and I had no one to help me. Of course, I had the people who were working for me but I missed so much having the love of my immediate family. You and your daughter made sure the businesses were kept in order. Even when Larry had gotten sick, I didn't have to worry about a thing when you two angels were around. Even though Larry Sr. could be hateful at times, know he did love you both as I love you. Now I just need you to promise me this. Please always make sure Diana gets whatever she needs to succeed. Start by telling her you love her and you are always proud of her. She is a good girl and will become an exceptional woman.

I need you to tell her I am sorry. I should have been a better mother to my children the way you and Barry were to her. If I was then maybe, I could have embraced my grandchildren at least once. I am sorry Betty. I could have done more to protect your child as you and your husband always protected, my husband, my children, and me. I don't know if Diana has told you but if she did, I must say you are a woman of class. You could have left me high and dry and had someone hurt my child. Well let me just say you are impeccable. You have never held anything against me. No, you did not. You remained loyal. If you didn't know please tell Diana she will be blessed beyond measure because she kept the evil sins of my family to herself.

You both are my angels whether you know it or not. I can't apologize too much because Barbara and Bernard are beautiful. Don't get me wrong I love all of Diana's children. I just wished they had known I was family too.

I love you Betty and I can't change the past but I can help the future, so you should have everything you need to take care of those grandbabies and Diana. I thank God for giving you such a kind heart. I will never forget you my friend. I hope that one day I will see you again when we meet behind the pearly gates.

I love you my dear friend and thank you for loving me
Your dear friend
Elizabeth Landers

****

Diana made sure she kept her children focused on God. Despite the fact, they were hardheaded teenagers. She knew the importance of having a foundation in the home. All her children understood who God was and the power he held.

As time passes on children become adults and develop a mind of their own. Her children were definitely developing something. Diana knew that at some point she could not control everything, so she kept praying. Diana made sure she focused on her children, her businesses, and the community. Diana never focused on herself. She never took the time out to find happiness in the companionship of a mate. Since the day Diana had sworn off men, she never took the time out to notice if a man was even paying her any attention. What Diana did not know is men paid her attention everywhere she went. Of all colors and races, Diana was viewed as one of the most eligible bachelorettes in her town. Men envied her for her strength. She was a businesswoman but not like other businessmen or women, anyone had ever encountered.

She was compassionate. She had a kind heart. She would give her last if someone asked. Because she was so blessed early in life, her last never came to past.

She was of average height about 5'4 and weighed about 145 pounds. She had a beautiful caramel complexion and her hair was shoulder length never to be infused with chemicals. She straightened her hair once a week and usually wore it pulled back. Her clothes were always neat and followed the colors of the season. Nevertheless, it was Diana eyes. She had very kind eyes, light brown, full lash, and a tad bit slanted. She had the eyes of her father. She was gentle; all that knew her, and met her felt very comforted in her presence. Her walk was very strong as she commanded attention as she moved forward. Her head was always slightly tilted for she was always in deep thought. She was always thinking of her children and hoping for their success and dreams to come true. She wanted to live by the lessons her mother had taught her through the years. She wanted to lead by example and she would not tolerate any riffraff getting in her way of her focus.

"Excuse me ma'am."

Diana hadn't lifted up her head to notice the very virile figure standing in before her.

"Yes sir, how can I help you?"

"I am looking for some fabric for my mother to make curtains. I was told this was the best place in town to come."

Diana always had loyal customers from the local neighborhood but the voice didn't sound familiar so Diana decided to look up. She could not open her mouth but she could feel her heart pound. What she saw before her eyes was nothing she had ever seen before. He was over six feet tall and had a coco complexion. He was dressed in a white collared shirt. The way the shirt grab his chest she knew there was some sight to see if he were to remove it. He had big dark brown eyes. When she looked at him, she smiled but quickly turned away in embarrassment. He smiled back at her as he showed all of his pearly white teeth.

"Uhh…," she stuttered, "Yes sir I can help you. Georgina..." Diana called to her faithful assistant.

"Yes ma'am?"

"Can you help uhhh...? Mr. Uhhh…"

"Miles," he interjected.

She smiled to herself and said, "Can you help Mr. Miles?"

"No just call me Miles. Miles is my first name."

"Umm Miles can you please help Miles?" They both started to laugh. "Georgina can you please help Miles."

"Yes ma'am I can."

"Thank you, ma'am," he said as he noticed Diana blushing.

Diana could hardly breathe. This man was breath taking and never had she seen such an exquisite figure, as he walked away so poised.

"Bernice!" Diana yelled.

"Yes momma."

"Please come in here and help me cook dinner."

"Yes mamma."

"Where were you today?" Diana asked Bernice.

 Mom I told you I had classes and I had to stay after with a study group. Bernice was in her second year of junior college. She was studying to be a schoolteacher.

"I am sorry baby, I forgot. Where is your brother and baby sister?"

"They are all upstairs doing God knows what."

Diana smirked. Bernard was preparing to graduate from high school and Beatrice was getting adapted to her sophomore year in school soon to become a junior. Barbara was a different story. She fell in love her senior year and decided she was going to get married. Diana made every effort for Barbara to go to college. Barbara was so in love with Jeffrey Barnes and she refused to hear anything her mother said. Diana refused to argue with Barbara about any decisions she chose for her life. Diana just wanted Barbara to be happy. "If you like it I love it," Diana would say. Diana refused to have any issues tear apart her family so she just let Barbara do what she wanted to do.

Bernice was focused on being successful. She wanted to have the best; she wanted to be the best, at everything she did. She studied, worked with Diana, and she help take care of her baby brother and sister even if they were only a year or two behind her.

Diana rushed through the kitchen to get everything set for dinner. There was a knock at the door.

"Bernice, get the door baby."

"Ok momma."

Bernice opened the door and there stood a handsome stranger with a bouquet of roses in his hand.

"Good afternoon young lady is your mother home?" She paused and looked puzzled at the man staring in her face.

"Yes sir, she is. May I tell her who is here?"

"Please tell her Mr. Kingsbury."

"Mr. Kingsbury?" Bernice said still looking puzzled. "Please come in," she said hesitantly. Bernice ran to the kitchen to her mother.

"Momma there is a Mr. Kingsbury here to see you."

Diana looked mystified. "I don't know any Kingsbury."

She began to take off her apron and walked to the living room. When Diana walked in her heart began to flutter again. It was the same man from her store.

"Mr. Kingsbury?"

"Please call me Miles."

Miles handed Diana the bouquet of flowers. From the time Diana spoke to Miles in her living room, she knew she might have to retrace her plea to God not to send her a man. She had a yearning for Miles. A yearning she had not had in a long time. He made Diana smile. Diana smiled often when it came to matters of the world but this smile was different.

"How can I help you sir?"

Miles smiled with a peculiar grin. "Well I am new to town. I am here visiting my parents while I am on leave from the army. I feel almost embarrassed to ask this. When I was in your store today… I don't know. I just don't know. There was something about the way you smiled. Ever since you smiled at me, I have wanted to see your beautiful face again. I do not mean any disrespect Miss but I just had to see you again. I have spent most of my life traveling with a career in the military and not once do I get to enjoy the beauty of people. When I saw you today you reminded me of why I should."

Diana was taken back. She had nothing to say, because she could not believe her ears.

"Why… me?" asked Diana.

"Why not you," he retorted? "There is something in your eyes, please excuse me if I am to forward."

Diana just smiled and said nothing. Bernice saw her mother's face and politely interjected.

"Excuse me sir, my mother and family were about to sit down for dinner, perhaps you will join us?"

Diana was shocked at Bernice's forwardness. Bernice never spoke out of turn but today she seemed bold. Diana was happy she had asked because she was in such awe she would have never thought to. The man was happy she had offered and was more than delighted to stay for dinner.

"If that is ok with your mother, I would love to."

"Of course that is fine," Diana said politely. "Please have a seat it will be ready soon. Let me go into the kitchen and help Diana, I mean Bernice," she chuckled like a schoolgirl.

"No mama you sit down with Mr. uhh… Mr. Kingsbury," said Bernice. Yes mamma, please, please sit down, and sit with Mr. Kingsbury. I will finish dinner." Bernice was over excited about their unexpected guest.

From that moment on every day for the next few weeks, the children saw their mother's world change. She sang joyful songs day in and day out. She even danced in the living room where she forbids the children. "Momma is in love," they would say amongst themselves. Those were exactly Diana's sentiments. She was falling in love with Mr. Kingsbury.

****

Miles took Diana for rides through the country and city. He showed her life outside of the small town she had dwelled in for so long. They took long walks through the park. He was so gentle. He would hold Diana's hand, and escort her from place to place. He would never invade Diana's personal space. He treated her as if she was the only thing in this world.

"Diana I have something to tell you."

"Yes Miles."

"I need you to know, these last few weeks have been wonderful and I have enjoyed every minute with you."

Diana felt the bow of disappointment about to take place. She was not prepared to be rejected again. She stepped back away from Miles.

"But..."

"There are no buts Diana. I need to tell you how special you are to me. How special you are. I have been running from city to city my entire life. Whether it was my father traveling abroad or wherever the military has taken me. I looked at my mother and father the other day and realized after all these years they were settled. They were happy and I longed for the same settlement."

Diana looked confused. "What are you saying Miles?"

"I am saying I want to be settled. I have three more years left to serve in the military. When I finish I want to have someone special by my side. I actually want them by my side while I finish, and then I want to spend the rest of eternity with them. The only person in this world I could fathom ever doing that with is…."

Diana interjected, "What are saying Miles? Don't say anything if you don't mean it."

"Please Diana let me finish."

Diana felt the urge to run but she knew she needed to listen to this man. Diana thoughts ran with different emotions. She was not sure about what he was going to say. She trusted Miles and something told her he would never hurt her.

"Diana I want you to come with me to Europe. I want you to travel with me and be by my side. I want to wake up and see your smile. I want to kiss your warm lips, and hold you close to me every day for the rest of my life; for the rest of our lives."

"Europe, you want me to go to Europe? I am not shacking up with…"

"Diana, please wait." Miles got on one knee and said, "I would never insult a woman as wonderful as you just to travel abroad unless I made her an honest woman." Miles bent on one knee and pulled a small box out of his jacket. "Diana Green… Will you do me the honor of making me the happiest man of my life and marry me?" Diana was speechless.

"I love you Diana and I want to be with you the rest of my life."

"But…," Diana said abruptly.

"But what, Diana?" asked Miles.

"What about the business, what about the house…?" Diana could think of all the important things in her life, but more important than anything else in this world. She thought about her commitment. "What about my children?"

Diana loved Miles and Miles loved Diana. Diana wasn't really keen about leaving Beatrice and Bernard especially when they were so close to finishing their high school education. Miles proposed that Bernard and Beatrice live with their sister Barbara or live in the house under Bernice's supervision; they would not have to uproot. Bernard would be on his way to college soon and Beatrice would be her only child left.

Diana wrestled all day and night trying to figure out what would be best for her children. *I can't leave them. They need me, what if something happened.* No matter how she evaluated the situation she could not she would not leave her children.

"Momma what is wrong with you?" asked Bernice and Beatrice.

"What do you mean?"

"Momma we are almost grown well at least Bernice is and Bernard is going to college soon. You don't have to sit and wait with me."

"Momma," said Bernice. "I will care for Beatrice. We can manage the business and the property. Momma he loves you and you are so, so happy."

"Momma do you love this man?" questioned Beatrice.

"Yes baby I love him," answered Diana.

"Then momma you should go. You should find some peace and go. It is Europe momma. You have never been out of this town. You don't know what anything looks like outside of these city limits."

"You right about that," laughed Diana.

"So Momma, just go. We want you to go, and you need to go."

"I will think it over and talk to God." Diana said as she smiled at her children.

"Momma God wants you to go also."

"Yawl shut up speaking on the behalf of God."

Diana didn't really care about the property the house or anything else in this world but her children. She knew she loved Miles but she also knew the vow she made to God concerning her children. She knew God had blessed her in ways she could not fathom, and she always vowed to be by her children's side. She needed to see them off to college; she needed to see them reach their dreams. After she prayed, she had made up her mind.

Diana decided to meet with Miles and share her sentiments. She knew her decision was hard but she also knew what the decision meant. This was the first man she loved in a long time. She knew her decision would have to be discussed with Miles. She had Miles come to her home while the children were gone. When he arrived, they sat in the living room. Diana loved looking at Miles' handsome face. She reached for his hand and stared in his eyes. Diana began to talk to Miles about their next steps. Miles listened to Diana attentively.

"Miles, my darling, I need you to know something. I have thought about what we talked about the other day. I first want you to know, nothing in this world would make me happier than to wake up and see your face. You are something I never expected in my life. You are a good man, a humble man; you are a man who loves me. I don't think you know what this means. The last man that loved me in my life was my father and no man has ever loved me since. So I had to love myself because most women break when they don't have a companion, but I didn't. I told God I would sacrifice everything if he just allowed me to take care of my children. Then there you are, the only temptation in my life that would ever have me think about leaving them. I love you and I want to be with you for the rest of my life Miles Kingsbury. I need you to know that. I would travel from here to the ends of the earth with you because you have changed my life. I want to wake up beside you; I want to feed you, cater to you, and honor you as my husband. I want our dreams to be in accord. I want us to laugh together, cry together, and pray together. I don't want you to be anywhere else than with me. I love you Miles."

Miles smiled as he looked at the ring he had placed on Diana's finger. Miles was so excited that Diana had decided to come with him. He knew he could make Diana happy. He had fallen deeply in love with her. She was the only woman he had ever loved.

Miles said, "Diana I promise you…."

Diana interjected, "Miles…but… I can't leave my children."

Diana took the ring off her finger and gently kissed Miles on his lips. She whispered as the tears fell down her face. Her lips were trembling.

"I love you, I will always love you. Thank you Miles Kingsbury for changing my life."

****

As time passed, Diana began to think about her past decisions. The more she thought the more she understood she could not break any promises she had made to God. Her children were older now and she watched them grow into amazing adults. She felt God was pleased with her actions. Barbara, Bernice and Bernard had left and moved on, and now all off her attention was on her last seed.

Beatrice was beautiful, she was the youngest, and she always seemed to get all of the attention. This included attention from her mother. Diana treated all of her children the same to the best of her ability. There was something special about Beatrice. Diana felt it was because she reminded her so much of her father. She was charming. She would bat her eyes and command attention without saying one word.

"Beatrice, get in here," said Diana.

Beatrice was outside commanding the attention of the young men from down the street. Diana forewarned Beatrice of the attention she commanded. She believed one-day get Beatrice in trouble if she acted vain. It did not bother Beatrice at all.

"Momma please, I ain't given these boys nothing they just love to admire my smile."

"Okay you just better watch yourself. Pay attention to the people you hold time with."

"Alright momma," said Beatrice while batting her eyes.

"Girl, go head and stop playing."

Beatrice grabbed her purse and began to walk out of the door.

"Where do you think you are going?"

"I am going out momma. Talesha and Rashanna are going to go shopping and then to the club. I got a hankering to do some dancing."

"Girl you better get a hankering to dance and praise the Lord!"

"Alright momma I am not going to miss church. You know I got to get my praise on after I get my…," Beatrice laughed.

"Girl shut your mouth talking like that. I ain't trying to hear that. Go on out of here, be careful, but you better not be in this house after 11 o'clock."

"Eleven? Momma, come on now."

"Eleven or I am going to have a hankering to embarrass you."

"Ok, ok momma."

Eleven, eleven thirty, twelve, twelve thirty. Diana dosed off. When she arose in the morning she noticed Beatrice's bed had not been slept in all night. *Now where is that girl? Let me call Barbara.*

Barbara had moved out a few years prior when she married the love of her life. Diana picked up the phone to call Barbara to inquire about Beatrice's whereabouts.

"Barbara?"

"Yes momma?"

"Is Beatrice over there? She didn't come home last night."

"You know she is probably with them girls. Don't worry about it momma."

"Look, don't tell me what to worry about! She would at least call."

"Okay momma did you call Bernard?"

"How the heck would she be with Bernard? He is all the way up North at that college. She would not take her behind up there. That does not even make sense. Shut up Barbara, you just concerned about yourself! Could you call…?"

Barbara interrupted, "I don't even know why you would call her. She is living in lala land."

There was a knock at the door.

"Hold on Barbara I think that is her."

Diana went to the door and opened it immediately. She was going to slap her in face when she saw her, for scaring her to death. However, Diana knew she was not going to lay a hand on her.

"Girl, didn't I tell you..." as she swung open the door.

It was the police. Diana's heart stopped. When Barbara and Bernice arrived at the hospital, their mother looked as if she had just seen death. Her face was pasty and she looked as if she had been crying.

"Momma what is wrong is she ok? Is she, momma...is she?"

"No she is not. But the doctor won't let us in the back to see her."

"What happened momma," asked Bernice?

"I am not sure. I haven't seen anyone to tell me what is going on." Diana got up and began to walk down the hospital corridor.

"Momma, where are you going?"

"I am going to do the only thing I know how to do. I am going to talk to my father."

Diana went right through the hospital doors and stepped outside where the sunlight had disappeared and the clouds were thick. She looked up at the sky and began to plea with God. She wanted God to intervene and save her daughter.

Lord in all my life I have done all I know how to do. The only thing I have ever asked is that my children be safe and covered from the destruction of this world. So Lord, I ask that your will not be pressed upon this family, I sacrifice myself. Lord I sacrifice and submit unto you totally. Lord, save my baby. Remove the blemishes from her and lay the burdens upon me. (Tears began to well in Diana eyes) *Dear God I plead with you. I beg of you, save her.*

At that moment, the sky opened and the rain began to pour. Diana did move she didn't say another word. As rain covered her body, Barbara ran outside.

"Momma, get out of this rain. She woke up and the doctor said we could see her."

Diana looked at the rain and said, "Thank you father, whatever your will be done let it be done to me..."

Diana walked into her child's hospital room. There was an IV protruding out of her arm. She looked at all of the machines as she walked over to the bed. She grabbed Beatrice's hand and kissed her on the forehead.

"Hey baby."

"Momma," Beatrice said in a weak voice.

"Shh... Baby, do not say another word. I am just thankful you opened your eyes." Diana understood at that moment, how on time God was.

Now the doctor instructed Beatrice to be very careful with her diet and activities. Beatrice's test results showed she was highly anemic. Apparently, when Beatrice went out with her friends she became extremely dizzy and fatigued. She began to get chills and sweats and told her friends she was going to bathroom. When she didn't return, they assumed she had gone off with some boy she had met at the dance. Beatrice had passed out on the floor. One of the bathroom attendants, who called the ambulance, discovered her. She was immediately taken to the emergency room.

When Talesha and Rashanna found out, they felt horrible. They apologized repeatedly. Diana did not care how many times they apologized she just knew they left her baby to die. Diana did not want Beatrice around them ever again in life. However, Diana knew that she could not choose Beatrice's friends. Beatrice had been friends with those girls for most of her high school year's right through college.

****

Diana was so proud to witness Beatrice's graduating college. She had been sickly in her final semesters and there were days when she did not think Beatrice was going to make it. Beatrice decided she would remain at home close to her mother while she pursued Master's degree.

Time was passing by so quickly. Beatrice moved as quickly as the time. She really didn't care how sick she had gotten, she was determined to complete her education. Beatrice was about to start her final semester of graduate school.

"Baby you are going to have to slow down," Diana said to Beatrice.

"For what momma?" said Beatrice. "I can't let anything stand in my way. You already know how hard it is for a black woman. I am about to break boundaries. Momma I was sick years ago, so what. The doctor said I was not going to be able to complete school. Look at how wrong he was. Momma I am going to do what God leads me to do. I am going to be happy. God did not intend for me to sit around. Isn't that what you always told me?"

Diana was not going to dispute with her daughter. She had always encouraged her children to shoot for the stars. She admired Beatrice's determination and strength. She had a lot to live up to with her older sisters and brother being as successful as they were. Even Barbara, who wanted to be just a homemaker; she was happy, so why couldn't Beatrice be happy working toward her dreams.

Diana went into Beatrice's room to wake her up and Beatrice was in pain. Her skin was clammy and her mouth was dry. Diana was concerned.

"What's wrong baby?" asked Diana.

"I don't know momma, I am hurting. I hurt so badly. I have been throwing up all night and my body just aches so, so much."

"Ok honey, let's get you up. We are going to the doctor."

Diana thought, maybe Beatrice was pushing herself to much. Diana began to think of everything that could be wrong with her child. *Lord, I hope she is not pregnant. God only know what that child does when she ain't home. What am I talking about she is a grown woman. She is fine Lord she probably has the flu. She just needs to get some rest. She has six more weeks until she graduate. Maybe then, I can convince her that it is time for a vacation. She can even go out with those coo-coo friends of hers.* Diana smirked.

Diana took Beatrice to the doctor. They ran several tests on her trying to figure out what was wrong. Diana waited for the doctor to come in the room with Beatrice's test results.

"I am going to call your sister and brother."

"For what, momma…? I am fine, I am have a little energy."

Diana looked at Beatrice's arms where they were bruised from the nurse trying to find an entry to withdraw blood. Beatrice's also had to get her fluids replenished.

"Lord have mercy, you look like they have beaten you black and blue."

"Momma stop, you know I bruise easily. You always told me to sit in the sun and get some color, so no one could tell how clumsy I was, with all my bumps and bruises." They laughed at each other and sighed.

"You are going to be fine. But you have to promise me Beatrice after this semester is over, we are going to take a vacation. We are going to go somewhere nice."

"Vacation…? Momma what kind of talking is that we ain't never been nowhere on a vacation."

"Then maybe it is high time we do. You have done so well for yourself and we have never wanted for anything. I know business ain't like it used to be, but we have more than enough saved to take some time out for ourselves."

"You, me, Barbara, Bernice, Tracey, and Bernard, we have never gone anywhere together as a family and it is high time."

"Where you wanna go momma?"

"Girl I want to go to an island; no, no better yet to Europe, or France."

"Momma you want to go out of the country? When did you make that decision?"

"I don't know. Ever since Miles left, I always think about not going with him. I was so scared to leave you children I let him go. I have never loved a man like Miles, since your father."

Beatrice was stunned her mother had only mentioned her father once and that was because Beatrice had asked. She knew her father had broken her mother's heart but her mother never said one unkind word about him. Beatrice hoped one day she would meet him but it never came true.

"Momma you miss him?"

"Yes baby I do. I often dream about what it would have been like if I just would have…," Diana's head dropped.

"It is ok momma. Ok momma when I graduate I promise we are all going to go to Europe." Beatrice smiled.

While they were talking, the doctor entered the room. He had her chart in his hand and began reviewing the information. He looked at the two women and greeted them with a smile.

"Hello Ms. Green?"

Beatrice said, "Hello sir, how are you."

"This is my mother, she is Ms. Green also."

The doctor said, "Nice to meet you, ma'am."

The doctor proceeded to ask Beatrice a series of question. He began reading off his chart. Diana had a bewildered look on her face. The doctor's questions worried Diana. Beatrice just listened to the doctor attentively.

The doctor began to explain his findings, "Ms. Green you have a high number of white blood cells which become apparent when your blood sample is observed under a microscope. Frequently, these extra white blood cells are immature or dysfunctional. The excessive number of cells can also interfere with the level of other cells, causing a harmful imbalance in the blood count." He began to ask Beatrice a series of questions. "Are you experiencing symptoms of feeling sick to your stomach often? Having fevers, chills, night sweats and other flu like symptoms. Such as feelings of fatigue and have you notice any rapid weight loss?"

Beatrice sat back and wondered why the doctor asked her all of these questions. She had been experiencing most of the symptoms he had questioned her about. Beatrice became worried but she didn't want to alarm her mother who already appeared confused with what the doctor was saying. Beatrice did not understand the information about her blood.

"Yes sir, I have experienced some of those symptoms," said Beatrice.

"Well I have to run a few more test before I make my final diagnoses. I will give you a choice, if you are feeling fine after we get some fluids in you; you are free to go home. However, you have to come to my office first thing in the morning. If you are not feeling up to it we can run the test right now."

Beatrice did not understand. "Why do they need to run more test? What is wrong with me doctor?"

"Ms. Green I don't want you to worry I am just making sure we eliminate any possibilities. It could possibly be that you are under stress. I want you to take it easy for a few days.
I promise you after we run a few more test we will have an answer."

Beatrice did not know whether to go home or stay. She really did not want to experience any probing. She was already tired from the test and she preferred to go home. She asked her mother her thoughts.

"'Momma what do you think?"

"It is not about what I think. How do you feel?" asked Diana.

"Well I feel much better."

"Then let's go home baby. We will put this in the hands of God and we will go home."

"Ok Momma. Momma I love you."

"Oh baby I love you too."

"Momma, are we going to Europe and find Miles?"

Diana laughed, "I can tell you this we are going to Europe."

"Momma what is going on with Beatrice," said Bernice?

"Nothing to worry about, the doctor just wanted to do a few more test. I told your sister she needed to slow down. You know she is trying to be the president of the universe. Diana was not completely focused on what Bernice was saying. She was more enthralled with her grandbaby. "Come here to grandma," Diana said as the baby stumbled over her feet. "Look at you girl, you are getting so big."

"Momma stop it you are going to spoil her," said Bernice.

"And so what if I am. She is my grandchild. I can do whatever I want. Let's see what I have in this kitchen for you."

"Momma, when will she be home from the doctor?"

"She will be home soon Bernice."

Diana walked in the kitchen with Tracey in her arms. She was tired of all of Bernice's questions because she didn't have any answers. She was as in the dark as she was. Bernice didn't take the hint and continued on with her inquiries concerning her sister."

"Why didn't she want you to go with her?"

"Listen Bernice, it is not that she did not want me to go with her, she hopped her tail up this morning, and said Talesha was taking her."

"Momma you ain't worried?"

"Worried? My father has taught me to take my burdens to the Lord and leave it there. My faith is what keeps me focused you better get you a swallow of it before you drive yourself crazy."

"Well how much longer does she have in school?"

"Oh…I think about five weeks," said Diana.

"Momma she can make it up in the fall. She needs to slow down."

"Girl who are you telling, but you are preaching to the choir when talking to Beatrice. You know that girl has a mind of her own."

"You talked to your other sister."

"Who…?" Bernice played dumb.

"What other sister do you have other than Beatrice?"

Bernice played dumb as if she did not know whom her mother was referring to. Bernice did not want to bring her other sister up. Bernice and her Barbara did not always see eye to eye.

"Barbara! Girl, don't play with me."

"Yea I talked to her for a few but...," said Bernice as she rolled her eyes.

"Don't do it Bernice. Don't criticize your sister."

"Momma she is a waste she just thinks about herself. She is living in public housing. She didn't have to do that. She had the same opportunities as us and she wanted to settle."

"Listen Bernice, we all make our own decisions. We have to do what makes us happy and your sister has been happy for years. She loves that man and he does what he can so they can survive. Trust me I have offered her time and time again. I have even helped them out with a few things, even tried to purchase them a house, but she is very content. I am not going to force anything on her she doesn't want."

"Momma you are always protecting her."

"Bernice everyone is not like you. Leave her alone and let her be. You need to start paying attention to your husband."

"Momma, don't start."

"No you don't start, let ye that is without sin cast the first stone."

Bernice was furious because she always felt her mother always took up for Barbara even when she was wrong. Diana knew Barbara had not made the best decisions but they were hers.

"Child you have made mistakes as she has."

"But momma I have righted all my mistakes".

"Well... have you really? I want you to think about that real hard. Have you righted all of your wrongs?"

Bernice dropped her head and didn't say another word. She didn't want her mother dredging up the past. She knew her mistakes but she felt they were not as extreme as Barbara's was. Bernice's mistakes were more deceiving than Barbara's was but she would never admit it. Bernice had a tendency to be very judgmental when it came to her sister.

Just then, the door opened and in walked Talesha and Beatrice. Beatrice had a long look on her face. She cracked a fake smile when she entered into the room. She saw her niece and knew Tracey could lighten her spirit.

"Beatrice what did the doctor say?" asked Diana.

Beatrice ignored her mother's question, "Hey Bernice, hey aunties girl how are you?"

"Beatrice you don't hear me talking to you, girl, what did the doctor say?"

"Momma we will talk about it later, can I just visit with my niece first."

Diana felt the urge to snap after having a heated conversation with Bernice. She wanted to know Beatrice's prognosis. She wanted to know if her child was ok. Beatrice refused to talk to her mother and wanted to wait later to discuss the doctor's findings.

"Ok fine whenever you are ready to talk you let me know." Diana left the kitchen and Tracey ran behind her.

"Granma…."

"Girl what has gotten into her?"

"Nothing you know we were just arguing as we always do."

"Let me guess about Barbara?"

"Yes about Barbara."

"Sis you have got to let it go. You know momma is not going to let you talk about Barbara for any reason."

"Okay whatever. Now Beatrice what did the doctor say?" Bernice said impatiently.

"Listen we will talk about this as a family. I need to make a few phone calls so give me a chance ok. I promise sis I will tell you."

"Fine, fine you all are crazy. Let me get my child and go home."

"Girl you can forget it. You know she is staying here for the night. So if you are going home you can leave now," Beatrice chuckled.

"Hmm... I don't even get to make any decisions about my child now. Well isn't that special. I was about to ask if she had clothes here but I forgot the child has her own room. I will be back in the morning for Tracey."

"Alright sis, see ya..."

Talesha stood and asked Beatrice, "Are you going to tell them?"

"Yes Lesha I am but I have something to do first. Don't worry I am going to talk to them as soon as I get the whole family together. Now I just need to get through these next few weeks of school and I will be ok."

"Beatrice...," Talesha interjected.

"Look I am going to tell you one more time I am going to tell them but I have to talk to them together." Tears began to well in Beatrice's eyes.

"Oh girl, please don't cry."

"Lesha I am scared."

"I know baby but you are going to be fine. You better clean yourself up before you go in there to see your momma."

****

Beatrice had received her test results but she never shared them with her family. She didn't want to alarm anyone of her condition, especially her mother. As she continued to go through her treatments required by the doctor, she knew it was inevitable that her secret was going to get out. She decided she would bring the family together once she had made a decision about her next steps. She had just a few more weeks of school and she was determined to make it regardless of the possible outcome.

Beatrice invited the entire family over for dinner. She had to make sure she let her Bernard know in advance, since he had to travel. She cooked all types of food for her family. Roast beef, ham, chicken, potato salad, macaroni and cheese, cream potatoes, fresh green beans, homemade biscuits… She wanted them to feast as if it were the holidays.

"Something shole smells good in here." In walked Barbara and her husband Jeffrey.

"Hey sweetie," Diana said. "Jeffrey, how are you?"

"I am fine Ms. Green. What you done cooked up today."

"Honey I haven't even boiled as much as one collard. Beatrice cooked all that, yawl smelling."

"What?" said Barbara. "When did that girl learn how to cook?"

"Barbara shut up she has been cooking for years. She learned just like you learned, from me and your grandmother."

"Hello, Hello, Hello!" In walked Bernard.

Everyone was so happy to see him. Diana missed him so much but knew he had a prominent job. When he finished his degree in engineering, he was offered a job making six figures. She would have preferred him move back home but she knew he was making a good decision when he stayed. Diana greeted her only son with a big hug and kiss.

"Hey momma," Bernard said as he embraced his mother.

"Hey baby."

"Ok all we waiting for Bernice, and Tracey."

"Is James coming?" asked Barbara in a sarcastic tone.

Diana ignored Barbara's jesting.

"Hmm…" Barbara said.

Bernard said, "Momma what is the occasion?"

"Honey there is no occasion your sister just wanted us to have dinner together."

"Well that's alright! My little sister has grown up."

Beatrice walked out of the kitchen with a serving dish in her hand looking bone thin. She placed the dish on the table and greeted her brother. She and Bernard were extremely close since they were the youngest siblings. Beatrice ran to Bernard and hugged him tightly. He could feel her skeleton through her clothes.

"Hey big brother…!" Beatrice said elated to see him.

Bernard looked in shock at his very thin sister. He hadn't been in town that much since he graduated, and had only seen his family a few times. He called almost every other day. Bernard was shocked about how thin Beatrice had gotten. It was not because she was so large, but before her appearance was flattering.

"Girl you better get to this table an eat something. I hardly recognized you."

"Shut up, boy! You recognized me."

"Girl what done happen to you?" Barbara asked.

Diana interjected, "I wish someone would tell me, she around here eating like a bird throwing up all day."

"I knew there was a reason I dreamed about fish. Girl you better not be pregnant," said Barbara.

"Pregnant?" questioned Bernard. "Don't you have just a few more weeks of school and you done gone and got yourself knocked up?"

Diana yelled, "Wait a minute, Beatrice!"

Beatrice shouted, "No I ain't pregnant, yawl shut up! Where is Bernice with my niece?"

"She called just a few minutes ago she said she was on her way."

Beatrice wanted to finish getting the food on the table. Since Bernice was on her way she wanted to have all of the food ready so her family could eat. Bernice motioned for Barbara to help her in the kitchen.

"Ok Barbara come and help me set the table," said Beatrice.

"Set the table? I am a guest. Ummm….guest don't help set the tables."

"Come on baby sis I will help you set the table," said Bernard.

Diana was aggravated by Barbara's laziness. She knew how contrary Barbara could be. She just shook her head because she didn't want to say anything ugly. She gave Barbara a glaring stare.

"What momma?"

"Nothing, Barbara, nothing…" Diana looked at Barbara and shook her head.

In walked Bernice and Tracey. Beatrice just placed the last dish on the table when they walked in the dining room. Bernice removed her coat and went to greet her baby brother.

"Hey bro…" said Bernice.

"Hey sis, how are you." Bernard kissed his sister and picked up his niece. "Well…why look at this girl here! Give your uncle some sugar."

"Hey Barbara," Bernice said cutting her teeth.

"Hey sis," Barbara said nonchalantly. "Where is James?"

"Well James is parking the car, if you must know."

"Oh ok…"

A few moments later James, Bernice's husband entered the house. He removed his coat and placed it in the living room. He walked into the dining room where everyone was seated.

"Hey everybody," said James.

"Hey James," said everyone in unison.

"Alright everyone the table is set let's eat," commanded Beatrice. James said grace. They began to pass around the serving dishes filling their plates. They were all laughing and smiling at each other. They hadn't laughed in a long time, as a family. Diana smiled. It was nice to have all her children in the same house again. As they enjoyed the food Beatrice felt it was time to have a conversation with her family.

"Alright family, I called you together for a reason," interrupted Beatrice.

"You always trying to steal the show," Barbara busted out in laughter.

"Barbara shut up and let the girl speak," said Bernice. Everyone concurred.

"Well you all know I graduate in less than three weeks. I wanted to make sure we were all there as a family." Everyone nodded.

"Of course we are going to be there baby sis," said Bernard. "What did you think we were going to do? Momma would kill us."

Diana smirked. She loved how her children supported each other. She looked at all of their faces and realized she had sacrificed everything in her life for a good reason. Diana stopped thinking about her past and continued focusing on Beatrice.

"Well I wanted to have this dinner tonight before I graduated because there is a possibility we won't be able to have another dinner like this again."

"Girl what is you talking about? Are you leaving?" asked Barbara.

Bernice continued to talk to her family, "So to speak, I wanted you all to come together and just be with me as I am now, for one more moment in my life."

Diana became worried. She wanted to know what her daughter was talking about. She began to think that this had something to do with Beatrice's test results. She hadn't forgotten that Beatrice didn't share; she was just elated her family was around. Beatrice began explaining what the doctor had discovered after all of her test.

"A few weeks ago the doctor ran some tests on me and I went and got my results. I didn't want to talk about it then because I had to figure out how I felt about it. I decided bringing everyone together was the only way."

Everyone in the room was quiet. They wanted to know what Beatrice was referring to. They all knew she had gotten sick a few times, they just did not know how serious her illness was. Beatrice knew what she was about to share with her family could change the whole dynamic. She didn't know any other way to say it. Beatrice let out a heavy sigh and shared with her family the doctor's diagnosis.

"I have, well I have... leukemia. That is why you see all the weight loss and why I have been so sick. Right now, I have gone through all of the treatments. Between the radiation and the chemo....I just don't know. My body doesn't seem to want to fight this cancer. I am getting weaker. I have been pushing myself for these last weeks because I am determined to finish my degree. I wanted to do this one thing before...."

Diana interjected, "Shut up shut up right now! Don't you even start talking like that! We can get a second opinion."

"Leukemia is what I have momma."

Diana became all flustered and upset. She did not know the ins and outs of the disease but she knew leukemia was deadly. She did not even want to think about death. She had lost so many people she had loved she was not even going to consider losing one of her children.

"Momma calm down."

"Don't you tell me to calm down! You don't tell me one damn thing. We are going to sit at this table, finish eating this meal, and we are going to praise God for everything, do you hear me, everything. There is nothing wrong with you."

Bernice stood up and walked over to her mother. She could see her mother breaking down. Bernice was stunned by the information Beatrice had just shared but she knew she had to hold it together for her mother. Barbara didn't say a word nor did anyone else at the table. Bernice went to embrace her mother and Diana began to yell.

"Don't touch me! Don't you touch me Bernice! Everyone leave me the hell alone!"

Diana got up from table and stormed out of the kitchen. They had never heard their mother swear one day in her life. There was silence at the table. No one said one word.

Diana stayed closed in her room for the next few days. She stayed up night and day, praying and tarrying asking God to forgive her. She begged and pleaded with God and did not believe this was her reality.

Beatrice knocked on the door. Diana refused to move or let anyone in the room. Beatrice persisted. She felt responsible for her mother's state of mind.

"Momma, please let me in."

"GO AWAY! GO AWAY!'

"Momma I am not going anywhere," said Beatrice. "I am coming in."

Diana was kneeled beside the bed arched over with her palms folded tightly. Diana had bags under her eyes. She hadn't slept for days. She looked at Beatrice and continued to cry.

"Momma, don't cry. Momma please, I am all right. I have talked to God over and over again and I have made my peace. I am not gone yet so let's make the best of these days."

Diana heard her daughter. She wanted all of her pain to go away. She wanted God to give her leukemia so Beatrice would not have to suffer. Diana heard a little voice, *Get up Diana you are stronger than this. It is time for you to be there for her. Enjoy her, hug her, and love her.* Diana embraced Beatrice and did not want to let her go.

****

It was a week before graduation. Beatrice was getting worse. She no longer could withstand her sickness. She was no longer receiving chemotherapy. Her body began to ache even more. She could not keep down any food and the doctors felt it was time for her to stay in the hospital so she could receive special attention. She had caught a cold and the doctor's feared her condition may worsen.

Beatrice had satisfied the requirements for her to graduate. She was now waiting for the honor to walk across the stage and receive her diploma. Her professors were made aware of her condition and fully supported her during this time. They assured her that she was going to receive her degree. However, Beatrice knew if she went into the hospital, she would never get the chance to walk across the stage to receive it..

"No mama, I cannot miss graduation."

"Baby you are not going to miss graduation. You are going to stay in the hospital until graduation day. If I have to walk across that stage myself, and get your diploma, I will."

Beatrice smiled at her mother. Beatrice was in so much pain it even hurt for her to be touched. However, her mother's hands were soothing. Diana massaged her legs daily just to keep the circulation moving through her joints. She fed her Jell-O since that was the only thing she could keep down. Diana stroked Beatrice's hair and looked in her eyes. Beatrice was Diana's baby.

The morning of graduation against doctors' orders Diana pulled a wheel chair up to her daughter's room. She had made a promise to Beatrice, and she was going to keep it. She was going to stand by her side until God said otherwise.

Beatrice looked at her mother and said, "Momma what are you doing?"

"I am doing what I promised. I called the Dean of Students and told them we were coming to get our diploma."

"Momma look at me I look awful." Beatrice was embarrassed by how her body had deteriorated.

"Girl we didn't work this hard to care how we look. You worked for this and we are going to get your reward."

Diana pulled the cap and gown out of the bag and in walked Bernice and Barbara. Beatrice was their little sister and they decided they were going to stand together as a family. Bernice and Barbara had set aside their difference because they realized how important family was. Their bickering was not going to take away the pain they felt. So they decided it would be better just to extend love to each other and their baby sister. Diana felt some relief. She couldn't take any more devastation in her life especially when she needed to be strong for Beatrice.

"What are yawl doing here?" Beatrice asked in excitement.

"Did you think we were going to miss your graduation, girl you must be crazy," said Barbara.

"I can't believe yawl did this for me," Beatrice wanted to cry.

"Awe… please girl you are our sister, we love you, and we promised you we were going to do this together," said Bernice.

Bernice and Barbara fought back the tears looking at their baby sister. They couldn't understand why this was happening. Out of everyone to get sick they couldn't believe it was Beatrice. She was such a healthy, vibrant young woman.

The three women dressed Beatrice and took her to fulfill her destiny. Diana, Barbara & Jeffrey, Bernice, James & Tracey, and Bernard gathered in prayer before they took Beatrice to receive her diploma. They were there as a family. Diana would have had it no other way.

Ms. Beatrice Veronica Green, SUMA CUM LAUDE. Diana rolled her child across the stage to receive her Master's in Business. Diana did not shed one tear because she was so proud of her daughter and her accomplishment. Beatrice smiled at her family as she accepted her degree. She had done it. She had achieved her goal, with her family standing by her side.

After the ceremony, the family returned Beatrice to the hospital. Even in her excitement she was extremely weak. The family gathered in Beatrice's hospital room. The nurses thought it would be best if some of the family waited in the waiting room. The nurse became compassionate when she witnessed the loyalty of the family. She allowed them to stay and support Beatrice. At about 11pm they all decided to go home, except Diana.

"Momma," Beatrice said, "Why don't you go home and get some rest?"

"I am going to get some rest, but I am going to do it lying right beside you."

Diana climbed in the bed with her child and held her closely. She held her tightly and kissed her on her cheek. She held her little girl and refused to let her go. Beatrice was so grateful her mother was by her side. Beatrice was tired and her breathe began to get shallow. She was happy with the events of the day. She was proud she had endured all of her strife during her illness. Beatrice had never given up regardless of her circumstances. She held her mother's hand and smiled.

"I love you momma."

"I love you to baby…"

Beatrice died later that night peacefully in her sleep as her mother held her for the last time. Diana knew she had left and she felt when Beatrice had taken her last breath. She kissed Beatrice on the forehead and said a prayer for God to watch over her child in the heavens. Diana called her children in the morning. In a somber voice without a tear, Diana told her family.

"She is gone home to be with grandma and grandpa."

****

Diana let her children pick her up out of the chair. She looked in the face of her now three children and she stared. She wanted to tell them how much she loved them, but they already knew. Burying her youngest child had cause her to remember how precious her other children were that were left on earth. They all had tears in their eyes but did not ruffle a sound. They stared at each other for another moment.

Diana said, "I am ready. Let's take your sister to her new home."

As they lowered the casket in the ground, Diana smiled because in those few moments she realized she had her memories. She realized God had given her strength. Her minor break was over and she snapped back into reality when she recognized she still had three children left to love and care for. She placed a white rose on her daughters casket and she said good-bye, for the last time, to her youngest child.

****

"Ms. Green it is so good to see you. I am sorry it is under these circumstances."

"Mr. Turner?"

It was not the same Mr. Turner who read Mrs. Landers, Will it was his son Timothy Junior. He had taken over his father's law firm when he passed. He had been assisting Diana throughout the years with her estate.

"To what do I owe this visit?"

"Well Beatrice stopped by my office about a month ago before her sickness had escalated. She wanted me to give you this." Mr. Turner handed her a white envelope.

Diana looked at the envelope and told Mr. Turner, thank you. Diana returned home to an empty house. Her other children had gone to their designated homes. They all offered for her to stay with them but Diana felt they needed their space.

She looked around and she heard silence. There was no laughter. There was no aroma of food piercing through the walls. There was no bickering from children, no one claiming they needed momma at that moment. She remembered how lonely her mother use to feel. She had dedicated her entire existence to ensure her children were secure. She was wealthy. God had supplied all of her needs in spite of her heartaches. She began to have a fleshly moment and of questioned where God was in the empty house. She immediately rebuked the spirit of deceit, and confusion, and in her heart, she praised God.

She went upstairs to her mother's old room, sat on the bed, and opened the envelope Mr. Turner had given her earlier that afternoon. She was not excited to open it because she knew whatever it was it finalized she had buried her youngest child. Diana opened the envelope. There seemed to be two different sets of paper and as she unfolded one of them, the other set of papers fell to the floor. She picked them up, placed the additional set of papers on the cherry wood dresser, and began to read the letter.

Momma,

If you are reading this then God has decided to make me an honorary angel. You can wipe your eyes because I am not crying at this moment. I cried when the doctor told me, and I cried several days before I told you. I was scared I disappointed you. You always put your children first and after competing behind Barbara, Bernice and Bernard, I just could not fail. I was never going to fail momma because I knew how much us succeeding meant to you. The sacrifices you made in your life were like no other mother I have heard of.

When you told God you would put us, first that is exactly what you did. I want you to know, I love you for that. You provided me with a solid foundation and that is the best thing a parent can do. I know you couldn't control all of my actions but because of the foundation I knew in my heart I was going to always be grounded. I kept my head up even when I knew death was near because I trusted in the Lord. You and grandma taught me that, and I will never forget it. Besides it may be useful up hear in heaven. Perhaps I can use my degree for some of God's angels. Whatever work God has for me I will fulfill his purpose because I had a great teacher who pointed me in the right direction and handed me the best textbook of all, My Bible.

I have always loved you and I appreciate everything you have done for me my entire life. Most children are not blessed to have the mother I have. So many people have told me how lucky I was and I realized it every day of my life.

Now I want you to do me a favor. Months ago, we talked about our dreams of taking a vacation, and I want you to do that. You have spent your entire life taking care of everyone except yourself. Therefore, I have one dying wish. It is that you be happy, as you have made me. I love you lady, you are truly the best thing that has ever happened to me. I thank you for always being there for me. I never had to figure out where you were, because you were always right there.

Love,
Beatrice

P.S. I have enclosed a round-trip ticket for you to travel to Europe. You have allowed me to follow my dreams now you follow yours. Go find your destiny. Go follow your dreams. I promise I will watch over you every day while I am in heaven. I love you momma, just blow a kiss at the stars and I promise I will catch it.

PART III

Releasing a Good Man

Veronica
"Narcissistic?"

Walston

Releasing a Good Man

Despair, jealousy, and craziness
Remembering the mistake of not understanding your perspective
Has caused me a moment of, miss you
And I didn't realize it,
Until I stared at my reflection
The ugliness of my yesterdays...
How good you were to me
How you loved and held me in high regard

This is my moment of truth
When I admit I was wrong
And you were good
And I was bad

I wasn't like other women who gripe about what their man would or
wouldn't do,
Because you did everything
Fools come in all genders
As well as bashing

I could have been a better woman
With understanding and support
Which I should have offered you instead of the headache
Of intentionally sabotaging your train of thought
To be a better man

I wrapped myself in the emotion of making you want
What I wanted
And you already did
I just didn't understand

Now I am the one who is stuck in unhappy

Walston

Without realizing until hereafter
The happiness was at my finger tips
Therefore, I go on thinking of how it used to be
Or how it is in my world, now

Nevertheless, you do not feel or breathe me anymore
You do not absorb my spirit
Without haste you moved onto where you would be appreciated
The forwarding address

Oh the disgust of my disappointment
Finally the self-awareness of ...
Oh, I miss you

Veronica

Veronica entered the empty house and listened to the songs of silence and sorrow. After a strenuous day of working, she wanted to relax and forget about any heaviness parading throughout her life of hectic. She needed a release and wanted relaxation to curb her appetite from the stress. She knew she should be happy and her feelings should have hounded her spirit with joy, but they did not.

She continued to stare at the house with disappointment of self. She said, *hello,* all that answered were the echoes of the acoustics of the grand foyer as her Nine West heels gently clapped against the hardwood floors. Veronica felt tears attempting to well as she quickly ran to the finely sculptured kitchen to find her favorite bottle of Riesling. She opened the drawer to her stainless steel utensils and found the corkscrew on the right hand side of the drawer.

She inhaled the glass of wine. She carried the bottle with her as she returned to the hall. She walked over to her purse and grabbed the pack of Newport 100's and the engraved lighter. She looked on her desk in the foyer where she kept the same documents she had received months ago. She knew she could not live in the past but the papers reminded her of choices she had made. She grabbed the newspaper, which was dated for the weekend before, and somehow the announcement ran repeatedly in her head.

The engraved letters "K.R." caused Veronica to place the lighter in the crevice of her lips. "I need to stop, I can't do this, not today," Veronica whispered to herself. She walked up the steps, removed the perfectly pressed clothes, and stripped down to her naked skin. She walked into her master bedroom; all that was present were her reflections in the mirrors that surrounded her. Feeling a bit vulnerable, she grabbed her fuchsia silk robe from the closet and walked to the bathroom adjacent to her bedroom.

Veronica looked in the mirror. She did not adore the blank reflection. Feeling extremely somber, she grabbed the cigarette lighter and began to light the scented candles around the tub. She opened her

CD case and began to make a selection from the various female artists. As the bath water ran, she pulled out the Tealeaf & lavender mineral bath soaking beads, Vaseline Intensive Care bath and poured the mixture into the popping hot water. She took a sip from her third glass of Riesling. She could not believe she was on her third since she had moved from the kitchen to the bathroom in such a short period. She moved her ashtray to the side of jacuzzi size bathtub making sure she was able to enter the bathtub without stumbling. She removed her silk robe from her perfect chocolate mold and admired the body she kept fit daily. She turned on the jets in the tub and hit play on the CD player.

"Somewhere in my Lifetime," Phyllis began to sing and Veronica began to sink into her pity. She lit her cigarette and began to sing along with Phyllis. Veronica knew every word, every bar, and the chorus, as if she wrote the words for Phyllis.

Somewhere in my lifetime
You've been here with me
Oh so close to me
Somewhere in my lifetime
Somewhere in my lifetime
I have kissed your lips
Lips so tenderly
They've been kissing me
They were visions
Of so long ago
You know memories come and go
So they say
People say, yes they do
Let visions of what
Of what will be
Somewhere in my lifetime
It was you and me...You and me

Somewhere in my lonely dreams
You've been here with me
Oh so close to me
And I've been loving you
Somewhere in my lifetime
Somewhere in my lifetime
Somewhere in my lifetime
It was you...and....me...

As the song faded, Veronica began to cry. She began to think about the type of woman she had become. She began to think about the type of woman she was before; how she use to act, how she treated people, including her family friends, and yes him. Why did she treat him that way? She took another drag off her cigarette and a sip of her wine. The water appeared to beat her body. The force was not soothing and felt uncomfortable. Was this the pain from her heart, turning into physical pain? She watched the water splash and hit her body as she continued to have overwhelming thoughts of her actions. She picked up a set of papers she had signed two years prior. *Initial here* __*VBW*__.

She placed the paper, back on the side of the tub. Then she grabbed the newspaper, which was folded to the announcement page. She stared at the articles but paid close attention to the smiles of the familiar face in the photo. *Congratulations to Mr. & Mrs....* She giggled to herself as the tears streamed down her face. She pulled the Newport one more time, poured her fourth glass of wine, and hit repeat on the CD player. Phyllis began drowning out the noises in Veronica's head. She wept and wept as the music played. She closed her eyes and remembered her first encounter with her supposed forever.

****

"Excuse me," the mannish voice said to Veronica.

"Yes?"

"May I ask why you are sitting in this car by yourself?"

"What the heck do you care? Is that any of your business?" Veronica said sarcastically.

"No ma'am it isn't but I was just concerned. A beautiful woman like you should not sit in such a dimly lit area all alone."

Veronica looked around as she watched people walk through the parking lot. "I am not by myself," said Veronica. Veronica began to get annoyed at the young man. "What do you want?"

The young man ran out of words and had no idea what to say. He had never interacted with such a brash woman. She was sadistic and not sincere at all. She was not soft or delicate but he could see something in her eyes. Regardless of how hasty she was being, he still found her to be intriguing.

"Ok I thought so. So since I am not by myself and clearly you have nothing to say that makes any sense. So, I am going to ask you to get away from me."

"You shouldn't be like that."

"Be like what? Dude, you came up to my car! You do even know me. You have said nothing of importance. I have had a hard day at work, I need a drink, have to drive thirty-five minutes to get home, and I am hungry! So if I want to sit in this car all night, I can. I just want some peace for God's sake. Why don't you bother someone who wants to be bothered?"

Veronica continued to act belligerent toward the young man who was trying to get to know her. She could have cared less about his intentions. She was frustrated and had no regard for any men. Veronica didn't care about her brashness, she just wanted to vent. It didn't matter who was on the other side of her display of ugly.

"There were more than enough lonely chicks at the bar... Why don't you do go and see if they need some rescuing," said Veronica.

The man stepped away from the car. Veronica had finally pushed him away with her aggressive behavior. She did not care what she had said to him or how he received it. She did not want to hear any of his corny pick-up lines.

"Okay, Okay, I am sorry I bothered you."

Veronica refused to accept his apology and turned her head. She did not respond to the man at all. Veronica started up her car and pulled off.

Veronica walked in her house thirty minutes later. She was tired and wanted to get a few hours of sleep before she had to tackle her routine for yet another day. She could hear the sound of her mother walking down the steps. Veronica was not in the mood for her nagging questions.

"Veronica is that you?"

"Yes mama."

"What time is it?"

"It is 2:15..."

"What in the world girl?" Veronica's mother came walking down the steps. "Why in the world are you so late?"

"Momma I had to work a double."

"Why are you up?"

"What do you mean why am I up. My child is out all times of the night, has not called, and I don't sleep unless my children are in the house."

Veronica said, "Momma, what children? I am not a child and you do not have to worry about me."

"Look Veronica, do not tell me what to worry about, and as long as I am your mother I can do whatever I want."

"I know, I know but you should be asleep." Veronica kissed her mother. "Is daddy in the bed?"

"Girl please he was out at nine."

"You see momma, he ain't worried."

"Oh please he is worried he just doesn't say anything because you're his baby. For some odd reason he thinks you can take care of yourself."

"Momma I can."

Her mother gave her a quick sniff and said, "Girl you been drinking and smoking."

"Momma I work in a bar for God's sake."

"You right for God's sake. You don't even need to be working in there."

"Momma we have been through this a thousand times. I have to work so I can go to school."

"Girl you don't need money. School it is paid for…"

"So let me guess, you're going to buy the clothes and the new car too. Oh yea, and you're going to take care of my living expenses, right?"

"Don't get smart child. I told you your daddy and I will help you do whatever you need."

"I know momma but there is something about getting your own. You and daddy worked for what you have. You didn't let grandma do anything for you."

"She paid for my education; she helped your daddy and me, get this house. Your father and I did not feel the need to ask for any more assistance. Your grandma was too busy taking care of everyone else in this world, to take time out for herself. She had enough stress in her life when we lost…never mind."

Veronica's mother paused in mid-conversation. She began to feel a little anxious but quickly rejected the emotions. She continued speaking with Veronica about assistance from her mother.

"She gave me the things I needed but I had to initiate my blessings. Not to mention I made smart investments."

Veronica said, "I know just like you and daddy provided school for me, a car, and insurance. Momma I am forever grateful. But I am not going to watch you take your last and take care of me. That is why I work. Think about it, in less than ten years I am going to be self-made and sending you two on trips."

"Girl we can send ourselves. We are not broke."

"I know momma but I want to do something for you. I just don't want to take. Let me be who you raised me to be. Lord knows I live here too."

"I like you being here baby."

Veronica didn't have the heart to tell her mother she was in the market looking for an apartment. She knew it would break her heart since she had been living there for years. Veronica would be the last child to leave the nest.

"Look momma, get some rest we have to be up early in the morning and I have two classes before I go to work."

"Girl you better slow down. Why am I telling you that, you are just going to add another class and get another job?"

Veronica laughed at her mother. "Probably so," Veronica agreed.

"I love you momma."

"I love you too."

"Oh by the way you got a phone call this evening."

"Momma I don't care if he called."

"Who said it was he?"

"Momma, I know who it was, he has been calling all week. There is nothing he can say."

"Baby, don't be like that he probably just wants to apologize."

"Sure, so he can drag what is left of my heart with him. Mama I can't and I don't need to talk to him, even if he is saying sorry."

"Sweet heart you have to learn to forgive. If you don't you may not be able to learn to trust another man. You will be guarded and forget what it means to be loved. You deserve so much more. We live, we love, and we learn. I never told you being in love was easy just understand it is the purest thing we have in life. Someone, somewhere one day is going to want to share love with you."

Veronica looked in her mother's eyes and knew there was some truth to the words she spoke. She could not find it in her heart to let it flow in her understanding.

"Get some rest baby," said Veronica's mother.

"Momma I will you need to get some too."

Veronica got dressed and did not have time to eat breakfast. Her parents were already in the kitchen having their morning conversation. Veronica grabbed her coat, kissed her mother on the cheek and was about to walk out the door.

Veronica said, "Morning daddy, bye-bye daddy!" Veronica did not make time to hold any small conversations.

"Slow down girl didn't you just get in a few hours ago?"

"Yes daddy it is almost seven thirty and I have to get to class. Love you bye," said Veronica as she exited.

Veronica's father shrugged his shoulders. "That girl is going to run a hole in the ground. She doesn't even take time to breathe."

"I know, I know, she reminds me of someone I once knew," said Veronica's mother. Veronica's father looked at his wife and did not say a word.

Veronica arrived at school twenty minutes later just in time to meet with her professor before the class began. She wanted him to allow her to do her senior project without a group. Veronica was a not a sociable student and did not enjoy working with others.

Veronica greeted her teacher, "Professor…"

"Yes Ms. Walters, how are you this morning? I see you are here early."

"Yes sir I am. I wanted to see if it was at all possible to work on my senior project without being in a group?"

Her professor was puzzled by her question. He knew that the senior project was group effort. He could not understand for the life of him why she would want to do it all by herself. He did not know much about Veronica but he had noticed that she did not interact with other students in the class.

"Let me get this straight you want to work on your senior project which is going to take countless hours of research, and writing, by yourself. You could cut the time in half with the help of others. Are you mad young lady?"

Veronica's professor always admired her determination because she was the most driven student in his class. He figured her isolation was the reason she had such excellent grades. He never tried to show her favoritism but he knew she deserved some leeway. He just did not know if he could grant her the accommodation with the senior project.

"See professor, I am working late nights and it is very difficult for me to meet with people. I work thirty-five minutes away and for me to do the back and forth gets kind of hectic."

The professor was well aware Veronica could do her senior project with her eyes closed; however, he was concerned it might not shine a positive light in the class. Little did the professor know that no one wanted to work with the perfectionist? The project had to be her vision, and not a group idea. Not to mention, Veronica was not popular in her class because of her arrogance.

"Ms. Walters, I know you have the ability to complete this project by yourself, but because you also have to complete your thesis this semester, I believe I would be overloading you with work."

"No you won't professor I started my thesis last semester when I was approved to complete my Master's. You know I took a double load of classes; twenty-six credits, so I could make this possible. So I have it planned out I can…"

"Veronica slow down," the professor interjected. "What is going on?"

"Nothing Professor…"

"Then why are you in a hurry, why are you not enjoying college? You are never at any college activities, you don't socialize, you live off campus, and you work ridiculous hours. To make even worse you work at a bar as a bartender. Your whole life is a contradiction. It is as if you want to have every minute of the day filled so you do not have to deal with anything other than your tasks and goals. What are you running away from?"

"Professor, listen are you going to make me work in a group or not?" asked Veronica hastily.

The professor stood back and looked at the young woman who seemed to be impatient for no apparent reason. "For your final project you must work in a group. I will assign you partners during class time."

"Fine," she said and stomped away. Veronica smacked her lips in disappointment.

"Ms. Walters," the Professor called out to his student. Veronica acted as if she did not hear her teacher call her name. "Ms. Walters," called the Professor.

"Yes sir…" Veronica shifted around with funky body language.

"You better wake up or you will miss your true opportunities." Veronica rolled her eyes at her teacher and did not respond.

It was 2:30pm and Veronica was on her way to her job at the *Shasta Bar 'n' Grill.* She kept her change of clothes in her car. She knew she could not stop at home because it would slow her progress. Veronica thought about her three project partners.

Oh God they are the laziest in the class. He knew what he was doing. He doesn't want me to succeed. Everyone wants me to fail. I will show him. He does not have to worry about it. You haven't seen anything yet. Oh, they must not know. Oh, they are going to work, if they plan on working with me.

Veronica hit the gas and proceeded down the road to her job while cussing out everyone. No one was present to hear the slanderous words. Veronica pulled into the parking lot of her job and held tightly onto the steering wheel in preparation for what she was about to embark on for the evening.

"Hey Roney…"

"Excuse me Ms. Thang, my name is Veronica," she said sternly. "You must be new."

"I am so sorry. I heard Lisa call you Roney. I didn't mean any harm…"

"Ok you don't explain yourself just learn the name."

"I…I, am sorry," the young woman was tongue tide.

"You will be fine," Veronica said sarcastically as she proceeded to her station.

"Girl you didn't have to act like that," Lisa said.

"Girl please, she doesn't know me to be chopping up my name. She ain't been here three days. She don't know if I own this place or not."

"Girl please you wear the same uniform as we do," said Lisa.

"Lisa please…, Mr. Graftko wears this hot mess too. I could be his wife for all she knows."

"Are you on your monthly?" asked Lisa.

"Don't play!"

"No, you don't play Roney! Don't come up in here with all that today. That girl did not piss in your cornflakes, and the way you have been acting lately, I am going to assume you squatted over your own bowl. Check yourself Roney. Stop being mad at everyone! We didn't break your heart, we didn't treat you like crap, we didn't cheat on you, and we didn't leave you!"

Veronica felt an overwhelming feeling to burst, but her heart was harden and did not allow her to. *Fine, I don't need this.*

"I am going to have a cigarette and eat before my shift starts."

Lisa yelled, "You probably need to take the day off and go change your pad!"

Veronica rolled her eyes and walked out the door. "Whatever bitch," Veronica mumbled under her breath.

Veronica walked over to the corner store across the street. She was furious that Lisa tried to play her at work. She entered the store and immediately started to find her favorite comfort foods. She picked up a Coca-Cola, a bag of sour cream 'n' onion chips, and a chicken salad sandwich. She placed them on the counter, and asked the cashier for a pack of Newport 100's.

"That will be five twenty five," said the cashier.

Veronica went to grab her purse and realized in her haste she left it behind the counter.

Veronica screamed, "Oh my God, can anything else happen today!"

"Here you are ma'am," a familiar face leaned over the counter and handed the cashier a twenty-dollar bill. Veronica stopped and looked at the man's face. Veronica was embarrassed. She was not accustomed to a man coming to her rescue. She was flattered and had forgotten to show some manners at the man's kind gesture.

"You're welcome ma'am."

Veronica paused, "Thank you."

The cashier noticed the way the young man was looking at Veronica and said, "Hmm…, everything ain't wrong today."

Veronica looked at the cashier, said thank you, and began to walk out the store. The young man grabbed his change and walked out the door behind Veronica. He followed Veronica out of the store trying to get her attention. She was not paying attention at all. She was still playing the scene in the bar repeatedly in her head. Veronica had become flustered. She reached into her bag and pulled out her cigarettes. The man watched her every step. He did not know why Veronica was flustered but he wanted to get her attention.

"You know those things will kill you?"

Veronica stopped packing her cigarettes. She looked at her knight who had showed up out of nowhere and rescued her from embarrassment. Veronica did not have much to say to the man but she knew she could not be rude after his kind gesture.

"I know I have been trying to quit." She continued placing a cigarette in her mouth and tried to find a lighter.

He had gotten her attention. The young man noticed she was struggling to find something to light her cigarette. He began to laugh as he pulled a blue lighter from his pocket along with his pack of Newport shorts. Veronica knew she looked like a fool and could not help it. However, because the man was so charming she did not mind him witnessing her mishaps. She began to laugh also.

"You have a beautiful smile," he said. "You should smile more often." Veronica could not utter any other words but thank you.

"Well I will see you around," he said as he was about to walk off.

"Thank you again," Veronica said as she began to walk to the picnic table.

He did not even ask me my name. Oh God, I don't know his name either. Lord what has gotten into me. What is wrong with me? I let this fool cloud my judgment and I have been so nasty. I didn't even notice a man was being kind to me. I know I was raised better than this. Veronica mulled over her intriguing encounter with the nameless man. Veronica ate her food and returned to work.

When Veronica returned to work, her entire disposition had changed. She had pondered over her actions at her place of business and realized not only were they unnecessary they were callous. Veronica knew she was not angry with her co-workers; she was trying to deal with a pain she had not released. She wanted to make sure she apologized for her unruly actions.

"I am sorry Lisa, and Beverly. I don't know what has gotten into me."

Lisa laughed, "I know what hasn't gotten into you and that is probably why you are so evil." Beverly and Lisa both laughed.

"Girl shut up," said Veronica. "I am so sorry Beverly. I should have never spoken to you like that."

"It's ok," she said in a squeaky voice. "I…, I have bad days too."

Veronica looked at Lisa as they both looked at the one hundred and fifteen pounds of passive. They began to giggle to themselves. Beverly insisted on proving her point.

"I do, I do, I get angry and I sometimes scream."

"Oh ok baby, we understand." Lisa and Veronica said in unison while smirking at the young woman.

"But I do guys."

"It's time to work before our boss comes out here wondering what we are doing in a huddle and there are customers to be waited on," said Lisa.

The grill was packed and there was not any time for a break. Veronica began to get tired but she knew she only had one more hour to deal with the debacle in the bar, and then she could be on her way home to do it all over again. *What the heck is the bar doing this packed on a Thursday night?* As she was preparing the Cosmopolitan for table six, she started to think about the man who so generously helped her out of a bind.

God he was not that bad to look at, at all. Is it possible I need a tune-up and an oil change? Let me get my mind out of the gutter. Roney you do need some maintenance that is not a lie. She began to giggle to herself. *Forty-five minutes God let me get out of here so I can go home.*

****

Veronica said, "TGIF!!"

She arose for her last full day of work and school before the weekend. She looked at her daily task for the day. She needed to call her study group to set up a time to start their senior project. She began to think about her other tasks. *I need to get an oil changed before work.* Veronica giggled. *I probably need to see what is going on for the weekend. Who am I kidding it will be Monday by the time I write this list out. We will see…*

The bar was packed. Veronica was fixing drink after drink. She had worked for over seven hours before she was able to take her first smoke break. She wasn't angry at all because her tip jar stayed full all night. Veronica was tired and wanted to get home as soon as possible. She knew she would not be able to rest most of the weekend, she was just happy she did not have to return to the bar for at least two days.

"This was a long night," Veronica said to Lisa.

"You got plans this weekend?" asked Lisa.

"No not really, you?"

"Yes I do, with my beau," Lisa chuckled.

"Well I don't have one of those so I guess I will catch up on some work."

"Girl you have time to catch up because you want to. And knowing you, you probably have everything already outlined.

Veronica looked at Lisa as if she had been spying on her creating her task list. Veronica liked to have everything planned and in order. She couldn't help it if Lisa lived a spontaneous life. She thought being unorganized was reckless.

Lisa told Veronica, "Everything does not have to be perfect. You need an outlet. Let loose one time for Pete's sakes."

"Who is Pete?" said Veronica.

"I don't know but you better ask somebody."

"Girl, go home," said Veronica.

"You too, drive safely."

"I am. I am going to stop at the store, and grab me something to munch on for the ride home."

"At two in the morning? You know you don't need to be out here that late."

"I know but I also need cigarettes. I am just going over to the store."

"Okay girl love you, see you next week."

Veronica pulled into the parking lot and began to look in her mirror before she got out of the car. She knew she had to hurry and get on the road. It was only thirty-five minute ride, but going back and forth became tedious. Veronica never left her car without checking her appearance. Even if it was late, and the store was empty, she never knew whom she might see.

She heard a voice coming from her peripheral, "You look fine."

"What the... Are you stalking me?"

"I should ask you if you are stalking me. You come to my job almost every other day and I have only been at your workplace once."

"What do you mean?" said Veronica.

"It's simple I work here in the storage room."

Veronica smiled but did not want the young man to know she was happy to see him. She did not want to seem desperate or give off any unwanted vibes. She was not interested in making him her main squeeze but she loved the attention.

"What do you mean you have been to my job only once?"

"Oh… I see, you do not remember me. Remember you cussed me out in the parking lot when I told you, you shouldn't be sitting outside by yourself."

The light went off in Veronica's head. She remembered his face. He was the young man who had approached her car inquiring why she was sitting all alone. She also remembered she was not polite. Veronica was ashamed of her actions.

"Oh yea..."

"Oh yea," he replied. "That was me."

"Look I am so sorry."

"No need to apologize just because a brother ain't got game. It was my fault for being kind of corny."

"Ok my bad," Veronica said. "So are you working tonight?"

"Yea kind of, I will be off in about twenty minutes."

"That's cool. Let me run in here so I can get down the road."

"Hmmm… Let me guess a chicken salad sandwich, sour cream 'n' onion chips, Coke, and a pack of Newport 100's."

"Oh don't act like you know me… I might have gotten another kind of chip."

He laughed. "You don't have to get out of your car. Give me a second."

Two minutes later, the young man walked out of the store with a bag of all Veronica's requests. He remembered her choices from their previous encounter in the store. He had made it his business to recollect what she liked.

Veronica smiled at the man and said, "Thank you again."

"You are most certainly welcome, ma'am."

"My name is Veronica," she blurted out.

He was shocked at Veronica's outburst but found it endearing. He responded, "My name is Kareem."

"Kareem it is nice to meet you, formerly."

"Well you should be getting down the road, I always here you complain that you have to drive thirty five minutes, so I won't hold you."

Veronica did not want to leave him so abruptly. *Lighten up girl, this man is kind just enjoy his kindness. Give it a chance if only for a few minutes.*

"Kareem umm…, I hope I am not being too forward, but why don't you join me at the picnic table? I can eat my food…and maybe we can talk. Besides I shouldn't eat and drive it is a little dangerous."

Kareem retorted, "Now who has the corny pick-up lines?"

Veronica stuttered, "No, no, I am, I am…"

"I am just joking Veronica. I would love to join you."

****

For the next few weeks, there were no commitments, no expectations, just friendships. Veronica did not slowdown in her task but she did enjoy her time with Kareem. Every night after work, he waited for her with her bag of goodies, just because. He admired her as a woman because in his mind she was God's ultimate creation. He enjoyed being in his space. Although she was solely focused on friendship he could not help but think about the, what if's.

What if I hold her close, smell her hair, and admire her beauty. What if I taste her lips, wrap her in the imperfections of this world, and guard her as the most precious commodity. What if?

"Kareem what are you day dreaming about boy."

"Excuse me…, boy?"

"Don't play with me. You know what I am saying."

"Veronica?"

"Yes Kareem…"

"What do you want?"

"I am not sure but I do know I don't want to gain any weight from all these sandwiches and chips you feed me night after night," Veronica said laughing.

"No Veronica, I am asking, what do you want in a man?"

Veronica had not thought that far ahead. She was happy to be in the company of a man who did not ask her for anything. She was happy he could not hurt her because she had made up in her mind she was not getting involved for any reason. Veronica had no thoughts of a relationship, which involved her feelings.

"Uhh…, I don't know, I haven't thought much about it."

"Well what do you want to do?"

Veronica did not pay attention to what she was being asked. She was so focused on her own interest. She did not understand the intent of his questions. She didn't embrace the intimacy Kareem was offering. She continued to eat her snacks as she began to answer the questions.

"That's easy. I am going to graduate in a few weeks with my B.A. in Sociology and complete the Master's program all at once. Then, I am going to get rid of this job at this jute joint, make six figures, run a corporation, shop until I drop, eat rich food, and build me a house that has a huge bathroom. Oh yea…it must have a Jacuzzi size bathtub. Yea buddy… with jets, and it must have a place for my wine glass and fruit."

Everything Veronica mentioned in relation to self. She didn't mention love, children, or family. Somehow, Kareem was not turned off at all. He appreciated her ambition and vision. However, Kareem wanted her to see him. He wanted her to see them as one.

"That's what you want?" asked Kareem. Kareem stared at Veronica and noticed how naïve she was that she didn't even recognize he would make it his life's goal to get her everything she requested.

Veronica took a bite of the chicken salad sandwich too concerned to see the man sitting before her. She was so comfortable with Kareem she did not care if she appeared to be a glutton. She was not trying to impress him or win him over. She never had a friendship from a man like Kareem. She had never been in contact with the opposite sex unless they had a hidden agenda. Veronica forgot about beguiling man who had previously taken advantage of her female attributes.

"Oh my goodness it is late... I need to be getting down the highway. Are we doing this again?" She asked the disappointed man.

"Yes dear we can do anything you want."

Veronica got in her car and started the engine. She began to check her mirrors and failed to look at the manly figure before her. She placed her seatbelt across her chest and turned her head to Kareem who looked as if he wanted to tell her something. She knew he was gentle and kind but she would not look far enough into his soul to see if he was the one who was destined to be her forever. Kareem did not want to let her pull off without saying anything about his feelings. Although he was tempted, something inside him resisted to ask her the questions on his mind.

Kareem asked, "Hey Veronica when is your next day off?"

"Honey please I never have a day off trying to complete Roney's mission in life. Why do you ask?"

"I want to show you something special."

"Oh do you now. You want to show me something. Whatcha you gonna show me?"

"It would be a surprise lady."

Kareem lied. He knew he would be able to put something together once she gave him a specific date. He wanted to give her something she never had. Even if it was for a private moments, Kareem wanted to figure out how to make her dreams come true.

"Okay sir let me look at my calendar and I will let you know. I have exams coming up. I need to focus on getting them done so they can hand me my paper. I have been looking for a job and with my credentials; I should be getting offers knocking down my door."

"Girl you are too much," said Kareem.

"I know but that is why I am so fierce." Veronica snapped her fingers. "You know you love it."

Kareem smiled. *I do love you Veronica.* He wanted to express the sentiment but knew it was not the appropriate time. He hoped that one day he would be able to tell her everything he felt. He was going to make it his life's work to make her fall in love with him.

"Okay so same time same place. To the bat cave I go." Kareem pinched Veronica's cheek and patted her door as she began to drive off.

****

Veronica's mother was shocked to see her daughter with a different attitude. Veronica was coming in later each night for the last six months. Veronica was not herself. She appeared to be content and not stressed. Her mother wanted to know what had been altered in her life. She and her daughter were very close. She knew she was going to get the information out of Veronica one way or the other. Her motherly intuition lead her to believe the opposite sex was involved. She identified that if this was the case then her daughter was relinquishing her feelings of loathing men. She had not seen her daughter happy with a companion in over a year. Veronica had hardened her heart after her last break-up.

Veronica's mother remembered how devastated she was when she discovered all of her lover's infidelities and discrepancies. Veronica was devoted to this man and never looked at another. Toward the end of their relationship, she had contracted an STD that he denied and tried to blame on her. He had also conceived another child during their four-year relationship that she did not find out about until after the two went their separate ways.

Veronica did not eat or sleep for weeks at a time. Her grades had plummeted to an all-time low. She was missing assignments and had fallen into a great depression. Her grieving caused concern in her family because Veronica was always strong and resilient. One day out of nowhere the light went off and Veronica bounced back into her old self. She never questioned the how, she was just thankful to God that he had put an end to her daughter's misery. The consequence of her bouncing back was she no longer cared about anyone but herself. She became extremely selfish and self-absorbed. Veronica's only concern from that point was how to make Veronica better. Her mother although concerned, prayed day in and out for her daughter to be delivered from this new spirit that tiptoed into her sub-consciousness.

When she took notice to the change of Veronica's behavior she was sure God had yet again answered her prayer. She was a bit skeptical but if her daughter was off her high horse, and smiled most of the day then she was satisfied. She wanted to know whom he was the man who had made a change in her daughter's heart.

"Who is this young man who keeps you out all times of the night?"

"Mamma...nobody, he is just a friend."

"A friend, huh...? I ain't ever had any friend keep me out all times of the night."

"Please... how did you and daddy meet?" Veronica laughed.

"I have you know I met your daddy at a church function."

"Momma, please stop it with the church function. You tell that lie too often. You met daddy after you and your friends left the church convention and went dancing."

"What...? How you know that missy?"

"Remember momma, grandma Di shares stories with your children too. You know she loves her grandchildren. She especially likes to tell us stories of yesterdays. I do not know why you like to pretend you were born into a perfect world and had a perfect life.

Saved, sanctified, wrapped up, tide up ,and filled with the Holy Ghost…whatever…," said Veronica.

Veronica's mother laughed. "Girl your grandma has no business telling you my business."

"Momma, you don't have any business like you tell me."

Veronica's mother wanted to take the focus off her and said, "Okay Veronica, who is he?"

"Who?" Veronica asked trying to be absent minded.

"The young man out in the boonies," said her mother.

"Oh Kareem… He is cool we talk about life and dreams; he buys me a sandwich, chips, and a soda every night. We just talk."

"Just talk, Veronica…? Don't play games."

"Momma trust me if I were getting some I wouldn't come back home. I don't think you are aware of the cob webs…"

"Look I don't need to know all that."

Veronica's mother was well aware that her daughter was grown but she did not want to know all of her personal business. She just assumed she was doing something ungodly since she did not have a permanent frown or tight look on her face. It did not matter anyway, what could she say about her fully grown daughter, engaging in an intimate act. It was not as if she was doing it under her roof. Not to mention Veronica's mother knew how easy a woman could be tempted in the hands of a man. Especially if he was fine and charming, that would cause even more distraction and destruction.

"Listen momma I can't tell you the story in halves," Veronica laughed. "He is nice but he is aware I have been hurt. He is just an average man trying to make a living."

Veronica did not want to make a big deal about who Kareem was. She knew her mother was secretly praying for her to find a man. She did not want to disappoint herself, or her mother. She felt that indulging at this point of their friendship would cause a conflict. She had subtle feeling for Kareem but not enough for her to fall back in love.

"Well what does he do?"

"Uhhh… I know he works in the convenient store part time. I am not really sure what he does."

"Veronica, than what on earth are you all talking about in the middle of the night?"

Veronica responded, "My favorite subject momma."

"What is that Veronica?"

"ME!"

"Girl you ought to stop."

"Well he asks."

"I am sure you go on and on about you all day. Don't make the man sick of you."

"What do you mean get sick of me; he is the one that initiated the conversation in the first place."

Veronica's mother wanted to slap her silly. She knew her daughter was too intelligent to play this stupid. She knew her daughter was vain and self-absorbed but she also saw how happy this enigma was making her daughter happy. She knew he could not be that bad to hold Veronica's time.

"Girl are you naïve? You don't even know when a man is interested in you?"

"Interested? Momma, you just have to meet him."

"Well that would be fine. Your daddy and I would love to meet him."

"Momma no…! I don't want him to think."

"You don't want him to think what? He is your friend right?"

She had finally struck one of Veronica's nerves. Veronica's face turned childlike as if she was embarrassed to answer. She had seen that expression before and realized at that very moment her daughter was interested in this man no matter how much she denied it.

"Momma, don't start."

"What? Veronica I just said I wanted to meet the young man. I am not getting you married. I just want to meet the young fellow."

"Okay momma, after graduation, at the cookout. He had asked me when my next day off was."

"Why did he ask you that?"

"Oh nothing he said he had surprise for me."

Veronica's mother began to giggle to herself. She loved how a mother's intuition worked. She had Veronica pegged at her first smile. Veronica was interested but guarded. She never wanted to let her mother know she was a tad bit vulnerable. She was going to continue to guard her heart at all cost. However, even if Veronica was going to play the role of a dumb blond her candid mother was going to speak her mind regardless of Veronica's reaction.

"Hmm, your *FRIEND* has a *SURPRISE* for you… OH… ok. Veronica let me just say this before you go to class and do whatever it is you do in twenty three hours."

"What momma?"

"You're STUPID!!! Have a nice day baby." Veronica's mother walked off shaking her head.

****

Veronica Beatrice Walters, Suma cum Laude! Veronica walked across the stage and had a huge smile on her face. She had been waiting on this day for six long years. She now held her B.A. and Master's in Sociology. Her next steps were preparing to do some hands on training. She had completed her internship at a boys juvenile home her junior year. In her senior year, she was able to do some clinical work at the *Fabridge Mental Institution*. Veronica had a dream to manage her own in home counseling office and open up a group home for boys and girls. She had big dreams and wanted to do big things.

Veronica's parents waited for her to get out of the crowd of thousands who had also graduated. Her family knew how hard she had worked to accomplish her goals. They knew their daughter was determined and was going to succeed in spite of any adversity.

Go Roney it's your birthday not for real, real but for play. Veronica danced around playfully as she approached her parents. Her parents

150

were the reason she worked hard. She came from a strong family. They supported both of their children in whatever they wanted to do. However, they were not prepared for all the vicissitudes with their girls. Nevertheless, they were never going to give up on their hopes for their children.

"Oh baby I am so proud of you!"

"Thank you, momma and daddy."

"Where's the rest of the family?"

"Oh they went to the house to change their clothes and are getting ready for the cookout."

While they were in mid-conversation, a young man began to walk toward Veronica with a bouquet of white roses. Veronica's mother noticed the young man but Veronica was too busy running her mouth getting cameo photos taken of her. Veronica's mother stared at the man as he walked toward them. He had on a cream shirt with linen pants. His mustache was neatly trimmed and a pair of designer sunglasses covered eyes. His skin was caramel and you could smell the Polo oil, mixed in with sweet pearls of sweat. Veronica's mother called her name.

"Roney, Roney!"

"Yes mamma."

She pointed in the direction of the fine stature walking toward them. He was smooth and sexy. He walked with such confidence and commanded attention of young women around. This young man only had one focus and one destination. As he approached Veronica's mother still stared
in shock and awe.

"Uh do, do you know him," said Veronica's mother.

"OMG…! You made it! Hey dude what is up!" Veronica said to the man.

Her mother looked at her as if she had lost her mind. *What is up? This is coming from a young woman who just received her Master's. Sweet merciful Jesus*! Her mother shook her head in embarrassment. She knew she had taught her child to be lady-like but she actually acted as if this was one of her homeboys. Her mother began to hope this was not the man, the friend; she had been sneaking off with at night. She thought the man who had her attention had allowed her to be more dainty and feminine. Veronica acted as if he was just another guy.

Veronica embraced the young man but caught a whiff of his essence and immediately let him go. *Lord have mercy, what was that?* She realized she had never embraced Kareem. She had also never seen him look that scrumptious. She always saw him in his work uniform, and even though he was always attractive, seeing him out of his element sparked something in Veronica. She tried to play it off after she embraced him and focused on him meeting her parents.

"Veronica, who is this?" Her mother asked while she was tapping her foot.

"Oh my bad…, Momma, daddy this is Kareem. Kareem Robinson."

"Oh so you are the friend?"

"Yes ma'am I am the friend," Kareem laughed.

"How are you young man?"

"I am fine."

Her mother said under her breath, "My God, yes you are."

"Did you bring me flowers Kareem? You shouldn't have," Veronica said sarcastically.

"Well I didn't, these are for your mother."

"Hey… oh hey friend, I like him Roney." Veronica's mother said cheesing from ear to ear.

Veronica was stunned. What type of move was that, she thought? She had never been around a man who acknowledged either of her parents with such class. She was a bit disappointed he did not bring her a gift because she longed for the attention. Instead of showing she was disappointed, Veronica was about to roll her eyes and her father interjected.

"Hello young man," said Veronica's father.

"Hello sir."

"Now I know that you didn't just show me up in front of my wife?"

"Ughh…no, no sir," Kareem was speechless.

"Boy I am just joking." Her father started to laugh, "It is nice to meet you."

Veronica's mother looked at her flowers and was so impressed with the young man. She was hoping her daughter had some sense. It was more than obvious this young man was interested. She figured she was going to make Kareem feel as comfortable as possible. She believed at some point her daughter would wake up and take notice to this man.

"These are beautiful flowers, thank you baby."

"You're welcome ma'am. Veronica asked me to come to the cook out. I hope it won't be a problem."

"Not a problem at all. You are more than welcome."

Mrs. Walters grabbed Kareem. They began to walk off arm and arm. She was always flirty. She knew a woman's responsibility was to let a man know he was appreciated. All her intentions were innocent and in the interest of Veronica. His thoughtfulness deserved a warm embrace and she wanted to know a little more about him. Veronica was shocked and began to shake her head. She knew her mother would take over. She was a little jealous but enjoyed the fact Kareem was so comfortable with her family, and he had just met them. Veronica and her father just stood there shaking their head. They began to laugh as they watched Mrs. Walters and Kareem head to the parking lot.

Mr. Walters looked at his daughter and bellowed, "Yo momma!"

"Yo wife," Veronica retorted. They both laughed and followed behind arm and arm.

****

Veronica's celebration was fantastic. All of her family was present and Kareem fit right in. Veronica was happy to share her day with her family and friends. She could not believe she was finally finished college. Veronica was already contemplating her next steps.

Her mother had cooked a heap of food while her father watched the food on the grill. She made potato, macaroni, and seafood salad. She also made baked beans, deviled eggs, ham biscuits, jambalaya, corn bread, fresh rolls, and a host of deserts. Of course, Veronica's mother needed to be in control of everything and made sure the cookout did not skip a beat.

"James! Get some more coal from the store. We don't have enough ice for the drinks either."

"Yes dear."

"Sir I don't mind running to the supermarket," Kareem interjected. "What else do you need?"

The man his daughter had brought home impressed James. He was refreshing after his encounter with Tracey's husband. He had seen his girls go through too much heartbreak. Kareem was refreshing. He just wanted his children to be happy. When they were younger, he knew that as a father he could only shield them from the terrors of the world for just a short while. When Tracey became pregnant although he did not like her choices in men, he was going to support her in all her hearts desires. After witnessing Veronica's last heartbreak, he wanted to see a permanent smile on his baby girl's face. Looking at Kareem, he knew there was something good in his spirit.

"Where are you going Kareem?" asked Veronica.

"I am going to the store for your pops."

"Okay honey I want you to meet the rest of my family when you get back."

Honey? Hmmm... Kareem smiled to himself. That was the first time Veronica had ever said anything endearing to him.

This is my Grandma Diana, my Aunt B., her husband, Uncle Jeffrey, Uncle Bernard, my sister Tracey my niece Brystal, this is my fat little nephew Jo-Jo, my best friend… Kareem had met everyone in the family. He felt as if he was already family. All embraced him.

The party was just starting. People were laughing, telling jokes and taking pictures. Veronica was so excited how her family always rallied together during family events. She was happy her parents were able to let loose even though they were strict Christians. They did not drink hard alcohol but they allowed beer and wine to be served at the cookout. They were totally against other alcohol but Veronica convinced her mother to serve fruity drinks like strawberry daiquiris. She even agreed to make few virgin ones for her mother and her father's enjoyment.

"Momma…! We need music."

"Music?" questioned her mother.

"You know Rev. Walters don't want to listen to no music."

Mr. Walters heard his wife and said, "Now Bernice let them kids do what they want it is Veronica's day." Veronica grinned and playfully poked her tongue at her mother. She knew her daddy's only purpose was to make her happy. It may have caused some confusion between her parents but she was the baby. She usually got what she asked for.

It's Electric…The, the, the….Electric slide…

"Come on here Rev. Walters don't act like you don't know how to do this."

The family danced and sang until about 8pm. Kareem was attentive to Veronica's interactions with her family. He saw how happy she was. He quietly watched and admired her in her natural element. He thought her beauty was timeless.

"Hey you," Veronica said.

"Hey miss lady."

"You okay."

"Yes I am okay. I am just enjoying the view."

"You're crazy," she smiled. She noticed something in Kareem's eyes she had never noticed before. She saw his heart smiling. Veronica did not know if he was smiling at her or the atmosphere.

"Well I guess I will save your surprise for another time." Kareem knew Veronica could not stand to wait.

"No, no! I want it now."

"I don't have it with me now. We have to go to your surprise."

"How far away is it?"

"Hmmm..., about thirty five minutes."

"You are joking right?"

"No ma'am I am not joking. But we can wait."

"No honey you can wait. Can you give me enough time to freshen up and we can go."

"I'll wait on you for however long you want me to."

Veronica was without words but said, "Okay, give me about twenty minutes."

Kareem waited for Veronica to get dressed. He was excited about her surprise and hope she received it with an open heart. He had carefully planned the events and made sure nothing was going to go wrong. He wanted Veronica to embrace new possibilities.

"Where are you taking me and why do I have to be blind folded."

"Look girl, are you going to complain the whole time?"

"Yes..., because I can't see."

"Veronica!"

"What!!"

"Do you trust me?"

"Hmm don't ask me that."

"Seriously Veronica, do you trust me?"

"Yes Kareem I trust you. Are we stopping?"

"Only for a few seconds... You will be able to get out of the car in just a few."

"I don't hear anything. Boy, are you trying to kidnap me."

"Yes I am. I am trying to steal you away from all the monotony. Kareem waited for a response but only saw a smile on Veronica's face. "Okay we are here."

"Why doesn't it feel like we have stopped and what is that noise?"

"It will only last for a second. Sit tight I am going to get you out of the car."

Veronica stepped out of the car and trusted Kareem to guide her steps. While Veronica was blindfolded, she began to sniff the air and said, "It smells like water, is it about it rain?"

"Listen here woman you just need to wait." Kareem guided Veronica to her final step. "Here hold on to this."

"This is a cold piece of steel what the…" Veronica continued to complain.

"Okay you ready..."

Kareem removed Veronica's blindfold and Veronica could not believe her eyes. They were on a ferry. The sky was clear, the stars illuminated, and the heavens sparkled over the river. It was as if God had heard Veronica's heart. Her yearning to understand and see the essence of beauty was her blessing this night. Her heart was so full of emotions she did not understand why she deserved this moment.

"Oh my God Kareem this is beautiful. This is absolutely gorgeous." Veronica felt tears welling in the pits of her eyes. "Thank you Kareem, thank you so, so much."

Kareem looked at the pleasure in Veronica's eyes and at that moment, he knew she was happy. "I wanted to bring you to a place that reminded me of you. You are right, it is beautiful just as you were the first time I saw you. This is gorgeous, just as you are standing before my eyes. I wanted you to see what I see when I think of you every day of my life since you graced me with your presence."

Veronica leaned on Kareem's chest because there was nothing to say. Nothing to say, at all; she just enjoyed the ferry ride.

Kareem held Veronica and whispered, "It's not over I have one more thing to show you."

"Okay and I promise I will be patient and wait," said Veronica in a calm voice.

Veronica and Kareem returned to the car and drove off the ferry, into a small-secluded town. He turned down a dirt road and drove up to an obscure structure that could not be clearly viewed.

"I am sorry I just have to ask, where are the lights?"

"Ok I am sorry there are no outside lights but I have improvised. I need you to sit here for just a few moments while I make us a clear path."

"You are going to leave me in the boonies?"

"Sweetie you are in the car the bears won't get you. I will protect you," Kareem laughed.

"Bears…! Uh huh, Kareem stop playing!"

"I am. Just wait give me a few moments."

Veronica waited in the car and the structure began to become irradiated. It was a house. It was two or three story home, which resembled a plantation house. It was a little run down but the structure was beautiful. She saw Kareem heading back to the car. The house was Kareem client's homes that he was renovating. His client had agreed to let Kareem use it for his surprise.

"Come on its ready lets go in. I have to get a few things out of the trunk but I will take you in."

Veronica walked in and was astounded. The house was more beautiful inside than it was outside. "Are we trespassing?"

"No crazy we are not trespassing come with me." Kareem guided Veronica. The house was lit by oil lamps and there was old furnace in the middle of the room where she stood.

"Is that fire? You know it is spring time?"

"It won't bother you I needed to turn it on so I could heat up the water."

"Was someone here?"

"Don't worry about it Veronica, let's just say I had a little help to get this in order. Do you trust me Roney?"

"Yes, Kareem I already told you I did."

Kareem knew his next request might change the course of events because Veronica was so stubborn. However, he knew she would not be disappointed if she just indulged in his request.

"I need you to take off your clothes."

"What, I am not taking off my clothes."

"You don't have to be naked in front of me although I wouldn't mind."

"Kareem, I am not getting naked."

Kareem felt some resistance but he was prepared to improvise. "Okay… here is a robe."

Veronica was still hesitant, trying to figure out what he was doing. She looked at the garment and immediately thought it could have belonged to another woman. "This looks new Kareem, where did you…"

"Don't ask me any questions just go through those doors and remove your garments please."

Veronica was shocked at Kareem's assertiveness. However, because she knew there was a surprise for her she did as Kareem asked. She walked to the door, turned and looked at Kareem with a devilish smile. She wanted to make sure she did not appear to give him the upper hand. Being difficult was a part of Veronica's daily bread.

"You better be lucky I have on flip flops."

"I would have preferred stilettos," Kareem said as he began to laugh.

Veronica walked to the other room hesitantly. She was not sure what Kareem was planning. However, she trusted Kareem. He had shown her nothing but respect from the time she had befriended him. It was not like Veronica to trust any man. She knew what it felt like to give a man her heart. This was different. She did not believe she had to give her heart to anyone.

She remembered Kareem had always been her friend and she knew that in her heart he would never do anything to hurt her. Veronica did as Kareem had asked. She was not concerned about him seeing her naked because she loved her body. Consciously and unconsciously, she did not mind if he admired her body. Veronica walked out of the room in just the robe as Kareem had requested.

"Okay you got me naked, so what are we doing?"

"Come with me."

Veronica followed Kareem into the next dimly lit room, to her surprise she walked in, and there was a porcelain tub, a bottle of wine, and a plate of fruit. There was a beautiful fragrance in the air but Veronica could not recognize the scent. Everything was beautiful and the candlelight gave the room just enough illumination and added a sensual ambience. Kareem stood before Veronica quietly as she admired the scenery. He wanted her to be happy and the look of surprise on her face exited him. He wanted to adore her and for her to accept his invitation and selfless act.

"What is this? What did you do?" Veronica was shocked when she looked at how carefully the room was decorated. She did not understand but she wanted to find out exactly what Kareem was doing.

Kareem grabbed Veronica's hand and guided her to the tub filled with bath oils. He placed his hand on her robe and began to open it so ever gently. Veronica did not say a word. She allowed her nakedness to be uncovered. Kareem could not help but stare at her velvety physique. He grabbed her hand and motioned her to step in the tepid water. As she sat down his hand grazed her skin and goose bumps appeared on Kareem's arm. He tried to focus on his plans for the evening. He did not want her to think his focus was on the physical. Kareem snapped back into reality and began to focus on pleasing her. He opened up the bottle of wine and poured her a glass.

"Here you are."

She took a sip and watched as Kareem picked up a strawberry, dipped it in a bowl of chocolate, and began to feed her. Kareem began to speak. He wanted to let Veronica know how he felt about her, and what he would do for her in the name of love.

"You said you didn't want much. I cannot give you the corporation or the six-figure job. However, I can give you a house with a… well kind of a Jacuzzi tub where you can put your fruit and drink your glass of wine. I can make you happy. I can do whatever you want me to."

"But I thought..."

"SSShhh...You are not getting paid to think. I know I am not what you are looking for. But I can be everything you want if you just let me. You could learn to love me as I have grown to love you. I am your friend but I want to be your best friend. I want to wake up and see your smile while you lay beside me. I know you have been hurt but I promise you don't have to hurt anymore as long as I am here. I love you Veronica Walters, and if you let me, I will love you for the rest of our lives."

Veronica was scared but mesmerized by the thoughtfulness of this man. She looked in his eyes and could see his tenderness. She looked in his eyes and knew he was for real. However, she did not want to endure any hurt. She did not want to live through another moment of rejection. *What if this is different? What if I just took a chance?* Her heart wanted to, but her body wanted something else. Everything she yearned for was right before her eyes. Veronica caressed Kareem's lips and realized they were as tender as his heart. She lured him toward her moistened body and pressed her lips against his.

"Yes, but...will you make me happy?"

"I will do whatever you want me to."

Veronica and Kareem kissed a kiss, which left their hearts rumbling. He fell in the tub with her and caressed her soul until the early morning. Their bodies were in harmony. Her friend, and now her lover were fulfilling Veronica's desires.

****

Veronica had spent the last year enjoying her newfound relationship. Kareem spoiled Veronica and tried to make her every wish come true. The more Kareem did the more Veronica wanted but she was not as giving. Veronica was selfish. She believed Kareem should do all the contributing without any reciprocity. She secretly had issues trusting and totally surrendering to any man. She had not realized Kareem was not just any man. She and Kareem did not make any big steps. They chose not to live with each other or make any huge adjustments to their lives. She continued to live in her parent's home because of the values instilled in Kareem by his family. Veronica was a preacher's daughter and it was not acceptable for unmarried couples to shack up. Veronica would have shacked up with Kareem if he wanted her to. Nevertheless, she would have done this for selfish reasons. She wanted all of the attention she could get. Kareem hoped that Veronica wanted the same things he wanted.

Veronica's mother could see her daughter's selfishness piercing through. She hoped Veronica would be a little more empathetic but Veronica's egoism was more powerful. Veronica's mother tried to reach her daughter in a sensible manner so she could recognize how fortunate she was. She knew Kareem wanted to settle down but she never really knew what her daughter's intentions were.

"Married?"

"Yes mamma, married."

"He asked me to marry him? "And you said yes?"

"Yes momma I said yes."

"Hmm...You want to get married?"

"Yes momma I want to get married. He is absolutely wonderful."

"Yes he is Veronica. I know he is wonderful I was just trying to figure out when you were going to figure it out."

"What do you mean?"

"Girl you been seeing that man for about two years and you give a hard way to go every day. You complain you cry you scream you holler. You want this you want that, you want everything. And Kareem, well he just says, *Yes Veronica.* I don't know when he has time to breathe or think for himself when he is always running behind you."

"Momma you know I have had a lot of stresses with trying to get into school and this new job. You know that I am trying to be an excellent Social Worker. I am trying to have my own business and this working for others stresses me. I need my own office my own clients and my own space. I don't understand what is taking so long."

"Because Veronica, you are not patient at all. You have to start somewhere. Those people know you are valuable they know the work you do, but you do not have to kill yourself. I know you are driven. But when is the last time you took a few minutes for yourself? When is the last time you took time out for Kareem? Becoming a wife is a big responsibility. You have to find a balance."

"Momma he supports me in everything that I do."

"I know he does, but do you? Veronica this man has been working himself to death to make sure you are happy and content. You don't even notice. When is the last time you cooked a meal? When have you bought him something nice?"

"See momma there you go. Just last week I ordered him an engraved lighter. I plan to surprise him with that little token. But cook a meal? Momma who has time to cook, let alone eat? I usually just grab something and keep it moving."

"Exactly, Veronica he cannot do everything. A lighter Veronica please, I hope he plans to stop smoking. However, with a woman like you, he may turn to drugs. You do not even get it or understand what I am saying. All I am saying is just appreciate him."

Veronica's mother was getting agitated with her daughter's insanity. She wanted to whack her across the face in the hopes that it would knock some sense into her. She couldn't believe this was the child she had raised. She was already outdone with Tracey's actions and she was trying to figure out where she went wrong with Veronica. She knew being angry wasn't going to help the situation so she tried to change the subject.

"Okay, okay," said Veronica.

Her mother asked, "Where is the ring?"

"Oh I haven't gotten a ring yet."

"Umm… I don't understand then how do you know he wants to get married?"

"Because the other night he said we needed to talk about what our next steps were and I just assumed since he is always talking about it that he had some plans in motion."

"Girl...dear sweet, merciful, wonderful, kind baby Jesus please forgive me.... you are so stupid. I am going to check your DNA; your father must have had a stupid sister. No, you could be as stupid as your aunt.....Jesus listen to me! Roney, he has been talking about marrying you since graduation. It's been nearly two years Veronica and yesterday was the first time you heard him?"

"Well, yes it was the first time. Momma he understands me like no one else. He has been working on some big project for the last few months, which is apparently top secret, and he has just been hush, hush. So I don't try to bother him about it."

"Let me get this straight. He knows everything you are doing, what you breathe, eat, and sleep; and all you know is that he is working on a project. That doesn't seem strange."

"Momma please as long as a man works does it matter?"

"Veronica is he involved in something illegal?"

Veronica sarcastically replied, "Yes he is, as bout as much as daddy is. Please he is one of the squarest dudes you will ever meet."

"Then there is my point again you have to pay attention to him. I am not saying wait on him hand and foot; or be nosy, but be interested like he is with you."

"Okay momma I hear you. But you just watch he is going to show up with a ring and he is going to pop the question, and I am going to be Miss Veronica Robinson. I cannot wait. Him, and his stupid values have kept me up in this house with you."

"Veronica if you want to leave and get your own place by all means you can go," her mother said sarcastically. "I respect a man who does not believe in shacking up. I would think you would too."

"Does it really matter momma, I spend two to three nights at his house a week. It ain't like we ain't ever..."

"Veronica, okay maybe there are some sins he just doesn't want to commit. You know it is like talking to a wall with you. Do you think about the things that come out of your mouth? You have a respectable, caring, loving man, who is definitely God fearing, in your life. He does not beat you or mentally abuse you, and loves you more than apparently he loves himself. You don't realize what you have. But I will say this to you if you don't truly realize what you have you may open your eyes one day and it may be gone. Love this man, respect who he is, and what God has made him."

"Okay momma, okay momma I hear you."

Veronica wanted to change the subject. She could care less what her mother thought about her relationship. Her mother and fathers relationship always appeared to be so perfect. She believed her mother needed to stay out of her affairs. She was a big girl and Kareem didn't seem to mind anything she was doing.

"Momma where is daddy?"

"Girl down at the church with the deacons preparing for revival, are you coming?"

"Oh umm… well let me see…"

"Well Kareem said he was coming."

"Well yawl have fun I am going to be there one night, but momma I have so much work to do."

"Whatever Veronica when you are ready to get your soul saved God will be waiting. But I tell you this, I would not let my man be in the house of God and I wasn't at his side."

****

Veronica spent most of the day shopping. She was a sucker for a sale. Nevertheless, if she saw something she wanted regardless of the cost she would get it. Veronica always had expensive taste. She did not have to plan a girl's day out to do any shopping she was elated she had her own money to do as she pleased. Not to mention Kareem or her father would supply her with any monetary funds she requested.

She remembered what her mother had told her about being a better woman, and being more attentive to Kareem. She believed she was doing enough. Actually, she did not know what else to do. She knew Kareem loved her, and she cared deeply for Kareem. However, she did not want to be irrational with her decision-making. She wanted to make sure she would never go back to the cold dark place she was when her heart was first broken. She wanted to show Kareem some appreciation but unfortunately, she did not know what to do.

While she shopped, she wondered if getting married was the best decision for her at that time. Kareem had all the qualities of a good man and she wanted some surety. She had the longevity before but it didn't pay off. She wondered if Kareem would do the same as her previous lover. He too was sweet and kind, but he was deceitful. She remembered his smile, but he was not as gentle as Kareem. She always felt insecure with him, but never with Kareem.

Her mind was going back and forth and her flesh felt uneasy. She didn't know and she wasn't sure. She only knew what Kareem told her. She wanted to believe in him as he believed in her. Veronica refused to submit for any reason. She knew she had to take care of herself. She was prepared to throw the blows before anyone could hurt her heart again. She believed her way of thinking was the only logical way. Even if she had to fake it around others, she was going to make Kareem think she felt the same way. She was not willing to give up the spotlight. She knew how Kareem felt and how she was able to get him to eat out of the palm of her hand. She was going to remain number one in Kareem's heart even if he was not number one in hers. She decided she would visit Kareem after her shopping spree and show him all of the wonderful gifts she had gotten. She made sure she picked him up a little something just to let him know she was thinking of him.

Veronica entered his modest home. She had a key even though they did not live together. He wanted Veronica to feel comfortable coming and going as she pleased. He wanted Veronica to trust him, so he let down all of his guards to prove his sincerity.

"Kareem... baby you home?"

"Yes baby I am in my office."

Veronica walked in the room with several bags in her hand. Kareem had turned one of his spare bedrooms into a makeshift office. He generally worked from home when he was not out in the field. He was a contractor. He built homes, was proficient in home repairing, and handled contract bids for the city. He was quite the handy man. He never completed a four-year college, however; he did complete vocational school and received his certification. He worked as an apprentice under a construction company full-time. In his spare time, he worked as a stock boy at the local convenient store in the evenings. After his certification he decided that the part time job was no longer needed. He was financially stable.

Veronica looked at her beau as he had is head buried in plans and blueprints. She admired his determination, although she really did not know what he did. She watched him work countless hours and still make time for her. He seemed exhausted at times but he never complained or got angry. He seemed content. She was too wrapped up in her shopping spree to care about the loads of paper work he had on his desk. Veronica was always inconsiderate when it came to Kareem's matters.

"Look what I got today."

Kareem was diligently working on some paper work and his supposed secret project. "Sweetheart I will look at it in a second. I need to finish this paper work and I have a couple of calls to make."

"AAWWWEEE...but honey I got something for you also. I want you to see," Veronica whimpered.

Kareem looked at Veronica and could not resist how she caused him to sway. Kareem pushed himself from the desk and motioned for her to come and sit on his lap. Veronica smiled because she knew her every wish was his command.

"Okay baby, what did you get?"

Veronica began to go to the montage of bags, pulling out different trinkets she had purchased for herself. Kareem looked bewildered because he was waiting to see what she had purchased for him. He was not use to receiving gifts from his beloved. It never crossed his mind to ask for anything.

"You like this one, how about this…."

Veronica was going through her bags in excitement as if she had never been shopping before. She didn't even think about how Kareem was feeling nor did she ask. In reality she actually didn't care, she was only concern with matters of self.

Just nodding his head, he agreed with whatever Veronica said. Veronica made it to the end of all her bags. Not once did she pull out any items for Kareem. Kareem still waited patiently for his supposed surprise.

"Baby what did you get me?"

"Oh yea, give me a second."

Veronica ran over to her purse and pulled out a key chain with the name of his favorite football team. It was a sight for Kareem to see. He stared at the token with disappointment. Veronica did not even notice the glum look on his face. She figured he should just be happy that he bought him something.

"Isn't this cute? The lady said these are hard to find especially in the off season."

Kareem nodded his head and thought to himself, *a key chain she made me stop working to see all the money she spent and gave me a key chain?* He didn't want to seem ungrateful or unappreciative but deep inside he expected more. He grabbed the key chain from Veronica's hand and kissed her on the cheek. He had no additional comments and wanted to continue working.

"Okay baby I have to work. You know I need to get this done I have deadline."

Veronica remembered her mother had told her to be interested in what he was doing. She sat down in the chair next to his desk. She wanted to show some interest, or at least try to engage in his day-to-day activities.

"Oh is that your secret project you are working on?"

"Secret project…? What secret project?"

"The one you never talk about."

Kareem felt a little agitated because he knew every time he wanted to tell Veronica about his new business endeavors she just ignored him. He had no secrets from Veronica she was too preoccupied with her visions to ask.

"Veronica this is the contractor I have been working with for a year. I am trying to start my own business and if this goes through, I will have a contract with all the major businesses in the area. When we get married, God willing, we won't have to worry about a thing. I will my own crew and everything. I really want us to have everything we need. You don't even have to work if you don't want to."

Veronica had no idea what Kareem was working towards, and she was shocked. She knew he was always busy but she never thought he was planning to have his own business. This was the first time he had ever mentioned her being unemployed. Veronica became uncomfortable with the conversations because she had no plans to stop working.

"Your crazy… boy, you know I have to work, I love to work. You know I am trying to get my own business too."

Kareem could see that Veronica had missed the whole point of his remarks. He wasn't telling her she should quit her job, he was just assuring her that if she ever decided to take a break, he would make sure he would provide all she needed.

"Yes Veronica I do. I have been looking at offices for you to lease. I have also done some repairs on the buildings you have worked in. I have done some free-lance work for your clients. So…yes, I am well aware of everything you are trying to do baby. I am not saying you have to give up your dream I am just saying we will be able to afford to hire people to help us with the job, that way we can have time for us, and the kids."

"Kids...? Who said anything about having kids?"

Kareem was becoming more disturbed with the conversation. He was trying to figure out if Veronica was mentally conscious of the conversations even though she was physically present. He was astounded by the conversation they were having. He thought he had always made his dreams clear. He knew everything Veronica wanted, so why was she unaware of what he fancied?

"Veronica we always talk about kids."

"Yes I know, but you know I have nieces and nephews that I can just pick up if I am feeling a little lonely."

Kareem felt himself getting warm. He was not in the mood for any of jokes. Veronica knew Kareem desired to have children of his own one day. Veronica continued to have a baffled look on her face. Kareem was tired of Veronica's oblivious attitude.

"Veronica, we have talked about kids, getting married, and moving into your dream house for over a year."

"I don't know Kareem maybe we get wrapped up in the moment because the loving is out of sight, out of mind."

"What...?"

Kareem felt insulted. He was offended she had minimized their dreams to pillow talk after their intimate moments. He felt a moment of disgust. He stood up and walked toward Veronica trying to get her full attention to what he was saying. He gently grabbed her hands and looked into her eyes.

"What are you talking about Veronica? Everything I say to you comes from my heart. I love you and I want to be with you for the rest of my life. I want us to live in a house with kids, even get a dog and cat. I want your family to come over for cookouts. I want to laugh and cry with you. That is what I want from you. Do you want the same thing?"

A glum look came over Veronica's face when she assumed Kareem had planned the rest of their lives. She felt like she was asked to surrender to his control. Veronica's trust was oozing out of her pores. She saw Kareem differently. She felt that he was being aggressive and not willing to understand her position. Her face was still and lacked any sincerity but she did not want to appear uncompromising. Veronica gave Kareem a bogus smile as if she understood what he was saying.

"Why of course I do, baby. Whatever you want I want," she said hesitantly. "Now, come here baby and give me a hug."

Kareem embraced the love of his life not really knowing if she was being truthful with him. He held her hoping she would somehow feel the same way. He wanted this woman, in spite of her disposition and attitude. He loved her; he had always loved Veronica, and always would.

****

Veronica was alone at Kareem's house preparing to leave. She thought about the conversation they had days before. She did not know what to do. She wanted to talk to someone about the conversation but she was baffled. She needed someone else to agree with her. She felt as if she was the victim of fraud and Kareem was trying to get over at her expense. Veronica refused to allow someone get the best of her and be the brunt of another man's joke. She was going to maintain the upper hand at his expense and refused to suffer any loss. She gathered her belongings and made sure all lights were off and everything was secure.

She was about to walk out of the door the phone ring. She was going to let the answering machine pick up the call but in an impulse, she grabbed the cordless. Veronica answered the phone in haste.

"Yes…"

"Hello, may I please speak with Kareem Robinson?"

"Uh… he is not here at the moment can I take a message."

"Yes this is the inspector for building 15, there is a leak, and it needs to be handled before the close of business day, or it will not pass inspection. Can you please have him call me at 434-847-7489?"

Veronica did not have a pen on hand. She did not want to be bothered with the trivial information and cut the individual off before he completed his statement. She had things that were more important to her on her mind. She deemed Kareem's business to be his and not her concern. She did not want to be rude but she found herself hurrying the caller off the phone.

"I am on my way out the door and I don't have a pen. Can you call right back and put the message on the answering machine. Thanks bye-bye."

Veronica had not waited on a response from the caller. She hung up the phone abruptly. Veronica walked out of the house and shut the door behind her.

Veronica walked into her mother's house. She sat down her bags and took off her shoes. Veronica walked into the kitchen where her mother was. Her mother was preparing dinner and singing in the kitchen.

"Momma how was revival?"

"Oh you should have been there, it was outstanding. The spirit was all over the building last night. Did Kareem tell you?"

"Tell me what?"

"That he plans on getting baptized in a few weeks."

"Baptized…he ain't said anything about getting baptized."

Veronica was thinking about their previous conversation. Kareem never even mentioned he went to church. She felt she did not know who Kareem really was. He never invited her to church with him and he never mentioned anything about revival. She considered that this was a part of his scheme to get her parents to believe he was interested in God. What Veronica failed to realize is that he had mentioned revival and going to church countless times. Veronica had not paid him any attention. Her fixation on not trusting him had spawned into a bigger evil.

"You know what he has been talking about Momma?"

"What? Veronica he has been talking about what?"

"He has been talking about having babies?"

Her mother was surprised and responded, "Babies?? Veronica please, yawl are not even married yet."

"Momma I know, how is he talking about having kids and he ain't even put a ring on my finger. I thought it was kind of crazy too.

Veronica was glad she had gotten her mother's attention. She was hoping her mother could make sense out of the conversation she and Kareem had, had. She knew she could count on her mother to listen. Her mother was shocked by what her daughter was telling her. She knew there had to be a misunderstanding because her daughter had a habit of blowing things out of context.

Veronica went on and on about how Kareem did not want her to work. How he wanted her to stay home with the kids once they settled down. She told her mother that he seemed to have their life already planned out. Veronica believed Kareem was trying to stop all of her dreams without even consulting with her. She was appalled he was already talking about having kids. After telling her mother listened to her daughter's version of the truth, Veronica appeared to be unsettled. She knew her daughter had not listened to a word Kareem said and she was just being selfish yet again. She knew her daughter just wanted to have her way and was going to make herself out to be the victim.

"He just wants me all out of shape. I think he wants me barefoot and pregnant. Kids! Kids, how dare he...!" Veronica hissed.

"Veronica, slow down girl," her mother said. "I don't think he is crazy. Are you even listening to yourself? Are you positive this is what he said and meant?

Her mother did not believe a word her daughter was saying. She knew there was more to this story. Veronica had a way of leaning to her own understanding. She knew Kareem. She had watched how her daughter misconstrued information and made him feel as if everything was always his fault. She wanted to try to reason with her daughter but once again, Veronica looked like a deer caught in headlights. At least she pretended to be lost in confusion.

"Veronica, I am saying…."

"What?"

Veronica's mother threw her hands in the air. She had enough. She did not want to talk to Veronica anymore. She found herself getting frustrated with the overly educated buffoon. Veronica was playing a dangerous game and her mother did not want any part of her foolery.

"You just don't get it at all do you? You are so crazy and self…"

"Momma what…?"

Veronica continued to look lost not understanding the point of the conversation. Veronica felt her mother did not understand her side at all. She thought her mother was going to take her side. Clearly, Veronica had picked the wrong person to try to convince that Kareem was taking advantage of her. Her mother was getting all bent out of shape and was tired of her daughter. Veronica had seen her mother perplexed but at that moment, she had never seen her mother look as if she wanted to attack her.

In frustration her mother screamed, "Never mind Veronica! Never mind..I can't believe you're this ignorant and naive…..AARRGGGHHH!!"

Veronica could not believe her mother's outburst. She had refused to see her side and apparently, she was conspiring with Kareem too. Veronica looked at her mother and could not understand why she was not supporting her feelings. *She just doesn't get it; she wants me to be broken too.*

Kareem was on the phone when Veronica walked in, screaming in a panic. She had never seen Kareem like this before. Kareem was clearly irritated. He was having an in depth conversation with a caller. He seemed to be confused about the information he was receiving on the phone.

"Why wasn't I notified? What do you mean you called? I have not spoken with anyone. Those contracts have to be completed before twelve o'clock tomorrow. What do you mean you can't get anyone out there today? Fine it doesn't matter. I will do the work myself!"

Kareem had found out one of the buildings he was working on did not pass inspection. Not to mention there was a leak that needed to be repaired immediately before it damaged some of the foundation. Kareem did not have time to figure out why or when the circumstance happened. He hurried himself out of the house. Kareem slammed the phone down and walked passed Veronica without even saying a word.

Veronica's feelings were hurt. She didn't know why Kareem was acting so frantic. Kareem never got angry, or at least she had never seen him enraged before. She never realized her inconsideration to take a simple message, was a part of the problem. She concluded that this was Kareem showing his true colors. He was not the man she thought him to be. She opted to go back to her mother's house and give him some space. Veronica picked up a few of her belongings, left out the house, and did not bother to call Kareem to see what concerned him. This was another opportunity for Veronica to be there for her man, and yet she failed again.

Veronica picked up her cell to answer a call from Lisa. Lisa had missed Veronica working at the bar but she knew Veronica was not going to bear that scenery after she graduated. Even though she missed Veronica, Lisa did not miss her standoffish attitude she brought to work from time to time.

"Where are you on your way to?"

"Oh I need to get to the office and get this work done," said Veronica to Lisa.

"Where is Kareem?"

"Girl, I don't know he ran out of the house a few days ago fussing at someone. I was not going to bother him he seemed upset. He will call me when he gets himself together. I have been home."

"What was wrong with him?"

"Girl I don't even know, he was fussing with someone on the phone about some contracts. You know if I don't have anything to do with it, I mind my business."

"Girl you know that's right."

"I will call you when I am finish my work but I don't know how long that will be."

"Alright girly, I will call you."

Veronica was at the office for over five hours a little longer than she had expected. She had thought about going to see Kareem but did not want to be the first one to break the ice. Kareem had run out on her, and treated her disrespectfully so why should she have to be the one to talk first.

She figured she would go to her mother's house to get a home cooked meal since it was a Saturday and she knew she did not intend to cook any food. She remembered her mother said she would be throwing something together that evening and that usually meant it was going to be a feast. It never had to be any special occasion because Veronica's mother just loved cooking.

Veronica's took her focus off the meal and back to Kareem not speaking to her. Veronica had not spoken with Kareem for almost forty-eight hours. She knew she did not have an argument with him, and they did not have a fight, so she wanted to know what was up with him not calling. Veronica began to feel some kind of way when she thought that Kareem took his frustrations out on her. She became heated while she was in thought. Never once thinking she had played any role in his sudden wrath.

What the hell is he doing that is so important? I do check on him every day even when I am not having such a great day. I am stressed too. He is not the only one with all these things on his plate. He is selfish. That's right, selfish. He is more concerned with his paper work and his contracts. Now he just wants me sitting in a house waiting all day long while he works on God know what. What about my dreams? What about what I want? I am not going to be tied down and follow someone else's dreams and I can't have my own. He doesn't want a wife, he wants a trophy and I am so sorry, I have worked too hard in my lifetime to settle. I am not doing it! Women are always loosing themselves for the sake of a man. Women are always sacrificing themselves and forgetting who they are. Oh hell no not me! I am not letting a man physically or mentally abuse me for any reason. I am worth so much more than that. If he wants to be with me then he is going to know that I am running this show. He can either roll with me or roll out! Because I would rather be by myself.

Veronica had made herself so upset she didn't even hear her cellular phone ringing to answer the calls. Veronica began to think about her sister Tracey and all the debacles she had encountered in her marriage. Veronica pulled into the driveway of her mother's house angered about all of the thoughts that had just vexed her spirit. She had gone from Miss happy go lucky, to Miss I am woman, hear me roar.

Veronica turned the key and walked into her mother's house, indignant, with a chip on her shoulder, which she had created. She did not care about eating. She was not concerned with anything other than the thoughts she had created. She did not want to hear her mother's mouth nor did she want to answer any questions if she had any. She wasn't in the mood for people who did not have her back. After her and her mother's last conversation, Veronica doubted that her mother was on her side.

"Hey baby," said her mother.

Veronica did not even pay attention to the tone in her voice. She seemed disconcerted and her responses were short. Her mother's smile seemed phony. Veronica was troubled and no one had done anything to her.

"Hey momma…"

"Veronica," said her father.

"Yea daddy..."

"What is wrong with you?"

"Nothing I am just tired."

"Come in the living room for a second," Veronica's mother motioned.

"Ma look, I just want to go to bed, I am tired."

Veronica's mother became pissed with her attitude. She had slaved over a meal and she knew it was all done for her. She was becoming intolerant of her bratty daughter. She knew Kareem was planning a surprise for Veronica and now she was about to mess it up.

"Veronica…," she heard a familiar voice call her name.

Veronica totally agitated, about nothing walked into the living room and there stood Kareem. He walked over to greet Veronica with a kiss. Begrudgingly she allowed the affection.

"Hey you, what is going on?"

Veronica looked at all the faces in the living room staring at her and became condescending. She didn't care that she was abrasive. She did not care that Kareem was there. She felt like throwing a tantrum.

"Nothing, nothing at all…"

She had not stopped to think, why Kareem was at her parent's house. She was fixated on her conjured dander and did not even notice that the dining room was prepared and decked out with the best china. She wanted everyone to see she was distressed. She wanted everyone to feel as miserable as she did.

"Baby is everything ok?" asked Kareem.

"No it isn't!"

Veronica began to burst into tears. Her mother and father had no idea what was wrong with their child. Her father shook his head and looked at Kareem. Her mother rolled her eyes and was about to comment on Veronica's childish displays. Kareem grabbed Veronica and held her tight.

"Are you okay baby?"

Veronica's mother motioned for her husband to leave Kareem alone with Veronica so that he could do some damage control as Veronica cried like a five-year-old child. She followed behind him. Tears were streaming down. Veronica's cry became uncontrollable.

Kareem had no idea why Veronica cried he just wanted to ease her pain. Kareem held Veronica and began stroking her hair.

"Alright baby, it will be fine whatever it is, I promise."

Veronica pushed Kareem away. She had so much to say because she felt her feelings were entirely his fault. He had put so much pressure on her. Veronica had made herself upset with Kareem because of her own insecurities and selfishness.

"Is it? Is it going to be fine? You just don't understand how bad I want this. I want so many things in life and it does not seem like I have any support. Everyone wants me to focus on something else other than myself."

Kareem had a puzzled stare on his face. He was at a loss for words. He knew he had not spoken with her for a couple of days, but she appeared ok when he last saw her. He began to think he had done something wrong. He never wanted to disappoint Veronica. He had made it his business to repair all of her bumps and bruises. Kareem could not figure out what he had done this time.

"Baby what are you talking about?"

"You just left me; you didn't call me, or have any concern about what was going on with me. You left out of the house in anger, and I have not heard from you. You did not call or contact me. You left me alone."

Veronica's bows of doubt had manifested into her own understanding of the days and events that had just past. Kareem looked at Veronica in confusion. Kareem was trying to figure out how he could fix Veronica's distress. He thought that maybe it was time to place her with different scenery.

"Can we take a ride?"

"I don't want to take a ride. I am tired I am worn out I have been beaten up all day."

Veronica did not want to make it easy for Kareem. She wanted him to suffer for her mistakes. She wasn't trying to hear anything he said. Kareem wanted to make her see he was committed to making her happy. Even in the midst of her stomping and kicking Kareem wanted to soothe his annoyed vixen. He lowered his tone and tried a different approach. He gently grabbed her by the shoulders and began to give her full eye contact. He wanted her to see his sincerity. He wanted her to know he wanted to fully compromise and make her feel at ease.

"Okay baby, okay. I am sorry you feel this way, I am so sorry I didn't call you. Trust me everything is going to be fine. I had some things to take care of and I have been working night and day to make sure they got done."

"You left me," said Veronica.

"No, no baby I didn't leave you. I stormed out because I had an emergency. Look I want you to go and clean yourself up. Your mother has prepared a wonderful meal for us and I want you to enjoy it. I have a surprise for you."

Veronica only heard the words, *surprise for you*. She didn't hear what caused him to leave. She was so self-absorb and self-centered; she was only concerned with herself. Not once did she ever become self-aware of her narcissistic attitude about the debacle she had created.

"For me?" questioned Veronica.

"Yes baby and I promise you will understand. I am so sorry baby, I don't want you to feel like I am not here for you. I promise I will never do that again."

Veronica had managed to change the entire houses attitude all due to her created drama and misunderstandings. Kareem did not even realize he was apologizing for something he did not do or create. He just wanted to make sure she kept a permanent smile on her face even if it was at the cost of his own. Veronica walked upstairs to take a shower and clean herself up. She had made her point her was going to submit to her and not the other way around.

"Is she alright Kareem?" asked Veronica's mother.

"I think so. I think she is a little stressed and had a mental melt down, but she will be okay. It may have just been a busy day at the office."

Veronica's parents felt embarrassment because of their daughter's action. They felt awful for Kareem. They knew his intentions and heart were pure and true. They knew he only wanted to keep Veronica content. They also knew a man could only endure but so much from these insane actions.

"That girl and her drama," said Veronica's mother.

"She gets it from her mamma," responded Mr. Walters.

Mrs. Walters rolled her eyes at her husband. She knew her attitude was not as grotesque and oblivious as her child's was.

"She didn't get that mess from me, she is a spoiled brat."

"Spoiled? Then she definitely got it from you," Rev. Walters said chuckling.

"Keep playing James."

"She is alright but she can be a little dramatic," Kareem laughed at the seasoned couple.

"You remember son that is the beginning of your, *for better or for worse*, you better get ready."

"'Yes sir I know but I believe there will be a lot more for better. The worse we can always get through as long as we have God."

"That's what I am talking about," said Rev. Walters. "I knew there was a reason why I liked this boy."

"Stop calling him boy," said Mrs. Walters.

"He is fine ma'am, he is fine."

****

Kareem decided the dinner was too overwhelming to show Veronica his surprise. He explained to her parents he would designate another time when Veronica was not as upset. Her parents agreed. Kareem waited a week later to show Veronica what he had planned.

Kareem planned to take her away from her stressful environment during the workweek. He knew it would be difficult for her to agree but he felt his surprise was important enough to put all other entities on hold. He picked up Veronica from her parents' house before she went to work. He first had to mislead her in order for her to agree. He told her he was going to chauffer her to her destinations for the day. He even called her office and explained his intentions so she was covered while she was with him.

"Where are we going Kareem?"

"You will see."

"Do we always have to do this? Why don't you just tell me, dangit…," said Veronica irritated.

"Baby, why don't you just wait and see?"

"Kareem you know I have tons of work today. I have reports to turn in and you insist on us joy riding. I want to know why we are joy riding?

Kareem you know how important my work is to me you know and what I am trying to do."

Kareem had enough of the whining. He knew what he had to show Veronica would change her entire attitude. He didn't have time to listen to her protest. Kareem began to become assertive so Veronica could see how serious he was. This was a rarity because he was always on the receiving end of Veronica's so-called assertiveness.

"Shut up!"

"What…," said a startled Veronica.

"Shut up!" Kareem said sternly. "Yes I know how much work you have to do; but I have something to show you, and it is important for me. It is important to me for you comprehend just what this means. Your work is going to be there. You are going to get it done. Why…because you are the most driven women I have ever met. You know what you want, and God knows you are going to get it. I am asking. Can I just interrupt your world for a while? Matter of fact I am not asking. I have to show you and it deals with you completing your work. That is all I am going to say about it. So now Veronica, shut up and wait."

Veronica felt the need to express her feelings but she secretly liked when Kareem was dominant and he always had such wonderful surprises. So why not just let him rant. Veronica didn't know what had come over Kareem. Instead of submitting to his request she felt the need to continue to inquire about their destination. She wanted to continue to get him riled up. Another sick game she liked to play at the expense of his feelings.   Kareem ignored Veronica and was set on continuing with his plans.

"Why…?" Veronica started to ask.

Kareem just turned his head. He refused to answer any of her questions until they were close to their destination. She became agitated that Kareem wasn't listening to her at all.

"But…," Veronica said as he continued to ignore her.

Kareem did not turn to give her any eye contact. He pulled up at a convenient store but did not turn off the engine.

"Oh we are stopping here?"

"Yes."

"Oh now you want to answer me."

"Only long enough to blind fold you."

"You are not about to blindfold me!"

"Oh yes I am now turn around girl and stop playing."

Veronica still had the will to put up a small fight. She never wanted to appear weak. This game was unnecessary because Kareem never saw her as a weakling.

"Girl..?? Don't play with me boy." They both laughed.

Veronica felt the car stop and heard the car door open. She wanted to know what was going on. She then remembered the last time she was blindfolded and how the surprise was more than she had hoped for. She knew he had something wonderful for her so she might as well play along.

"Ok darling, let me help you out."

Veronica grabbed Kareem's hand and allowed him to guide her up a supposed walkway. She wanted to say something but nothing that ever came out of Veronica's mouth was positive or constructive.

"Oh, we are not in the sticks and woods, so I suppose."

"Veronica don't start just walk with me. I need to say something to you before I remove the blindfold."

Kareem stood with Veronica's hand in his. He guided her and made a sudden stopped. Kareem had rehearsed his thoughts over and over again but decided he would just speak from his heart. He held Veronica's hand tightly while she stood blindfolded. Veronica was a bit confused and unaware of what Kareem was about to say.

"When I first met you in that parking lot I knew there was something special about you. Even when you turned me away with your sass and rudeness, I said to myself you were the one. I knew you existed somewhere in my lifetime. From the moment you showed up at my place of business frantic and did not have your purse, I knew it was fate bringing you close to me. Veronica you have been somewhere, in my lifetime. When my nights were lonely and I just needed someone to talk to, we befriended each other, and talked until the sun came up. It was then I knew that you were the, somewhere in my lifetime. You were my vision, you were my destiny. The first time I kissed your lips and held, you in my arms I knew there was not another in this world meant for me other than you. I was happy with you. You were driven, smart, and feisty; you had a fire in your eyes most men run away from."

Veronica's heart began to pound because she knew deep down inside that Kareem meant every word he was expressing. No one had ever said anything remotely close to the words he was conveying. She began to let down the walls she had created. She began to question her unruly actions. She allowed Kareem to continue without interrupting him.

"I have so many memories of you just in a short time. I believe I have memorized your every move. Now today after I have listened to your spirit speak to mine I know it is God who has placed you in my life for a purpose, for a reason. You are my destiny Veronica, you are my lifetime and I want you to know I want to spend a lifetime with you."

Veronica felt Kareem moving.   She did not know what he was doing.   Kareem was positioning himself for her to see what he had done for his treasure and soon to be lifetime. Kareem was calm but excited because he wanted Veronica to be exhilarated over his kindness.

"What are you doing I can't see," Veronica questioned?

"Take your blindfold off."

Veronica was shocked. She did not know if she should stare at Kareem, what he was holding, or the beautiful image she was standing in front of. She could not speak. She could not catch her breath.

"I, what, uh Karee…"

"Veronica Beatrice Walters will you do me the honor of becoming my lifetime."

"Yes, yes I will."

"Yes Kareem I will be, no I am, your lifetime."

Kareem had finally gotten his wish. The woman he loved had agreed to be his forever. She was going to honor him and become his wife. He could not have asked for more. Veronica grabbed Kareem pulled him off his knees and kissed him as if it were their first time.

****

Veronica could not wait to tell her parents the wonderful surprise Kareem had given her. She knew her parents would be happy she was finally getting married. She on the other hand was surprised at the house he had built for her. She thought her ring was beautiful but to receive her dream home was what she treasured more. Deep down inside Veronica was still not sure if she wanted to marry Kareem. She just wanted to share with her family what he had done for her. Veronica did not realize her parents were already aware of what Kareem had planned.

"Momma you should see it, look at my ring… but you should see it. I have never seen anything that beautiful in my life and it is mine. It is all mines! Mamma you should…Oh my God it is a dream. But momma, look at my ring."

Veronica's excitement did not move her mother. She had seen the house and the ring. Kareem had asked for their blessing weeks prior before he unleashed his breathtaking surprise. The plan was to have Veronica and Kareem over for dinner, and he was going to make a similar speech as he did when he proposed. Due to Veronica coming home and having perplexed fits, the plan had been deviated. Veronica's mother had planned an elaborate meal because she knew how important the proposal was to Kareem. Her daughter brought the foolery and drama to the joyful event.

Veronica's mother was so outdone with Veronica's actions that night; she was concerned if Kareem was even going to go through with the proposal. However, she saw the love Kareem had for her demented daughter. She almost felt sorry for him but she hoped in her heart her daughter would change and see the light.

"Veronica calm down for God's sake! That's why I cooked all of that…ugh… blaming food girl!"

Veronica's mother was pissed. She could not even get excited about the engagement. The sacrifices Kareem was making for Veronica she knew would never be reciprocated as long as her daughter continued to live in her own little world of Veronica.

"Girl you are going to make me cuss and lose my religion. You are so clueless or at least you pretend to be. You are so wrapped up in your own whatever, you did not even notice. Kareem spent most of his time putting you back together, it was too late, and so he told me and your father there would be a more appropriate time."

Veronica ignored everything her mother had said to her. She didn't care because she felt her mother should not meddle with her happy moment. Veronica was fixated on what she had received. She didn't believe her mother was always right. She was going to do what she wanted, and no one was going to steal her moment of joy.

"Momma did you see the house? It has a Jacuzzi and a beautiful kitchen…"

"Why are you so concerned about the kitchen, you don't cook?"

"Oh my God... I have to call Tracey. I have to call my sister and tell her the news."

Veronica's mother rolled her eyes and held her hand back again from slapping Veronica across the face. Her child was testing her yet again. She refused to let Satan get the best of her in this situation. She wanted to focus on planning her child's wedding. She knew something good could come out of the calamity. She still wanted her daughter to be happy regardless of her oblivion.

"Girl she already knows, everybody knew except you. Get a grip. She and I were talking about when you should get married."

Veronica paused. She had forgotten there was a wedding to plan. She was obsessed with her dream house but not with planning the wedding. She was still in the middle of working on her life goals. She had talked about marriage on several occasions with Kareem but after their heated conversation, she had placed the thought on the back burner. She had decided on her own to get all of her ducks in a row before she said, *I do*.

"Oh I almost forgot."

"How did you almost forget did you not get a ring?"

"Yeah...But I had gotten so excited about the house, and the ring is beautiful..."

"Oh so you forgot about getting married."

"No I didn't." Veronica was lying.

"Veronica what is wrong with you? You think this man has put his heart, blood, sweat and tears into all of this, not to get married. Do you want to get married Veronica?"

Veronica paused and could not answer her mother. She realized she did not. She wasn't ready to get married. Even if Kareem was a good man, she was not ready to commit to him for forever. She wanted all of her dreams first. She knew in her heart she made a mistake by saying, yes, but she had been wrapped up in the moment. Actually, she focused on the house and could not have denied his request.

"Veronica! Are you out of your mind? Are you crazy? Did you not just tell that man yes!"

Veronica sat down and still did not answer. Veronica mulled over and over again, about how beautiful the house was. She even loved the ring but she had so much more to do with her life. She had so many goals. Maybe she could think all of this after her promotion, take care of her financial situation, finish her second Master's, and then get married. It would only be about three years. They could have a long engagement she thought. They could have a long engagement and then she could take all the time she needed to plan the wedding.

"Veronica! Are you listening?"

"Yes mamma. We will talk about it later. We don't need to do any planning right now."

"Veronica, Veronica Walters!"

"Momma I will talk to you later I have to go and take care of some stuff for the house."

Veronica walked out her mother's house abruptly. She did not want to discuss the matter any further. She just needed to talk to Kareem to get him to understand and go along with her plans. She knew he would understand. He did whatever Veronica asked she believed her request was a respectable compromise.

****

"So what did you and your mom's talk about?

"Nothing much, you had this thing planned the whole time?" .

"Yes I did," Kareem smiled. I wanted everything to be perfect for you."

"Boy you are so crazy."

"What I tell you about calling me boy," Kareem laughed. "Well I know you and your mother have so much woman stuff to do with planning the wedding. I talked to your father and he agreed that we would split the cost. I had to fight him on that. He is so traditional."

Veronica was trying to figure out how to tell Kareem her plans to deviate. She saw how excited Kareem was so she wanted to make sure she was virtuous when she was about to make her appeal.

"Veronica…? Veronica did you hear me?"

"Yea baby I heard you."

Kareem sensed something was on her mind but he knew planning a wedding could be stressful. He didn't want Veronica to worry about anything. He wanted to give her, her hearts desires.

"Look you pick out whatever you want. I was going to furnish the house but I know my place, so I figured you and your sister would want to do that also."

Veronica was still silent. Kareem became uneasy with Veronica's silence. He didn't know if she was about to throw a tantrum. He wasn't sure where Veronica's head was at so he braced himself.

"Veronica?" Kareem said.

Veronica knew she could not continue to ignore Kareem. She did not know how to approach the conversation. She did not want to disappoint him. She knew how much getting married meant to him. She also knew how she felt, and she didn't want to be hasty in her decisions.

"Uh baby…, I was thinking. We can wait to get married. I can furnish the house. We can live together for a little while and I can plan the wedding later."

"A little while, move in together? Veronica you know I don't believe in shacking up. You know I want to be married before we live together. Why do you think we don't live together now?"

Veronica had an unknowing look on her face. However, she was not ignorant to anything. She understood Kareem's values. She knew what he wanted. She just wanted him to rationalize her request.

"Well you know I am working on my second masters, and the grant is about to go through for my group home. I have a few more months before my promotion, and I was going work with the company for a little while longer. I just wanted to take a little time to work out some of the technicalities, you know for the betterment of us."

Kareem found himself getting warm. He could not believe Veronica's request. He didn't understand where she was coming from. He had done everything she had requested. He had given her everything she had ever asked for. Kareem was confused; he no longer knew what Veronica wanted. He did not know whom he was talking too. She was not the same elated woman who had just told him, *yes*.

"What do you mean Veronica? Do you not want to marry me?"

"No Kareem that is not it."

"You said yes Veronica. You told me, yes, you wanted to get married."

"Baby I do, I just want to have everything in order when we do."

"Then why the hell can we not do it together as husband and wife! We can work on our dreams together. Why are you always trying to do things on your on and not include me?"

"I want to include you."

"Then what is it? What do you want? It sounds to me as if you want me to wait another five years. If that were the case then we should have waited period! Why have I done all this planning?"

Kareem was infuriated. He could not believe Veronica's excuses. He could not believe he had taken out so much time to make her life perfect. He knew he loved Veronica but now she was becoming unbearable. Veronica's audacity began to rear its ugly head. She felt Kareem was overreacting. He seemed uncompromising and controlling. She saw him in a different light. She felt as if he were the one being selfish. She couldn't believe he didn't understand. How could he not understand her point of view? She began to get upset. She could not believe he was acting in this manner.

"I don't know why you have done all this planning," Veronica sneered at Kareem. "I didn't ask you for none of this Kareem. It is you running around here making plans and not including me. You are mapping out our lives, naming our kids, and I ain't even pregnant. You are always planning and I listen to your plans."

"Dammit then you should have told me. I wouldn't have taken all this time and worked so hard, if I didn't love you. I thought this is what you wanted. I asked you what your dreams were. I put my dreams on hold for you. I have been working my ass off for the last few years for you!"

"I didn't ask you too. I never asked you for anything."

"You are delusional! You ask every day for something. You are demanding, you make requests, you through tantrums, and always have needs. I have obliged you in everything without one complaint. I did all of this just because I love you!"

"You should have asked me Kareem."

"I should have asked you what? What should I have asked you?"

"You should have just checked with me. People talk all the time I didn't know."

"You didn't know what! That I was serious, I wasn't just some nigga in the street pretending. That I wasn't some sorry man who speaks and does not have a follow through! What, what was I supposed to do?"

"I don't know. I don't know."

"So you don't want to marry me?"

"Yes I want to marry you!"

"You just don't want to marry me right now? You want me to wait another five years or so until you have completed all of your dreams and I am supposed to forget mine."

"That is not what I am saying. You can work on your dreams too Kareem."

"You don't understand Veronica, you are my dream!"

There was a quiet pause in the room. Kareem fought back the tears. He could not believe he was standing next to a woman who had his heart and soul. He had put her before everything else in his life and until recently, he had put her before God. Just like that, just like man, he realized he was failed.

"Kareem…," said Veronica.

Kareem could not answer. He felt disappointment and hurt run though his body. Kareem was crushed. His heart was broken. He closed his eyes and said a small prayer. He knew he had to make a decision. He knew he was about to make a choice which was going to change both of their lives. He opened his eyes and looked at his supposed lifetime. He looked in her eyes and no longer recognized the woman he had fallen in love with; she was an enigma.

"Kareem...Kareem why can't we?"

"Because we can't... No Veronica your right, we can wait. We just won't wait together."

Kareem fought back the tears as they flooded his tear ducts. Kareem walked out of the house and Veronica just stood. She had no response. She only had feelings of numbness. She watched as Kareem left, never to turn around, or return to aid her.

****

Veronica had been at her mother's house for four months without a word or call from Kareem. Her mother knew her daughter had made the mistake of her life. She had warned Veronica about letting her heart harden to the possibilities of love. She had told her the ramifications of her selfishness. Clearly, Veronica did not take heed to her words of wisdom.

Veronica acted as if Kareem never existed even though her insides were being torn apart. Veronica refused to admit her wrongs in the situation. She refused to be the blame in the choices she had made. She figured Kareem would get his act together and understand her side. She knew he loved her at one point and could only be out of her presence for a short period. She was confident he just needed time to think. She believed in her heart he would come around at some point.

"Veronica you got a package."

"What mamma!"

"You have a package. The UPS guy dropped off a small box addressed to you."

"Who is it from?"

"I don't know open it up and find out."

Her mother was not about to tolerate anything from her after dealing with her foolishness over the last few months. She felt some sympathy but it was minimal because she knew her daughter had caused the fiasco. Veronica's mother left the package in the foyer for her to retrieve. Her mother refused to care about what Veronica had received and returned to the kitchen.

Veronica picked up the box. There was no return address. There was an envelope attached. Veronica took the package to her mother's living room to open. Veronica opened the letter.

Dear Veronica,

I know we have not spoken in a while and I thought it was time I broke the silence. Since the day I left the house, my heart has felt as if it were stolen. I didn't know how to get it back so I needed to leave. Maybe I was wrong I am not sure. I just know I have loved you and will probably always love you. A wise person told me, if you really love something, you should be able to let it go and it will find its way back to you if it truly loves you back. I don't know if we could ever find our way back to each other so as a man I know I must release you. You have your dreams, and visions; and I cannot impair you or myself in the hopes we will be on the same accord. Just know I would have given you the world and anything else you asked for. I just wanted you to give me all of you in return. Now I know that was too much to ask for in return. I will never forget you, and what you meant to me.

I have enclosed some documents you will need in order for you to be able to move in your dream house. No, I don't want the ring back. I want you to have it all. At least there will be a comfort in my spirit knowing you will have a piece of your dream and I could at least give you that. I am satisfied with knowing, "Somewhere in my lifetime it was you and me."

Love you forever and always
Kareem Robinson

Veronica opened the box and looked at the deed to her dream house. Kareem had signed it over to her. All she had to do was initial the paperwork. He had given her dream. Veronica did not say a word or release a tear. She didn't mum a word to her mother or make a comment about the letter she just read. She knew it was not Kareem that released her. She realized at that moment that she had released a good man.

****

The CD player stopped the water was now lukewarm. Veronica refused to move. Two years had passed that Veronica had lived in her dream house alone. She looked at the deed and remembered Kareem's selfless act. She lit another cigarette and wanted to drink her cares away. Nevertheless, no amount of alcohol could harbor the agony she was felt. The bottle was empty and all she could think about was his smile. Veronica became ill as she engaged her loneliness.

She knew at that very moment that it was not a dream. She realized she sacrificed her happiness to follow her own dreams, absent of love, and for what. She had the car, the house, and the Jacuzzi bathtub. She had a successful group home and completed her second Master's Degree. However, Veronica had a void she could not fill.

She picked up the newspaper article one more time to see the faces that appeared to have the dream that use to be hers. *Congratulations Mr. & Mrs. Kareem Robinson.* The picture of the young woman was not the image of Veronica. Her smile not familiar but the apparent happiness made Veronica sick to her stomach. *Who is she, where did she come from?*

Whoever she was, apparently she was more capable of loving the man who once professed his undying, and unconditional love. Veronica assumed that while she waited patiently Kareem would come to his senses. She looked at the cheesy engraved lighter she had purchased for Kareem. She never gave it to him because she was always so clueless of being empathetic to his needs. The present had left her mind and she had it on her possession the entire time. She knew the only thing she gave Kareem was her stubbornness and unruly behavior.

She realized she was wrong and Kareem was now gone forever. He was now someone else's for better for worse. He was now someone else's lifetime.

"Oh God, she cried. What did I do? What did I do?"

Veronica did not move from the cold water as she wept in agony. Her heart ached, and her eyes closed. She reached over to the CD player, pushed repeat button, and hit play.

Somewhere in my lifetime
Somewhere in my lifetime
It was you...and....me........

PART IV

Decadence and Divinity

Bernice
"Deceitful?"

Decadence and divinity

So you smiled at me on a Monday
I shied away
Denying your flirty flaunts of interest
But persistence was your name given at birth
And persist you did
Thank you…

I held your hand on Tuesday
Tickling the sensations of felicity
And embraced the unknown,
But felt the surety of its rightness

Wednesday we walked wistfully
Through the fields of what if
And waltz right into the helix of happiness
Ignoring obsolete
And embraced the refreshing

Thursday you held me in your arms
Hearts beating rapidly in harmony
The eruption of temptation caused a thermal dysfunction
To my understanding
Of what "at first sight" really meant

Finally
Friday we shared our first kiss
Echoed the melodies of an angel's harp
As we danced mirthfully around the union
Of an undisclosed promise of forever

Saturday we completed our task of consoling the void
As our souls collided

Creating the perfection of a blended spice
Entangling our soft hues which
Resembled the nougat a sweetness

Sunday we blessed our matrimony
And its timeless wonder
Our breath saturated with the whimpers of I love you
Causing an unexplained tremble
That would forever leave a "foot print" a remembrance
Of your existence

For it was seven days
Of sunrise and sunset
Decadence and divinity
A season of rescue & restoration
For he was
Her destiny
Her little piece of heaven on earth

Bernice

Bernice sat on the cold table waiting for the man in the lab coat to return to the room. She had been feeling ill for the last few weeks. Bernice could not help but think that perhaps she may have had the same ailments that resembled flu like symptoms. Nausea, fever, loss of appetite chills etc…

I wish the doctor would just come and give me something so I can get home. Bernice was nervous and she could not figure out why. She had been in the doctor's offices before but today she felt uneasy. Her body was going through a hormonal transformation, which was affecting her concentration.

Bernice looked around the room and noticed all the gadgets. Her husband was at work and she knew he would not be home until nightfall. She didn't feel the need to make any phone calls. Calling him would just make him worry.

Bernice's spirit was somber. She had a yearning for something. She needed to feel at ease. She wanted to run away and frolic from responsibilities. She was tired and exhausted because her life was a commitment but not to herself. She knew with the career decisions of her husband she had to sustain a façade that may be the reality of others, lest her own. Was she sure, this is what she wanted to do? Did she want to commit her life to such tedious responsibilities? *What would it be like if I left it all, she thought?* What would it be like if she gave it all up? She could not. She chose this life. She was in a binding contract. Bernice had uttered the words, *I do.* She took a vow of, for better or for worst, till death do them part. Since Bernice had no thoughts of killing her husband, she knew when she made the commitment in front of God that she wouldn't break her contract.

Bernice knew she had let go of the adventure her spontaneity. But who was she fooling she had always lived a very square life. Her family had always criticized her. They believed she was a perfectionist. She listened to everything her mother ever told her. She did whatever she was told because Bernice did not break rules. Why would Bernice complain if she thought she had a perfect life? She was an educated colored woman. She was a schoolteacher who helped other young colored children become successful. She had a perfect husband who had committed his life to Christ. In fact, he was completing his education so that he could become a practicing minister. She knew he was called. She knew that God had a purpose for his life the moment they met.

She did not have to ask anyone for anything because she worked and focused on doing what was right. She didn't lie, drink, or curse. She studied the bible and prayed daily with or without her husband. She was supportive and submissive, all the characteristics of a good preacher's wife. She had her life mapped out the moment she was able to think for herself. Paying close attention to the mentors in her life, she vowed to excel. She valued the women in her life. She was always thinking of what could happen if she had a profound effect on people. Bernice made sure she extended a kind word or hand to help those less fortunate. She had made up her mind that she was not going to make the same mistakes as her sibling before her. She wanted to lead by example so her other siblings thirsted ambition as she had done. *But can a person really be perfect, Bernice thought? Can a person hide the obvious even if she doesn't mutter a word?*

Bernice knew who she was supposed to be. She also knew whom people thought she was when they met her. Everyone adored who Bernice was because she appeared to be grounded and of sound mind. She was a strong woman and she exhibited traits most women wished they had. No one could ever find any fault in her except herself. She hid away from truths that were buried and held her heart with fear. Bernice thought and thought of her life as it passed her by but her conscious would only lie upon the thoughts of her special secret. A secret she would vow to take to her grave because it would cause her shame.

What would they actually think of me? I will not dare give them a reason. What has happened has happened. I cannot change the past I can just move forward. Besides everyone has at least one secret.

While Bernice was wrestling with her consciousness, a young man in a blue jacket and folder in his hand began to approach her. He seemed extremely friendly. Although he was not a man of color, he was blown away by Bernice's beauty. Most men were. She was a gorgeous. Her hair was long and silky. Her frame was exquisite and she had curves in the right place. She had eyes like her mother. They were slanted and entrancing. Her eyes intrigued any man who gazed at Bernice.

"Hello Mrs. Walters, are you not feeling well today?"

The man looked very familiar but she was well aware that she did not know him. Nevertheless, his smile so warm and it just seemed so familiar. Bernice was in remembrance of the months, which had past. She wanted to relieve herself from her significant moment. But Bernice's subconscious was just playing a cruel joke.

"Mrs. Walters," the young man said twice. Bernice continued to drift into the yesterdays of her secrets past. Her subconscious was taking over. She saw the doctor's mouth move but she didn't hear a word.

****

"Bernice!" Mrs. Lucas was calling her name but Bernice was working diligent. "It is time for lunch. You know we only have an hour before those children come off of that playground," she giggled.

Bernice was steadily grading papers that were not due for at least two days. She always consumed every moment of her day with work. She rarely found time to eat. She was so task oriented she forgot about the necessities of her day.

"I am coming Shanell. I am coming. I just want to get this work done so I won't get behind."

"Bernice it is Monday we haven't even gotten into the week. You need to relax. This is the time. It is almost the end of the school year.

Grades are not due until the end of the week. What is wrong with you?"

"I just need to keep busy. James is out of town, the house is to quiet, and I am all by myself. I just like to keep busy Shanell."

Bernice missed her husband and she did not have the noise from the classroom in her home. She didn't know how to take advantage of her time alone. All Bernice knew how to do was work, work, and do more work.

"I hear you girl but you are going to work yourself to death."

"Well you know I have to have my life in some type of order because James is trying to expand his church and he has all these wonderful ideas. He wants a men's group, a woman's group, and community group. He has his vision all planned out I have to make sure we are well organized and put together. You know the job of a preacher's wife is never done."

Bernice was proud of her husband and his work. She wanted to be supportive. She knew in order to have an excellent marriage that she would have to be an excellent wife. Her husband appreciated her hard work at home and in her career. She refused to let him down due to a few minor details.

"Bernice I got that but on top of that it is not like you are not helping your mother with your sibling. You help everyone and do not take time for yourself you just need to sit and release. Don't let life pass you by."

Bernice laughed, "Girl I don't want to pass life by."

Shanell had struck a nerve. Bernice knew how hectic her life could be but she believed she had everything under control. She never thought much about what she wanted because she believed deep down inside God had provided her with her hearts desires.

Bernice believed in family and being of service. She watched her grandmother and mother service their community her entire life. Bernice had nothing but respect for hard work and she believed in order to succeed that people had to stay motivated, determined, and under the grace of God.

"You know my mother still has her businesses and she is always having issues with people trying to buy her out."

"Girl your mother is one of the smartest women I know and she is not going to let anybody just walk in and take away what she has worked so hard for."

Bernice knew what Shanell was speaking was the truth. She just wanted to be there in case her mother needed her. Bernice always stretched herself thin. She never once complained and did everything in humbleness.

Shanell wished Bernice would let loose and let her hair down for once. From the moment she met Bernice, she noticed Bernice was focused. She was never judgmental which was a bit intimidating to the other staff members. Even though she never gave anyone a reason to question, her intentions they always did because they could not believe an individual could be that empathetic and sincere.

"Look we are talking right through lunch and you still haven't eaten. So what did we accomplish?"

Bernice grinned.

"Okay, let's just take a walk."

Shanell and Bernice walked to the playground to where the kids were playing. Children playing kickball, sliding down the slide, jumping rope and all they could hear was laughter.

"Look at them girl," Bernice said. "They have it so good; they don't have a care in this world. I remember what that use to be like."

"You do?" Shanell said. "I figure you started working when you came out of the womb."

Bernice laughed. Bernice remembered always being driven. She watched as her grandmother and mother worked diligently. Her siblings were just about the same age. Then one day God sent a wonderful blessing to her family and her mother now had the fortitude to work smarter. Bernice knew it was nothing but God, her mother's faith was solid, and she never wavered for a moment in spite of any adversity. Bernice knew how hard it was for her mother. She knew how faithful her mother was. She also knew that nothing was perfect.

Her mother made sacrifices for the sake of her children even when it came to her happiness.

"You are strong like your mother. What about your father?"

"Girl I don't even know who he is and my mama never mentions him."

Bernice had never asked who her father was. There was never a male figure around. She had her mother, grandmother, school and church. Bernice desired at times to know but she felt it would be an insult to ask her mother. She believed if her mother wanted her to know then she would have told her. She never did, so Bernice never asked.

"How many sisters and brothers do you have?"

"Four," said Bernice.

"Four..., and there was never a man around the house?"

"Never a man I can remember, not once. I am sorry that is not the truth. There was one few years ago, I think about the time my brother was graduating."

"What happened to him?"

"Girl it is a long story, but I think that was the first time I saw a different light in my mother's eyes. She was always happy but there was something different about her. Then I met James and moved out and we were married within a few months.

"A few months," Shanell looked at Bernice stunned.

Bernice had married James the moment he had asked. She did not want a big wedding so they went to the justice of the peace. They did not go on a honeymoon and as soon as they said, *I do*, they were back at work.

Yes, James was different from other men. He was ambitious, wanted to make a change, and that is what drove her to him. Because Bernice did not grow up with a father figure, she did not want to court any man for a lengthy period. He was into the church and it just seemed right at the time. Bernice never experienced any other man other than her husband.

Shanell was trying to figure out their attraction. Bernice never said anything about love or her emotions. Shanell did not believe Bernice was really in love with her husband as she claimed. Shanell wanted Bernice to give more details about why she had married him so she continued to pry.

"What do you mean?" said Shanell.

"We were similar. We came from similar backgrounds. We were in school together and he attended my church so you know we had the same values and that was important to me."

Shanell looked at Bernice and still saw no enthusiasm. "So it was a good arrangement per say?" said Shanell.

"Don't call it an arrangement. I cared for James and he cared for me. We both wanted children, I wanted to be a schoolteacher and he wanted to be a preacher. We would both be helping people, kind of sort of..."

"So this was no love at first sight?"

"No I can't say that, but it fit. Like a missing piece to a puzzle, we just fit. Now, here we are."

"What about children.

Well we decided we would at least wait five years."

"Oh my God you all planned when to have children. Do you two, plan alone time also?"

"No," Bernice laughed.

"Then how do you control when you have children, you are not on anything are you?"

"The good Lord knows and you know we count."

"You count? Count what?"

"The days, crazy..."

"Okay I have had enough. You are living on a rhythm and a hope that you don't get pregnant."

"Don't say that. We want children. I love children but when it is time."

"Okay so what do you do if you get pregnant before your five year deadline?"

"Girl please it has been working thus far, we will be fine. If it happens it happens, but trust me, it won't."

Bernice's confidence dwindled in the conversation because she did not know. She knew she sounded foolish but she would never admit it. She wanted the conversation to end. Luckily, the bell rang and Shanell and Bernice returned to class.

Bernice arrived home at 4:45 pm. She looked around her house and realized it was empty. She realized her husband would be gone for the next seven days. Bernice reflected on the conversation she had with Shanell earlier that day. She began to think there was some truth to everything her co-worker said. Was she really missing something? Was there something absent in her life? God had blessed her in so many ways why would she not be happy. She had a wonderful husband and a supportive family. She had a good job and good friends. What could possibly be missing out of her life?

Bernice felt an overwhelming urge to cry. She had no apparent reason to shed tears. She began to think about the world she had created. She insisted everything be in order. If everything had order then there was structure and logic. Her house was flawless, her clothes were neatly pressed and dry cleaned. Even the designs in her home were color coordinated to match and accent each part. She had a garden with fresh vegetables, and herbs. She never deviated from her task list. Even when she shopped, she carefully calculated a plan. Bernice looked around her seamless life and wanted to scream.

Bernice grabbed her purse and walked out of the house. As she walked she had no idea where she was going, she just knew she had to get away. She yearned to get away from the monotony, the structure and the order. If she did not know any better, she would have believed she had served in the military under strict rules and guidelines.

Bernice walked about two blocks until she came upon a park. The park was near a construction site, which made it difficult for children to enjoy. Usually they went to another neighborhood park so they were able to run freely. She saw a park bench and decided to take a seat.. She sat down and began to mull over the thoughts, which had just breached her perfect sanity. The tears found there ways to escape the thresh holds of her tear ducts. Once she started, she could not stop crying. She hoped no one had seen her outburst of emotions. Her heart was heavy and she seemed confused about her choices.

"Are you okay?" a sound voice said to her.

Bernice was too mortified to respond so she kept her head tilted. How did someone find her like this? She thought she was all alone. She wanted to have her breakdown without an audience.

"Ma'am, are you okay?" the voice persisted.

She wanted the mysterious voice to leave her alone. She nodded her head hoping the non-verbal response would be sufficient. The voice seemed to have disappeared. As she lifted her head out of her hands, she saw a hand outstretched with a white handkerchief dangling in front of her. Not knowing what to say or do, she immediately, in embarrassment grabbed the handkerchief and began to wipe her soiled face.

"Thank you," she said as her mouth quivered.

"No problem."

The stature standing before her did not move. She did not intend to lift her head for him to see her disheveled face. At this point Bernice did not care if the unannounced stranger continued to stand. Instead of taking heed to the silence of the tousled woman, the young man began to speak.

"Why are you crying pretty lady?"

There is no way Bernice felt pretty because she was aware of what she looked like when she arose in the morning. With watery eyes and possible traces of snot, she knew that she was a sight for sore eyes. She knew that at this point she would need to respond because assiduous man did not budge.

"I am okay sir..."

"If you were okay you would not have filled my handkerchief with your tears of sorrow."

Bernice realized that this individual was not going to leave. She proceeded to lift her head. There stood before her a dark skinned, colored man, in dusty clothing. Strong cheekbones and deep almond features were noticeable. He had a neatly trimmed goatee and full lips. The attractive man appeared to work in construction. Even covered in filth there was something extremely gentle in his eyes. His build was succulent; strong shoulders, flat abdomens, and trimmed legs. His body appeared to be cut with a certain precision. Bernice was able to notice all of his features even though he was fully dressed. Bernice felt proceeded to try to clean up her face. Without a request, he sat beside her on the park bench. Bernice's body felt an uncomfortable quiver. She was not sure what the reaction was but she wanted him not to notice.

"So, are you going to tell me what's wrong, pretty lady?"

"Please sir, I don't even know you."

"Well here is how I see it. I do not know you and you do not know me. Nevertheless, there was a reason why you decided to sit in this park right here today, at this very moment, and cry as I walked by. So that is more than enough reason for you to take the time out and share with me why someone so beautiful, would cry so openly outside, while staring at God's natural wonders. These are not tears of joy."

Bernice felt the urge to tell him everything on her mind but she couldn't. She just stared in his eyes. His eyes were warm, and caring; she had never seen anyone's eyes that pierced her soul the way this man's did. Bernice could not talk for a force, which took over her every sense, drew her in.

"Did someone die?"

"Uh…, no they didn't."

"Then what's wrong?"

"I don't know. I became overwhelmed with all of these feelings and I just started to cry."

"So in other words you are having a moment?"

"Yes I am having a moment."

"Well sweetheart just like everything else in this life, this moment too, will pass. So if in this moment, you must cry, then you cry. I will sit here with you if you like while you cry, and I don't have to say another word. I will just listen to the sound of your whimpers and watch your tears, while they hit your beautiful brown skin."

He cannot be for real. He is to full of himself. Bernice was astounded by his words and yearned attention. She felt special and noticed. She felt all of her insecurities dwindle at the hands of this stranger. She didn't feel the need to refuse any of his requests. She also didn't feel the need to cry anymore. Her heart was a bit heavy and if she decided to cry she was assured it would not be in vain. She loved the silence. She adored looking at his smile.

"Okay," Bernice said as she turned and looked at God's wonders while listening to the songs of nature.

Bernice did not know what she had agreed to but she had no objection. Bernice and the young man sat silently on the park bench while her sporadic tears fell, until the sunset. As the sun departed he walked her to the side walk and bid her good evening never to ask her name, nor did she his.

"Thank you, kind sir."

"Goodbye and good evening, pretty lady."

That was Monday afternoon.

****

Bernice could not concentrate after the events of yesterday. Her mind was focused on her recent encounter. Shanell noticed that Bernice seemed a bit misplaced. Shanell was certain something had happened and she hoped she hadn't offended Bernice.

Shanell Lucas was a nosy, busy body. Most people could not believe they were friends but they had a natural bond. Bernice treated her like a kid sister even though they were close in age. Shanell couldn't understand Bernice for the sake of her life. She was thoughtful and caring but didn't have much more depth. When they first met, Bernice was quiet and extremely focused. Bernice appreciated Shanell for who she was; even her flaws, and did not judge her even though most of the faculty steered clear from the hyperactive adult. Shanell wanted Bernice to come out of her shell, and made it her life's work to pursue this task.

"Are you okay?"

"Huh…, why do you ask?"

"You seem distant. You just don't seem like yourself."

"I am fine Ms. Lucas, everything is okay," said Bernice in a condescending tone.

"Then why do you seem to be here in flesh but not in spirit? Please don't tell me you are snapping out, girl. Girl don't tell me that all of this chaos you call organization is finally getting the best of you."

Bernice laughed, "No it is not. I am just in thought, nothing more, nothing less."

Bernice knew she could not share the happenings of yesterday with Shanell because she may have asked unnecessary questions, which Bernice could not answer. She loved Shanell but she did not like the way she always tried to pry into her personal business. Bernice never wanted to give Shanell too much information. She knew Shanell would never do her any harm intentionally, so she never gave her ability to strain their relationship.

Bernice did not know what light the stranger had turned on in her, but she knew this was a new feeling she had never had before. The mysterious man had caught her attention. She felt drawn to him and found it hard to concentrate.

Shanell continued to rattle off in Bernice's ear. She knew Bernice was not going to open up instantly. Since Bernice was being secretive about her thoughts Shanell figured she would change the focus of the conversation.

"Look here we have one more week of school, I know it is a bit lonely but maybe you should just concentrate on getting your grades completed. This may help you relieve some of your stress."

"I am fine crazy, and yes, I will probably finish grading these tonight."

"Okay lady, are you sure you are okay?"

"Yes girl I am fine, I am alright."

Bernice had an urge to walk by the park again just to see if what she had experienced was a dream or reality. Something in her soul felt as if it were forbidden. Bernice walked to the park reluctantly. *What am I thinking? I haven't done anything wrong. This is ridiculous I am condemning myself. Someone reached out to me and I wanted to thank the kind being who was there. He was God sent.*

Bernice had convinced herself of things that didn't matter. She didn't want to believe that someone other than James had cause a twitch in her spirit. This was different. James was the only man Bernice knew. She had never looked at another man other than James. James was very thoughtful and kind. Bernice knew that with all of his wonderful qualities he lacked a certain passion. She was aware James had never really sparked a fire in her. She just knew he was a good provider, a loyal man, a man of God.

Bernice made it to the park only to find that it was empty. Bernice began to talk to herself. *What am I doing? This is absolutely crazy. There is no one here, and I don't even know what or who I am looking for. Bernice you are going crazy. Who does this, and what exactly am I doing?* Bernice continued to mumble to herself as she looked at the empty park bench. *Go home Bernice get your head out of the cloud.*

"Who are you talking to?" The voice came from behind her.

Bernice knew the voice and it caused her heart to beat rapidly with anticipation, and hope, it was he who stood behind her. She brushed her clothes off and braced herself to turn around. She was a bit bashful but she wanted to match the voice with the face once again.

"Hey pretty lady," he said. "Who are you talking to?"

Without a thought, Bernice turned around to the virile stature and with a twinkle in her eye and said, "Myself..."

"Pray tell, what are you talking to yourself about?"

She let out a girlish laugh without a response. She knew she could not tell him she was rationalizing their encounter. She was not swift enough to make up a bogus excuse. Bernice just smiled and did not verbally respond.

"What are you doing here today? Please don't tell me you are crying?"

Bernice was a little embarrassed about her previous display. She knew she had no reason to cry. If he needed her to cry, for him to stay longer, she was prepared to shed some tears.

"No sir, I just went for a little walk after a long day of work."

"Well then Miss, since you are here and I am here, why don't we have a sit down. Take a load off and sit a spell."

"Sit a spell? My, my sir you are a little country."

"Really"

"Really," Bernice laughed.

"Um...," Bernice said. "I have a question?"

"Let me guess," the man said. "Better yet, let me answer, William, William Burrows."

"Burrows?"

"Yes ma'am, but you can call me William, or Will for short."

Bernice giggled because Will had answered the question that was on her mind. So she waited and anticipated he would ask her the same. She cleared her throat to get his attention.

"Is everything ok?"

"Yes, but do you not want to know mine?"

"I do know yours," he said gently.

"How do you know my name," Bernice looked in amazement.

"I called you by your name yesterday."

214

Bernice was still confused because she knew she never exchanged names with the man. Or did she? She knew couldn't have because of all the crying and whimpering she was doing. She mulled over the events of yesterday but she could not remember all of the conversation. She was too busy staring in awe. Will reminded her.

"Pretty Lady," said Will with a slight grin on his face.

Bernice chuckled. "Yes I do appreciate the compliment but my birth given name is Bernice; Mrs. Bernice Walters."

"Nice to meet you Mrs. Bernice Walters," emphasizing the Mrs.

Bernice looked startled trying to figure out how to respond since Will, did not glitch at the point of her being spoken for under vows.

"So Mrs. Walters what do you do?" said Will.

"Please call me Bernice. I am a 6th grade school teacher."

"A teacher, hmm...," said Will. "That is why you look so studious."

"Studious..., please..."

"Yes ma'am you walk around with your minuscule heel, mid-calf skirt, buttoned blouse, and a sweater neatly worn on your shoulders. It was either that or a preacher's wife," Will begin to laugh.

Bernice laughed also but chose not to verify the allegations of her being a preacher's wife. Somewhere in her rational Bernice chose not to think about her current roles and responsibilities, she was drawn to the company she kept at that moment. She knew it was a bit deceitful but she knew she did not have to divulge all of her personal life to this extraordinary man.

Will and Bernice decided they would talk. They did not talk about anything to personal. They just enjoyed each other's company. Bernice and Will laughed, smiled, and talked the afternoon away.

"Excuse me pretty lady, when was the last time you have been on a swing?"

Bernice looked astonished because she could not remember when she was on a swing. She wasn't sure why he asked but she felt his question to be very endearing. He had asked her about something, which she had never given much thought to.

"Um… I am not sure."

"Come with me," said Will as he grabbed Bernice by the hand.

He guided her over to the swings. They appeared a bit warn and dusty. Bernice was shocked by the touch of his hand; as large and overworked as they appeared his touch was soothing. His palms were a bit calloused but even the calluses did not feel harsh against Bernice's hand. Will took Bernice to the swing and motioned for her to wait. He pulled out a white handkerchief from his pocket and dusted off the seat. He placed a perfectly clean handkerchief on the seat after he removed the dust.

"I can't have you messing up that nice skirt of yours, pretty lady. Now you should be able to take a seat."

Bernice smiled. Bernice grabbed the sides of the swing and took a seat. Will laid his hands over hers and began to motion the swing forward. Bernice felt herself glide back in forth in the air with an overwhelming freeness. She acted as if she were a schoolgirl on a playground. She was smiling inside and the out. She allowed the wind to hit her face. Her thoughts of being organized and responsible were in the wind. She felt something she had not realized she was missing; she was happy.

That was a Tuesday.

****

6:30 am

"Oh my goodness…!"

Bernice jumped up and screamed. She had overslept. In the years she had been working, she had never slept past 5 am. She was always up at 5 am to read, pray, and plan her day. This allotted her enough time to make James's breakfast and her coffee. They would listen to the radio for the latest news updates, but not this morning. Bernice had woken as if she did not have any responsibilities.

She knew she had to leave the house promptly at 7:30 so she only had an hour to get herself ready. She turned the shower on and ran back to her room, opened her closet trying to figure out what she would wear. She had to make sure it didn't need to be pressed because she knew she would not have enough time to get to work. For some reason she could not think clearly about what she was going to wear, so she decided to take her shower.

As the water hit her body, she thought of how beautiful yesterday was. Will had changed something in her that she never realized. She smiled from ear to ear and began to hum a tune. She did not know exactly what she was humming she just knew she was full of bliss.

Bernice arrived at Stuart Middle School at 8:05 am a little after breakfast was served. She opted not to go into the teacher's lounge. She did not want to be any one to think she was late. *Technically, she would have only been late if she had arrived after 8:30.*

She rushed in her classroom to prepare for the day. Luckily, there was not much to do because it was three days before summer vacation. The awards ceremony was at nine. She knew she did not have to present any awards but it was mandatory that the faculty and staff be present. Mrs. Walters just did not feel like it today, she could not stay focused at all.

"Mrs. Walter's," a head poked in the classroom.

It was Judy Marshall, one of her students. Judy had struggled when she first entered into Bernice's class. However, Bernice identified her weakness and put in extra efforts to watch her succeed. Bernice was aware of the struggles of parents, this was the reason she became a teacher. She wanted to help those who did not always have the resources.

Judy's father was terminally ill, which left her mother to work and fend for the household. Her mother worked countless hours and was not always able to give her children the attention that was needed. Judy had six brothers and sisters. Coming from a large home, Bernice knew the importance of family. She knew how much it meant to stick together.

"Hey darling, are you coming into class now?"

"Yes ma'am I just wanted to say, um…here you go." Judy handed her a little box. "Thank you so much for all you have done for me this year." Judy smiled at her teacher.

"Oh sweet heart you didn't have to do this."

"Yes I did because you are one of the best teachers I have ever had. I am going to miss you when I go to the 7th grade. I wouldn't be going to the 7th grade if it weren't for you."

"No baby that was all of your hard work and dedication. I was there to support you."

"Mrs. Walters you help me with my reading. Now I understand all of my work. My grades have improved. I do not feel… you know, dumb anymore.

"Judy, don't ever say that. You were never dumb baby. We all have challenges; and we all learn, and process information differently."

Judy smiled. "When my momma didn't have time to do this sort of stuff, you know, because she is always working. But you were right there. I know my momma does the best she can, but I am very thankful for you."

Bernice looked at Judy and felt the urge to hug and kiss her. She knew the challenges the young girl had faced. Bernice was happy to make a difference. She made sure she gave as much attention as she could to all of her students.

"Open it Mrs. Walters."

"Sure baby."

In the small box, there was a handmade bracelet. It was made of yarn and had rainbow colored beads intertwined. This was a thoughtful gift, which came from the heart. It made Bernice think about the absence of children in her own home. She knew one day she would have children of her own who would bless her with joy the way her students did.

"Oh sweetheart this is absolutely beautiful. I am going to put this on right now."

"Let me help you Mrs. Walters."

Bernice held out her arm and let Judy place the bracelet on her wrist. She began looking at the trinket. She was honored to be wearing it. She extended a big hug to Judy to show her appreciation. Bernice fought back the tears and released the child from her embrace. Bernice felt extremely special.

"Ok sweet heart it is almost time for the others to come in."

The students began to enter the classroom all excited about the last three days of school. Bernice was excited, hoping she would see Will later on that day. He was her special present, which she had to share with no one else. She imagined he would be her little secret. No, harm no foul. *I will just enjoy my time until James comes back. Then this foolishness with me acting like a schoolgirl will cease.* Bernice began rationalizing her behavior.

As the children gathered in the room there were bows of noise all throughout the classroom. Shanell poked her head in and noticed Bernice sitting at her desk in lala land, while allowing the kids to continue with their shrieks and banters. Shanell was flabbergasted. Little Miss Organized was letting the crazies run the asylum. She instantly knew something was wrong or troubling Bernice and she was determined to find out what was causing this supposed breakdown. Shanell had no idea Bernice was preoccupied with thoughts of the unmentionable. Bernice was so focused on her thoughts of Will she was able to tune out all of the noise that surrounded her. All she could think about was the tone of his voice, and softness in his eyes.

"Are you ok?"

Bernice looked up at Shanell startled because she had no idea why she would ask her such a thing. She looked like she was caught with her hand in the cookie jar. Bernice pretended to shuffle the papers on her desk.

"Yes...uhh..., why do you ask?"

"You don't hear these kids? Cause I can hear them in the hall."

"Okay class, settle down." Bernice said.

"Yes, Mrs. Walters," the children said in unison.

"Girl you never let the kids make noise. I can hear them in the hallway."

"Please," Bernice said. "They are just excited. It is the end of the school year. They have nothing to do other than talk about the summer ahead. I will keep it to a minimum lady."

Shanell was startled because she knew exactly how strict Bernice was about her classroom.

"Oh... okay," Shanell said to Bernice.

Bernice wanted to scurry Shanell out her classroom. She didn't want her to start with her game of fifty questions. She knew it was almost time for the assembly so she focused her attention on the students.

"Children we are going to the auditorium in just a few moments for the awards ceremony and we do have to keep he noise down."

"Okay Mrs. Walters..."

Bernice had her class line up in a single file. She grabbed her papers from her desk. She wanted to make sure that she finished grading all of her papers so she wouldn't have to spend any additional time in the school building. She had already planned, when the bell rung for the half of day at school; and the children ran out that she was running right behind them. She had no time to waste for there was something special waiting for her on the outside.

During the assembly, Bernice was still preoccupied with thoughts of Will. He had promised to meet her after she finished her day. She didn't know what else they could possibly talk about but she was willing to sit in silence just to be near him. She had forgotten about her husband. For the moment, she did not forget about her vows. She knew as long as she and Will were out in the open that she could not be tempted to indulge in any of her lustful thoughts.

The assembly seemed to be endless. She was tired of hearing the children's names called for various awards. She became a bit agitated when the principles guest speaker was rambling about nothing. *Oh, God he might not be there. Of course, he will be there; I told him that I had a half a day at school. He said that he wouldn't be too busy and that we could meet.* Bernice became worried. She just wanted the bell to ring and be dismissed from her day. *No, he will be there.*

When the bell rung Bernice did just as she planned and ran out of the school building. Mrs. Lucas tried to stop her for conversation but Bernice would not let her deter her from her plans. She walked right pass her never to stop and just threw up a hand saying goodbye.

Bernice arrived at the park only to find Will was nowhere to be found. The anxiety began to set in. She was wondering if she had missed him. She had planned her thoughts around this moment and would not have been happy if he didn't show up. *Where could he be she thought?* While Bernice was about to perspire she turned around and faced the street. Just then, a 1972 mint green Thunderbird pulled up right in front of her.

"You looking for me pretty lady?"

"Why… I was waiting… you said you were going to be here." Bernice did not want to sound anxious and tried to play coy.

"I am here now, are you ready?"

"Ready…um…. I thought we were going to talk in the park."

"We are, just not this park, get in."

Bernice conscious was telling her that it would not be appropriate to get into a man's car because someone may see her. She paused. Will noticed Bernice had a confused look.

"I don't know if I should."

"What are you scared of, that someone will see you?"

"No I am not scared, I just…"

"Then get in, I won't bite you, I promise. I just want to take you away for a little while. Is your... excuse me, is Mr. Walters home."

"No, no he isn't Bernice stuttered but you know the neighbors, people..."

"Okay, just sit tight give me five minutes I promise I will be right back."

Bernice was confused when Will sped off. She looked around to see if anyone noticed her. She didn't see or hear anything. She knew the park might be inundated with children at any moment. Then she thought about the construction. She knew they would probably ventured to the other park in the neighborhood. *Stop worrying Bernice. You both are just friends. You are not doing anything wrong. James has to talk and associate with several women in the church and you never say a word.* She began justifying the actions she was about to take. Just then, she noticed Will's car pulling in toward her. He handed her a bag through the passenger window. She opened the bag and to her surprise there was a pink scarf and sunglasses inside. Coincidently, the scarf matched the design in her skirt.

"Now unless someone is being extremely nosy, no one should notice you at all. I promise we will be away from these parts in no time."

She began to get excited. Nothing was going to keep her from spending time with this man. Regardless of the supposed friendship, she appreciated his thoughtfulness of her discretion. As she hopped in the car she proceeded to put on the head covering and shades.

"My God you could put on anything and be beautiful."

She blushed as Will began to speed off.

Bernice had no idea where she was going. The country side was beautiful. She admired the trees and the fresh air as it hit her face. She felt free. It felt like an adventure only shared between the two of them.

Will began to slow down. There was nothing in sight but nature.

The ambience was breath taking. Bernice saw the beautiful colors of nature and smelled peace. Her spirit felt harmonious and in tune with her surroundings.

"Where are we?"

"I call this my quiet place. I come out here to think."

Will got out the car and Bernice began to open her door. Will rushed to the passenger side of the car. He didn't believe a woman should ever have to open her door if there was a man near. He was old fashion and believed a woman should be escorted.

"Let me get that."

"Why thank you sir," said Bernice grinning as she stepped out of the car. Bernice was amazed with his kindness and attention.

"Where are you taking me?"

"I am taking you to see something that resembles you."

"What?" Bernice asked.

"I am taking you to see something beautiful."

Bernice and Will arrived at a small pond and witnessed small ducks floating on the water. It was surreal. There were different colored flowers, which surrounded the pond. Everything looked alive. It put her in mind of a romantic Garden of Eden. There were weeping willows, which surrounded the pond that appeared to be bowing at Bernice. There was a small bench like figure near the pond.

"Here sit down," said Will. "No wait a minute and he pulled out a white handkerchief and laid it on the bench. There you go my lady."

"This is beautiful," said Bernice. "I have never been here."

"A lot of people don't come here at all if you can believe that. I come just to take time out to enjoy God's silence and beauty. That is why I love it."

"I thank you Will, this is magnificent."

"So are you going to tell me more about you?"

"What do you mean you know something about me?"

"You know about me but we don't really know each other."

"What do you mean?" Said Bernice.

"What do you dream about ? What are your goals? How long have you been married? Do you have any children, what are their names? What do you teach, what do you love?   How did I get the honor of spending this time with someone so beautiful?"

Bernice was overwhelmed with the montage of questions. She began to blush. It was a bit embarrassing for her to talk to Will about such personal things but he was so convincing. She grabbed her wrist that held her gift from her little friend. Will reached for her hand admiring the craft and began to gaze into her eyes. She felt she could be honest with him without divulging anything too private. She had never asked him anything personal but so many questions were unanswered. She knew if she had asked him about his personal life, it would open up doors she was not willing to travel right at that moment. Telling Will a little about herself was not going to harm anything; he already knew she was spoken for.

"I haven't been married that long. I have three siblings, two sisters, and a brother. My mom lives a little ways from here but I do see her as much as I can, and I try to help her with her stores. I don't have any children but I love children that is why I became a schoolteacher. I love peach cobbler. I don't know why I am here. I just know that something seems so different when I am with you, and I can't explain exactly what it is."

Will was intrigued by Bernice's girlish qualities. He knew she was a grown woman but she acted innocent and shy. He loved the way she blushed and became flustered when the conversation was placed in her corner. Will, got a little closer to Bernice so that he could hold onto her every word. Bernice interjected as Will moved closer.

"I am happily married."

"I didn't imply you weren't. So… where is your husband?"

"He is… oh God… I feel embarrassed."

"Don't be."

"He is out of town for this week doing some work with the church."

"Does he work with the church?"

"Well yes... he does," Bernice began to stutter, "He is a....a preacher."

"So that explains it." Will laughed.

"What...what do you mean?" Said Bernice.

"Nothing bad, just like I told you, you had that look. He smiled. You have not told me why you are here. What is that look in your eyes?"

Bernice did not know what to say and didn't answer. She didn't know why she agreed to spend time with Will. She was happily married, or so she thought. She didn't want to tell him his eyes, and his scent overwhelmed her. She didn't want to tell him she was drawn to him. She just turned her head. Will didn't want to pry. He wanted her to enjoy her time with him. He didn't care about her circumstances. He was drawn to Bernice, as she was drawn to him. Will turned her head to face his. He looked in her eyes and smiled.

"Then don't worry about what it is, let's just enjoy the moment. Let's just enjoy right now."

She looked in Will's eyes and felt refreshed and un-judged. He had touched her soul. He was tender and his stroke was soothing. Even if her actions were questionable, she appreciated being in his company.

"Thank you for not judging me."

"Why would I judge you? I am going to enjoy you because I have you all to myself right now. Excuse me for being selfish."

Bernice smiled. "I am being selfish too, because I want to be here with you also. I am happy... not that I am not always happy. You just give me a different kind of happiness."

"Then why not just be happy."

"I will as long as I can spend the rest of the day with you."

Bernice smiled at Will. He grabbed her hand kissed it lightly. They enjoyed the setting and continued to talk and laugh the afternoon away.

That was on a Wednesday.

****

"Two more days until these brats go home and are out of my hair."

"Girl…they are not brats," said Bernice.

"Listen I don't know what has gotten into you but these children can work a nerve." .

Bernice laughed, she knew Shanell's statement had some truth but she could care less. It was less than *48 hrs.*, before she didn't have to deal with Gods little gifts, for at least two months. She would have her summer without grading papers and time constraints. She also knew she had to prepare for whatever duties James needed her to perform.

"Girl, remember when you were a child?"

"I know but my parents adored me," said Shanell. I was their only child."

"Then that explains it," Bernice laughed.

"What do you mean that explains it."

"Girl because you don't have any friends," said Bernice jokingly.

Shanell did not take kindly to the statement. She knew she was considered a busy body but some people did like her. Bernice did not mean any harm and could see she offended Shanell.

"I have friends, plenty of them."

"Awe girl, I was just picking. You know I love you."

"You love me? Awe, you are my big sister."

"What, big sister?" Said Bernice sarcastically.

"Yea, yea, you're my big sister. Remember you are a few months older than me."

"Ha, ha," they both laughed.

Shanell and Bernice had combined their classes together so that they were able to watch a film. They had reserved the projector from the library earlier in the week. They weren't thinking too hard about keeping the kids busy. They knew it was easier if they just put their heads together. Other teachers banded together and did similar activities just to relieve the stress on each other.

"What are we doing for the school party tomorrow?"

"Well…each child is to going to bring something from home."

"So they can all be high off of sugar?"

"Don't forget to mention salt and caffeine, which is why we only have a half of day, so when we send their behinds back home to their parents and they can deal with their craziness."

Bernice and Shanell continued to laugh. They knew giving the children goodies would get them hyped. Bernice didn't mind because she had already started baking all sorts of goodies in anticipation of the celebration. She needed to find something to do with her energy at the end of her day after being swept away by Will's charm.

The children took notice and felt that their fun time was being interrupted by the cackles of their teachers. They sometimes felt the teachers caused more disturbances than they did. A few students were having a hard time hearing the movie and decided they would get the cackling teachers attention, respectably.

"Shhh…," the students said in unison."

The teachers looked at the children and laughed again. They hadn't realized they were causing such a disturbance in the room. They decided to step into the hall and continue their conversation. Bernice pulled two chairs in the hallway. They were able to leave the door cracked so they could monitor the class.

"Bernice, can I ask you something?"

"Sure you know you can ask me anything."

"Do you miss James?"

"Do I miss James? What kind of a question is that?"

"I just want to know."

"No you just don't want to know. So…I would love for you to tell me why you asked me such a question about my husband?"

"Well to be honest with you, it's because you haven't said a word about him thus far."

Bernice hadn't mentioned her husband since Monday. She hadn't noticed but Shanell did. Bernice would usually make small conversation about James but never anything to personal. Nevertheless, "her husband," was a part of her daily conversation. Bernice did not even express she missed James. She was not having any small talk about "her husband," that week.

"He has been gone since Sunday and you have not said anything. Maybe I am crazy but most wives that have a husband out of town cannot wait until he gets back. You don't even seem sad or in a moment of miss you. You did earlier this week. What has changed?"

Bernice knew that if she did not respond, Shanell would rip her apart. That is what nosy women did. They asked a question, wait for a response, and then chop it all up with their theory; always looking for something that wasn't there. The problem was Shanell was right. Bernice did not miss her husband. She wasn't even thinking of her husband even before she met Will. Once she met Will, James left her subconscious and consciousness. She was well aware she was married; however, her focus was not on her husband. Bernice realized even in her vows she had said, "I do" to a stranger.

"Girl you are crazy! You know I miss James. He will be here Monday."

Bernice told Shanell that James planned to stay for one of the minister's services and it would be too late to travel. She suggested he come home the following morning. Bernice's body clenched when she realized she was lying with a straight face. People around her had done it so often, and she often criticized people who did not utilize the truth. Now Bernice was doing the same thing. She again found herself being deceitful. She wanted to cease the conversation and she knew if she did it abruptly, Shanell would see into her fabrications.

"So how is he Bernice?"

"Who, how is who?"

"What do you mean who? We are talking about James," said Shanell.

"Yes girl we are. What is going on with you today Shanell? You got loads of questions today."

"I am just saying, since the last moment you and I spoke about James, a change has come over you."

"Is that what this is about," Bernice said agitated. "Are you still saying I am overworked and I need to take time for myself?"

"No, no I am just saying that I think you need to focus on self."

"Then don't worry Shanell, trust me, I am taking time out for me. James is doing what he needs to do, and I am doing the same."

"Okay if you say so but I just can't put my hand on it,"

Then, just keep your hands off, Bernice thought. "Thank you for being concerned but I am fine. James is fine, we are fine."

The bell rung and Bernice was in a hurry to leave. She remembered Will said he would be working. She was disappointed she could not see him that afternoon. She felt some dismay in her heart because she knew the week would be over soon and to miss a day with, Will, might cause her to go insane. She wanted to cherish every moment she was allowed. She knew she had to compensate for the time she was going to miss today.

Bernice entered her home realizing there was no one to greet her. The loneliness was unsettling. Walking to the park was not an option either. Her reason for going to the park was preoccupied with work. *What am I going to do this afternoon? I have completed all my paperwork for the end of the year. The house is clean. Maybe I will cook, but why cook there is no one here to eat it.* As Bernice mulled over her thoughts she realized, not one of them, was in reference to her husband. All of her cognitive foresight was on a man who did not belong to her. *I can't do this right now. I need to see my mother.*

Bernice did something she didn't liked to do. Tired of doing the norm, she decided to step out of her comfort zone. Bernice rode the city bus daily. She preferred to be escorted to her destinations unless it was an extreme emergency. When James was not available, she had no choice, especially when the bus wasn't running. She grabbed the car keys to James's car, her purse, and walked out of the soundless house.

****

She knocked on the door and awaited an answer. A shocked, beautiful fair-skinned woman opened the door. She was use to only seeing Bernice when she called ahead of time. Since Bernice had gotten married she had not visited, as often as, she had liked. She was dependable and present when she was needed, but her time for leisure activity was limited. Everyone's needs, she tried to fulfill, but her husband's career was her priority.

"Girl what are you doing out here in the middle of the week?"

"Nothing, I just thought I would take a ride."

"A ride Bernice…" questioned her mother. "Girl you don't even like to drive. If the bus or your feet can't get you there, you usually stay planted." The lady started laughing. "We don't see you unless James brings you here, or unless I need help."

"Momma, what is wrong with me just popping up to come and see you."

Bernice's mother observed her daughter's body language and peculiar look on her face. She knew she had something on her mind, she just did not know what. She immediately became concerned and tried to lighten the conversation.

"You know… it is going to rain?"

Bernice was aware of the forecast. That is why she was wearing a light rain jacket. In the event she was caught in the storm, she wanted to be prepared. She wasn't planning to spend much time at her mother's house but she knew she had all afternoon to kill some time.

"Yes momma I do, that is why I came here before the storm had a chance to hit."

Bernice did not give her mother full eye contact. She seemed a bit antsy and anxious. She wanted to give her a hug just to relieve some of her heaviness. She didn't want to move too hasty, because she knew her mother would begin to ask to many questions. All she really wanted to do is enter into a familiar setting.

Coming home always eased Bernice's mind. There were so many rooms to choose from she thought of just hiding out in one, and getting away from the reality of the world. Then there was the smell of food that frequently lingered from her mother's kitchen. A home cooked meal was something she appreciated. Bernice could cook but there was nothing like her mother's southern cuisine. Bernice felt safe. Her mother motioned for her to come inside the house.

"You know I was going to let you come in, get in here girl…" she chuckled.

"Where is Beatrice?"

"Girl please, she ain't here. She is probably somewhere trying to figure out how to take over the world. Barbara just left here a little while ago."

Bernice responded nonchalantly as if she didn't care if Barbara was at her mother's house. Bernice adored her little sister, Beatrice, but was annoyed by Barbara; however, she loved them both. She didn't agree with the life choices Barbara had made. She knew how hard her mother had worked to make sure all of her children received an opportunity, and Barbara chose to take an easier route. Bernice did not want to be judgmental but she knew deep down inside how much it hurt her mother.

Bernice watched as her mother began to shuffle around the house in excitement. She was happy Bernice had come to see her. Bernice had just expressed to her mother that she didn't need her to go through any trouble for her visit. All she wanted to do was be in her mother's company.

"Can I make you some tea?"

"Yes please, I would love some."

Bernice's mother directed her to the kitchen and pointed for her to have a seat at the kitchen table. Bernice sat down. Her mind was so preoccupied that she had forgotten to removed her jacket.

Bernice's mother noticed the bemused look on her daughter's face and was hoping she was going to receive an explanation. She knew there had to be more to this surprise visit. Bernice visited but it was usually to run errands, check on her siblings, or her mother. But she always called. Popping up and a storm was brewing created a lot of questions. Her mother did not want to pry but she wanted to help settle her daughter's spirit.

"Is everything okay with James?" Said Bernice's mother as she served the hot tea.

"Yes momma, James is fine."

"Are you here to tell me that I am going to be a Granma?"

"Mamma no, I am not even close to being pregnant. Please, James travels too much for us to even try to have children."

"Then what is it?"

"Mamma can't a daughter just want to check on her mamma."

Bernice appeared was uneasy. She knew her mother could sense something was wrong. She did not want to tell her mother she had thoughts of another man. Bernice's mother was Christian who believed in the commandments, all ten of them. She knew deep inside her mother would not approve of these feelings.

"Really Bernice, you live thirty minutes away, you don't like to drive, you have a phone in your house, but you wanted to check on your little old mamma. What's wrong Bernice the phone don't work?"

Bernice looked at her mother and just wanted to tell her everything she was experiencing, but she did not know where to start. She did not know what to say. She wanted to share the secrets of the forbidden encounters, she had the last few days. She wanted to tell her how gentle Will was, and that she had never felt this way about any man, even her current husband.

"Mamma how do you know when you're happy?"

Bernice's mother looked puzzled. Her mother thought that this was a peculiar question to ask. Her mother immediately sensed Bernice was troubled by something, which dealt with her personal choices. Bernice's mother knew her daughter lived in a glass house and tried to make calculating decision to maintain order, and control. This was one time she noticed that Bernice had no control.

"How do you know when you are happy?" Said Bernice's mother. "Baby, I suppose it is not you, it is something that you feel in your heart. It is because God has placed something in you that in spite of all the happenings around you, you just feel like everything is ok."

Bernice was obviously looking for another answer because she had a blank stare on her face. Bernice wanted her to say more but she knew the conversation was ambiguous and did not outline any specifics. Her mother wanted her to come clean about her situation.

"Look Bernice, are you not happy?"

Bernice could not answer her mother immediately. Her mother began to give her full eye contact. She knew she could not deceive her mother as she had Shanell. Her mother had a way of pulling out the truth.

"I think so…"

"Well if you think you are happy, what would make you feel that you were not?"

"I don't know mamma. It has been just so crazy this week. I have had to think about things that I never had time to even ponder."

Bernice's mother looked at her troubled daughter. Bernice decided to explain to her mother in some detail what had transpired. She did not want her mother to know about the time she was spending with Will. She minimized their encounters, to only one incident. She shared with her mother in confidence knowing it would only be between the two of them. Her mother was surprised. First of all, she did not agree with Bernice making a hasty decision by getting married. But she knew Bernice had made this choice and had to remain committed. As far as her current issue, she did not care who Will was or what feelings Bernice had. She knew that adultery was a serious offense. Her mother was well aware of what the flesh could do when the spirit was not intact. Bernice's mother felt the need to explain to her daughter what would happen if she did not honor God's word.

"That is Satan; you have to much idle time. You know an idle mind is the devil's workshop. Satan is walking through the door messing with your mind."

Bernice's mother did not want to preach to her daughter but she knew that any time Satan was involved in a person's decision making that he would try his best to make a person of faith stray.

"He will have you question things that you never questioned before. He will have you think about things that never crossed your mind. He will place things in your life that appear to be better than what you have. The grass will always appear greener on the other side of the fence. That is the trick of the enemy."

Bernice knew exactly what her mother was talking about. She was feeling scorned. She knew her mother was right but she couldn't understand how such a gentle man like Will could be a temptation from Satan. Her mother saw her daughter was not absorbing her words and continued to try to get her to snap back into reality.

"Girl you have to stay stern in the word. You are a preacher's wife. You should be in the word daily. When the devil is causing this much confusion, you should be rebuking him right out of your mind. You cannot lose your focus Bernice. You have been so blessed."

"But Momma, what about when we make mistakes."

"Baby we all make mistakes. That is why we ask God to forgive us. We are not perfect. We live in the flesh. Sometimes we cannot control our flesh, but this is why we must always be in prayer."

"Momma I am scared…"

"We all get scared and we began to fear the unknown. Trust me when I tell you, the only thing we should ever fear is God. See this life is not a permanent for us, this is only temporary. We have to focus on living right. Don't you want to go to heaven?"

"Yes, ma'am."

"Then you have to be obedient and do what the word says. You have to shed the things that don't belong in your life. Remember we die daily, but just like Paul, we must humble ourselves to the Lord."

Bernice began to shake her head. She covered her face with her hands to stop any tears from falling. She felt like she couldn't resist the yearning in her spirit. Her mother grabbed her hands. She saw the sorrow in her daughters eyes. She became concerned that her daughter would break at any given moment.

"Tell the Lord what you are going through. Tell him what is on your mind because he will listen to you. Bernice… just know, he is always listening to you."

Bernice felt the tears well in her eyes. She was at a loss. She realized what the consequences of her actions would cause. Being unfaithful to her husband was adultery, and she knew it would not be pleasing to God. She was ashamed and embarrassed.

"Baby what's wrong?"

"Nothing mamma, my heart is just heavy; some things have become blurry, and I don't feel that I have a hold on anything right now."

"Baby you have to pick and choose your battles," her mother reiterated. "If it is too much then you need to give it over to the God."

"Mamma I am weak…"

"Yes baby we all get weak but in our prayers we have to ask God for the strength to endure another day. Now, I suspect that I do not know everything that is going on with you, and perhaps you do not want me to know. That is okay. You cannot control everything Bernice. Some of that you have to release. Whether you tell me now or later it doesn't matter."

"Mamma I don't want you to judge me."

"Judge you? Girl is you crazy. If you even really knew my life, you would understand that if I judged anything right now God would strike me dead. I will tell you this; I have been where you are. Bernice you are a wonderful daughter, and I love all my children. However, you have made it your life to live in the walls of perfection that do not exist. You have to have things in order, you must always be in control. Nothing is perfect. Not everything is going to go your way."

Bernice's perfect little world was caving in, as her mother spoke. Her mother had hit it on the head. Bernice was losing control of her organized life. She wanted to please everyone. She wanted everything to appear a certain way. While she adamant about creating this perfect world, she had lost sight of herself. Bernice's mother wanted to ease her pain but knew she had a responsibility to be candid with her child.

"Do not let life pass you by trying to please others. Just please God. Here is the thing, whatever mistakes you have made, and are going to make, God already knows, and he still loves you. Some mistakes you can control, and some things you do out of pure impulse. Regardless, you have to stay focus. Let me tell you something Bernice, I love you in spite of anything you do. I will never judge you. I have made mistakes, I have tried to right my wrongs, and the Lord keeps on working with me. He will convict you when necessary. Know this Bernice, in ever thing you do, there will be reaping for any seed you sow on fertile or unfertile ground. Why...because you are human."

Bernice allowed one tear to run down her cheek. Her mother grabbed her hand and held it tightly. Bernice's mothers grip reassured her that God was in charge no matter what. But Bernice still had mixed feelings. She still yearned to be with Will, if only to be in his presence. She knew the consequence of adultery but she questioned if it was still adultery, if there was no fornication. Her spirit let her know that she was in a compromising position, and that her resistance could not be withheld if she continued to walk into the lion's den. Bernice heard the thunder crack.

"Lord, I need to make my way home."

"Baby you should probably wait until after the storm."

"Momma it might last all night, and if I go now I may beat it."

"Bernice, did you hear anything I said?"

"Yes mamma."

"Bernice I am happy you came to see me. You should come over more often when you are not tied down with work. I would love to see you."

Bernice hugged her mother. "Thank you," said Bernice. Her mother was wise. She tried to instill in each of her children good morals and values. Even if they didn't listen, she knew she had at least taught them well. She embraced the kiss her daughter had planted on her cheek and smiled.

Bernice hopped in the car and made her way back to the city. She saw the dark clouds getting full and could smell the rain coming. *Lord just yet let me get close to home so I don't have to be in this storm.* God must have ignored her because at that moment the drizzling started. "Thanks God," said Bernice sarcastically. *All I have to do is stay focused I only have about fifteen more miles.*

The rain began to pour down just as she entered into town. She realized that she had forgotten her umbrella. Her jacket would just shield her body, it didn't have a hood. Bernice knew she was going to get soak and wet when she got out of the car. She decided she would try to park, as close as, she could to the door. If she had driven on the grass the neighbors would have thought she was crazy. She knew she could pull the car up as far as she could, in the driveway, but she would still have to make a run for it.

Bernice began to think about what the rain would do to her hair and became frustrated. She did not feel like using a hot comb tonight. Bernice pulled up at her house and realized the door looked much further than usual. She got together in her mind a plan of execution. She decided she would take her shoes off and make a run for it.

It was dark outside and she realized all the lights were off in the houses on the streets. Bernice thought about the superstitious old people. *Don't say a word be silent while the lord is doing his work.* Bernice began to laugh. She didn't even leave the porch light on for herself. She thought she would only be at her mother's for a short while. She stayed a little longer than she anticipated.

Bernice opened the car door, grabbed the keys, put them in her purse, shoes in right hand, and purse under her arms. Bernice got out of the car and began to run to the front door. The rain was coming down hard. She heard a voice echo from behind.

"Hey pretty lady!"

The rain was falling heavy. She made a sudden turn and looked at the figure standing on the sidewalk. It was Will, standing in the rain, soaking wet. His body was perfectly outlined as the raindrops hit his frame. Even through the rain, she saw his eyes staring deeply into her soul. She just stood there with her shoes in her hand. She had forgotten all about the precipitation. Her heart began to beat rapidly and her knees began to quiver. He said nothing and she said nothing.

He smiled. She was elated to see him. She remembered everything her mother had said. However, Satan was about to win this battle. Bernice didn't think once to rebuke her insatiable appetite for this man. She dropped the objects in her hands and proceeded to walk back down her front steps in a hurried speed. She walked up to him and looked him in his eye.

"You are what… *at first sight means*," she muttered.

She dropped her head and buried it in his chest. He wrapped his arms around her. The warm spring rain continued to hit there soiled bodies. They both were unmoved.

That was Thursday.

****

"Last day of school, yippee! Girl I never thought I would get here," Shanell screamed. "I need to rest and take care of me. Maybe there will be a man at the swimming pool as I trot around in my bathing suit."

"Girl you are crazy."

"That is easy for you to say," Shanell said. "You have a big strapping man that will be in your bed sooner than you can blink. I live at home with my momma and daddy."

"Shanell what happened to your apartment?"

"Girl, please, that is old news. I had to go back home to save a little cash."

"Whatever you say Shanell," chuckled Bernice.

"What… don't get grown on me lady, you didn't move out of your mother's house until the day you got married." Shanell redirected her questions. "Girl what are you going to do for the summer?"

Bernice stopped because she knew it all dealt with what James needed her to do for the church. She did not even want to think about her over crowded schedule. She wanted to remember Will holding her in his arms under the warm rain.

"Well you know, the usual," answered Bernice unmoved.

"Girl you need to go on an adventure. You don't have any kids. I am sure that the stuff for church can wait. Pastor's take breaks also."

"Shanell I will, but maybe in a couple of years."

"In a couple of years you will have hyper children running around the house."

"Just tell James you need a change for the summer."

"Girl it is not that easy."

"Of course it is. Since you have gotten married when is the last time you two just relaxed with one another."

Bernice felt her spirit getting warm. She didn't like Shanell's pushy attitude at this point even if she was right. She wanted to tell her to mind her business. She was already confused; and after her conversation with her mother yesterday, she did not want a double dose from Shanell.

"Look Shanell, I appreciate your concern but my husband and I have a plan, we will have more than enough time to do all the fun things that you are talking about. But we have an agenda that we are going to stick to."

Shanell felt the sternness in Bernice's voice. She knew it was time to back off. She had never heard Bernice be so vigorous in her disposition. Shanell sensed the uneasiness, but she knew when to keep her mouth closed. She could not help but feel that Bernice's attitude stemmed from other underlying issues.

"Okay, okay I wasn't trying to get up all in your business."

Bernice did not mum a word. She had made her point. If Shanell was not going to take heed she didn't really care. Shanell wanted to lighten up the conversation because she could see Bernice getting agitated with her.

"Well then lady, what are you doing tonight? Some of the girls are going to go out this evening."

"You and some of the girls that sounds fun but I think I will read tonight."

"Read? Girl school is out, we can drop by..."

"No!" Bernice barked unexpectedly.

"Okay, okay, I am sorry, I was just saying..."

Bernice caught herself because she didn't need Shanell asking too many questions. She knew her outburst would draw attention and more unnecessary questions. Bernice tried to clean up her response.

"I am just saying.... I have just a few more days to myself before it gets busy, busy, busy... I just want to take a warm bath, drink some tea, and read a good book. I am not in the mood for any company."

What Bernice really wanted to say is; I really don't want to have any company other than Will. She knew, she could not say that. Therefore, she just smiled and turned her head so Shanell could not read too far into her body language. Bernice tried to play it off.

"Girl, maybe another time," said Bernice.

Bernice went home and did not know what to expect for the evening. She didn't make any plans with Will. She didn't know how to contact him. He knew where she lived but she never asked him where he resided. The weather did not permit her to walk to the park. She didn't want to drive around looking for him because she felt the action to show signs of desperation. The phone rang....*Ring, Ring!!*

"Hello?"

"Well hello Mrs. Walters."

She recognized the voice on the other end but could not perk up. The voice caused her to become numb. She knew she needed to put on a happy face and pretend she was excited.

"Hi Mr. Walters," she retorted.

"Honey, how are you?" Said Bernice with a fake tone of concern.

"I am fine. I know I haven't been able to call that much this week but we have been truly busy, and it has been a lot of late nights. I knew you had to work. I anticipated calling you tonight since this was the last day of school. So... how is everything baby?"

"I am good."

James sounded so excited to speak with his wife. He had no idea she did not feel the same. He wanted to tell her all about the work he was doing. James was a good man. All he wanted to do was make Bernice happy. He knew it was a strain on her when he traveled as often as he did. He wanted to assure her he was doing it for the betterment of their life.

"Honey I have so much to share with you when I get home."

"Well honey, when are you coming?"

Bernice was hoping he had changed his plans from Sunday to a later date. She wanted to see if she could steal more time with Will. She was not concerned with any of his accomplishments at this point.

"I know we originally planned for Sunday night but there may be a delay."

"What sort of delay?" Bernice perked up.

"Well you know we will have service on Sunday but we have a meeting Monday morning, and we will be on our way thereafter."

"But honey I was expecting you home on Sunday I miss you." Bernice lied again.

"Sweet heart I know you do. I promise I will not be traveling that much thereafter, I am really getting things in order and the brother hood is so special out here. Lord knows this may be where we want to plant our seeds someday."

"James are you talking about moving?"

"No sweetheart I am not talking about moving now. It is just in the vision for when we expand. There so many people out here that need the word of God. There are so many people that have strayed away."

James did not realize his wife was also straying. Bernice thought about what she was saying, and realized she didn't care when James came home as long as it was after Sunday. She was secretly hoping he could delay even longer.

"I know sweetheart how important your work is. You will be home soon enough. I understand, that you need to do this. Take all the time you need."

"That is why I love you. Honey, you shouldn't be by yourself this weekend maybe you should call your mother, and spend some time with her, and your sister."

"I don't know honey, I may. I am not sure what I am going to do with myself. I do know that I am going to clean this house."

"Clean the house? The house is always spotless."

"How do you think it stays that way? I can change the sheets and mop the floors. You know I have a little laundry to do and I could always go in the garden."

"I know you will find something to occupy yourself. Well dear I have to go."

"No problem James."

"Bernice?"

"Yes James?"

"I love you."

"I love you to James."

Bernice hung up the phone remembering why she fell in love with James. He was a good man. He supplied her every need. He was a loving husband who was ambitious and always wanted more. So why, was she so tempted by this other man? What was it that Bernice longed for? Was she willing to take foolish chances? Bernice was overwhelmed with confusion. She wanted to pray but she didn't even know what to ask God for in her prayers. *Lord what is going on? There is no reason for me to feel like this.* She didn't think about other men because James was the only man Bernice knew. He was the only man she had ever dated. He was her husband.

Bernice began her chores. James was right Bernice's house was always spotless. With her being the only person there, there was definitely no dirt or dust to be found. Bernice removed her clothes from the washer and prepared to hang them up on the line. Bernice walked through her back door, through her little garden, and stopped at her homemade clothe line. Bernice thought about her commitment to her husband. *I love my husband. I love my husband.* Bernice continued to talk to herself. She tried to convince herself that James was the only man in her thoughts. She was now deceiving herself.

Bernice placed the sheets neatly on the line. She realized she was hanging the clothes with a possibility it might rain again. *Oh, it is just a few sheets. They will be fine.* As she walked in the house, she noticed that her back gate was opened. *Now who the devil left this open? Dog-on stray cats. They always are running around her sniffing for a meal or mice.* Bernice looked around and noticed her shrubbery was disheveled. *Lord have mercy is this from the rain. My pots are a mess. I need to get in this yard.* Bernice knew in a few hours the weatherman had called for rain so she hoped the sheets would dry quickly. Bernice was trying to decide if there was any point to leave them hanging. She knew she had nothing else planned so she might as well.

Bernice noticed her neighbors to the right were all packing up for the weekend. Mrs. Cunningham came out her house with her two bratty kids totting bags to the car. She did not hold many conversations but she decided to make small talk.

"Hey Eileen, are yawl leaving for the weekend?"

"Yes child, we are going down to Richard's momma's house for the weekend, they having a grand ole cook out. You know there will be plenty of food, and honey I love to eat," said Mrs. Cunningham laughing. Bernice was not amused. She could have cared less what her neighbor was doing but she made sure she engaged her with a smile on her face.

Mr. Brown on the other side was making sure the house was secure. Mr. Peter's was checking behind his house. The Smiths were loading their luggage in their station wagon. Everyone was doing something, except Bernice.

Loneliness began to fill Bernice. She thought about going to her mother's house tomorrow. She wondered why her neighbors were traveling in the afternoon. She remembered their children just got out of school. Perhaps they were trying to get an early start. It didn't make much sense to her; they could have packed up and left early in the morning. It did not really matter; it wasn't as if Bernice shared memorable moments with her neighbors other than minute conversations. Most of them held conversations with James.

Bernice smelled the rain so she prepared to go into her house. She grabbed the damp sheets and decided to hang them up in the house. The neighborhood seemed empty and she appeared to be the only one on the block. She decided she would take a hot bath. Before she proceeded to the bathroom, she looked around the empty house. It was to quiet and Bernice needed to break the silence. Bernice did something she had not done in a while; she put on an old Nina Simone record.

Nina began to sing and Bernice began to hum. She forgot how much she loved this music. She began to drag her feet and sway back and forth to the melody. She began to feel different and start to reminisce. She remembered her vibrancy, her soul full of undisclosed visions. She remembered what she loved, dancing, singing, her family, her existence, and the essence of being a woman. She loved the touch of her skin and the scent of her hair. She loved herself for who she aspired to be. She loved to dream. She loved the outdoors, and she loved the cool breeze against her face. She just loved, but somewhere in the midst of this loving, she realized as she danced wistfully around the floor that she lost sight of her love. She had given up a life of love for security.

There was no thrill, but things were in order. There was an array of perfections with no imperfect spontaneity. Being a teacher was a sure thing. Then her husband fit the mold because she did not want to take the chance on the average Joe who may have appeared to have a few challenges. There was comfort and security all around her, glassed in a fortress of the unbreakable; Bernice wanted to break, snap even. She didn't want or desire to be perfect anymore. She did not want to look down on how others acted or led their lives because they appeared happier in their dysfunction than she in her organized chaos.

She wanted something different. As she thought of all the things that could be different, she heard a knock at her window, which startled her. She went to the window and saw the face of her forbidden imperfections. She pointed him in the direction of the back door without a thought. She opened the back door and just stared at him through the screen. This could not be. Why did he show up that very moment? *Has my life led me to challenge everything that I sat in motion and called my perfect life?*

"Hi," she said.

"Hello," he responded.

"What are you doing here?" she said surprised at Will for popping up unannounced.

He took a step back when she responded. "Is there something wrong?"

Bernice was torn. She had made up in her mind she was going to focus on doing what was best for her family. She also knew that Will was exciting, refreshing, but forbidden. She wanted to scream. Why did he show up now? She could have balanced out her feelings but he had surfaced unannounced, and she felt vulnerable.

"Yes there is something wrong. I am a happily married woman that has everything. I have my ideal job, a beautiful home, and a wonderful husband. I don't want for anything; he and I have a promising future. But..."

Bernice could not get the rest of her sentence out. She felt overwhelmed. She wanted to resist. She wanted to rationalize. She wanted to send Will away. However, her heart and flesh would not allow her. She began to subside.

"But what?" said Will.

"But then, there you are, you came out of nowhere. You showed up and made me question everything I believe. You came, and you discombobulated my world. You don't even know me; you don't even know who I am. Just a few years ago, I would not have even let a man of your caliber hold a conversation with me, but you talked to me and you did not demand a thing. You are so sweet and gentle. You move things in me that I never thought could be moved. I am going crazy because I took a vow, for better or for worse. I am not even in my worse stages, but some part of me is yearning just to have you hold me. I am yearning to feel you for whatever time I have, at whatever cost, and this is foolish. No one gives up what I have. No one thinks for a second about whether or not to take these types of chances."

Will opened the screen door and began to walk towards Bernice without saying a word. He was covered with a scent of desire. Every word Bernice said was true but Will didn't care how he had turned her world upside down. He wanted her as much as she wanted him. He was willing to take any chance at all cost, just to be with her. He didn't care about who she used to be, or what she wouldn't normally do. She had him at the very moment her tear hit his handkerchief, and she stared in his eyes.

"I am not going to let you do this to me!" Bernice put her hands up to block Will from coming any closer.

"Bernice…" Will whispered.

Nina Simone echoed from the living room, "*Don't let me be misunderstood.*" Will walked closer to her and moved her hand so ever gently. She was seduced and could not resist him. Her flesh had fully taken over. He grabbed her wrist and pulled them to his waist. He pulled her body closer to his. He placed her arms on the small of his back as he caressed the crevices. She looked into his eyes and the tears began to well. He lifted his hand and wiped the tears from her cheek.

Then he placed the tips of his fingers on her lips and slightly opened her mouth. He took his hand, pulled her face close to his, and tasted the sweetness of her saliva. As their lips locked, there was a silence. The rain began to fall as their tongues became entangled. He began to kiss her neck and hold her as tight as he could. The sounds of Nina became more powerful. Will hoisted Bernice's body from the porch and guided her into the living room. Bernice interrupted the kiss and laid her head upon his chest as they swayed back and forth to slow jazz tunes. They swayed until the clock struck 11:30 pm. Then they stopped and gazed at each other with a longing in their eyes.

That was a Friday

****

Bernice and Will had dozed off on the living room couch. She woke up suddenly and realized that is was almost three in the morning. She did not really remember how they fell asleep she just remembered the sway caused a somberness around the room. She looked at Will who appeared so peaceful. She did not want to wake him. She decided that she needed to take a shower. She was exhausted. She knew she felt peculiar with another man being in her husband's house but she could not curve her lips to express concerns.

Bernice went upstairs to the bathroom and turned on the shower. She closed the door and removed her garments. She stepped into the shower and grabbed her washcloth and soap. The tepid water hit Bernice's body and she felt relief. She knew she could not lie beside Will without answering the desire that tingled in her unmentionables. She knew the shower was necessary because maybe she could wash the yearning away.

She looked at the water hit her nakedness. She didn't use the soap or washcloth, she just allowed the water to soothe her femininity in the hopes of a release. Her flesh ached for the sensation of the unfamiliar man. She then turned to the wall and leaned her head against the cold tile to balance out the temperature in her soul and inner thighs.

The curtain drew back. Bernice was not startled. She welcomed the body into the shower without laying eyes on his essence. She refused to turn around. Warm hands stroked her shoulders followed by supple lips kissing the nape of her neck. Then she felt a warm wet manliness on the small of her back. The hands ventured over her body and she realized she was about to indulge in sin. Sin completed with ecstasy that marveled the mind. She felt his warm hand reach into her inner thigh where her thirst had been hidden. She knew her lady friend was going to consume his manliness.

He turned her body around and cupped the bottom of her buttocks with both hands as her glided her up the shower wall. The water continued to hit the exposed bodies as their indulgent hues fused a perfect blend of caramel and coco. James had never; James would never take control over her body as this man was doing at this very moment. She moaned seductively as he lifted her face and demanded their eyes locked. He grabbed her bottom lip with his two lips, sucking them in the moment of passion. She clinched his back holding on tightly. Pants of breath began to steam, for she was about to reach a peak women whispered about.

Will had not released the pressure that was built up in loins. He picked up Bernice and secured her body against his. Will moved with Bernice safely in his arms and stepped out of her tub. She had no idea where he was taking her but at this very moment she didn't care. Will made it to the spare bedroom, which was picture perfect. He laid her on her back and sat strongly on his arms.

"Tell me what you want baby. I will do anything to you that you desire."

Her only response was, "Whatever you want ...." Bernice wanted will to consume her mind, body and spirit. He kissed Bernice passionately all over her body. He buried his face between her thighs sampling her nectar, which had never been tasted by any man. Bernice felt exhilarated. Her legs trembled and body jerked uncontrollably. Will pleased her without a question or thought. He knew she, and her body felt ecstasy. His plan was to make love until their bodies, and souls could no longer withstand their voracious appetite. Their bodies stayed entangled from the time the sun rose until the sunset that evening. There was no food no water just momentary breaths of rapture.

That was a Saturday.

****

Bernice arose blissfully but her body rendered physical exhaustion. Will was nowhere to be found but a melodious spell was lurking from some part of the house. Bernice went into the bathroom to take care of some necessary touch ups. She felt the need to shower because she had Will's scent covering her body but it loomed of a musty bliss.

She walked into her kitchen and there stood the man who had just stolen her innocence and perfection. He was preparing her breakfast. Bernice did not question how he found his way around her kitchen she just adored his sexy smile.

"Good morning beautiful," said Will, while smiling at Bernice. "I was actually going to bring this up to but it appears you beat me to it".

Bernice was still in shock and awe of the events, which had transpired in the last twenty-four hours. It played repeatedly in Bernice's head. No one had ever made her feel this way.

"This is your first time leaving the bed so maybe we should just eat in the kitchen."

Bernice was still in silence because her knees were still a bit wobbly. The flashbacks of passion over powered her ability to speak. She could still feel Will's hands all over her body.

"Baby, are you all right?" said Will.

"Yes I just. I just... I don't know."

"Well I have a surprise," said Will.

Bernice knew there was no way they were going to repeat the events of yesterday because her body would not permit, even though secretly she longed for it. A surprise from Will was all she needed. She knew whatever he had planned would be the cherry on top of their sensual encounter.

"Surprise...?"

"Yes we are leaving the house today."

Bernice showed no hesitation, she didn't ask any questions. She was willing to do and go wherever Will had commanded her too. Bernice smiled at the beautiful creature in anticipation of the surprise.

"I am ready whenever you are."

Bernice and Will got dressed and were ready to leave the house. Will had parked in an undisclosed location and he had Bernice meet him around the corner. He left first going out the back door. Bernice left out of the front and met him at the corner.

Bernice did not ask Will where he was taking her she just enjoyed the ride without a covering or sunshades. The wind blew gently against Bernice's face. She stared at nature and smelled sinful perfections in the air. Will drove them to their secret place.

"You know I love it here."

"Yes I do. This is where I brought you after our first few encounters."

"I know."

"I brought you here so you could remember. I want to ask you something Bernice."

"Yes..."

"What do we do next?"

"What do you mean?" asked Bernice.

"I want to take you away from here, away from all of this. I know that you have responsibilities, and commitments, but I don't care. I want you for myself. Yes, I am being selfish but I have fallen in love with you, and I hope that you would want the same."

Bernice was shocked because she instantly wanted to utter yes. Bernice knew in her heart this could never be. She didn't know if she could agree to be so irresponsible. Even after the events, which had taken place, she was still married. Bernice knew Will expected an answer.

"I…, I Love you to. The problem is I think I have fallen in love with you. The funny thing is I think I fell in love with you the day you handed me your handkerchief. If this were a different day, a different time, with different circumstances, I would follow you to the ends of the earth, because I know it is you that completes my soul. You are what I have longed for, for such a long time. Without giving my life a chance, I ran to the first sign of comfort. I ran to the first sign of security. I will not lie; I really, really care for my husband. In fact, I love my husband and he has been amazing. When I vowed to be with him, it was a promise. I never thought I would be standing here looking at you, wanting you, or needing you. I always thought that forever would be a place for my husband and me. Then you came on a cloud and scooped my heart into your hand. Now I don't know what to say or do."

Will wanted Bernice just to let everything go and take a chance but when he looked in her eyes, he knew that his selfishness was not going to make her break any promises. He knew she would never break a promise. That is why Bernice never promised him a thing. She was a woman of her word. She was a true woman of her actions. He knew that this was a destined moment, which was clearly forbidden, but his heart and flesh were toiling with separate rolls. He grabbed her hand and pulled her close because good-bye was going to be the next verbiage they exchanged. Will decided that the good bye was inevitable but it did not have to take place at that very moment.

"When does your husband return pretty lady?"

"Tomorrow," Bernice dropped her head.

"I may not be able to have you as my eternity but you will be my decadence for the time we have right now. You will always hold a place in my heart. You will always be my *pretty lady*."

Bernice looked in Will's eyes she knew that he was an admirable man even with the sins they had just committed. She knew they were caught up in the moment. They would not change it no matter how wrong it was. He held a special place in her heart. She also knew she only had a little more time and she would relish in the time that was left.

"You sir are my moment of divinity. You have captured my heart and soul. I will never forget you. I will never forget us."

Bernice and Will made love in that very spot all afternoon.

Shortly thereafter, Will took Bernice to the park where they had first met and he released her back to her life. They kissed for the last time. Bernice stepped out of the car and walked to the park bench. Bernice sat on the bench and watched as Will drove off. She remembered when her tears had started before their first encounter. She sat on that park bench and cried for the rest of the afternoon. Bernice realized there was no handkerchief to catch her tears.

That was a Sunday

****

"Mrs. Walters?" The doctor said again.

"Are you feeling ok? Do you want me to call your husband?"

"Uh no, doctor I am ok."

"You seemed to have dozed off into dream land."

"I am sorry doctor I have been feeling up and down for the last week and this flu is really getting the best of me."

"I understand Mrs. Walters."

"Well Doctor, are you able to prescribe anything to help me."

"Well you see Mrs. Walters that is what I wanted to talk to you about. I looked at your blood work and you are anemic. I am going to need to get some iron in you in order to withstand the next months to come."

"Oh my God…!" Bernice thought the worse. "Doctor I don't have cancer do I. I knew it I knew it. I knew this was not the flu. I don't smoke or drink how could this have happened? I eat right, I exercise sometimes, but Doctor, I can't have this."

"Mrs. Walters you don't have cancer."

Bernice let out a sigh of relief.

"Mrs. Walters you don't have the flu either."

"Well doctor if I am not terminally ill and I don't have the flu than what is wrong with me?"

"Mrs. Walters, you are pregnant."

"Pregnant? That is not possible. My husband and I are very careful."

"So you all use a contraceptive?"

"No sir, we count."

The doctor began to laugh. "Oh you guys use the rhythm method."

Bernice did not find it funny at all. She recalled the first time she had shared with Shanell her unorthodox method of birth control. She had also found it to be comical.

"Why are you laughing?"

"Because ma'am that does not guarantee you will be opted out of getting pregnant."

"I can't be pregnant we have so much to do. James and I had a plan. We were going to wait until the church was fully functional and I was going to stop working when it was time to conceive. This is entirely too soon."

"Mrs. Walters were you and your husband considering alternatives?"

"Alternatives…?" Bernice looked at the doctor puzzled. "Oh no never we would never do that. Doctor please, understand, he has been working so hard. He has been on the road off and getting pregnant was not in the plans. It is almost time for school to resume. My husband and I have only spent about three weeks together for the entire summer. The times that we have been together he has been very tired and almost not wanting to perform. It has been so few and far between I didn't think it was possible for me to get pregnant under those circumstances."

"Well Mrs. Walters I hate to tell you for most people it only takes one time."

"Doctor this baby will be in the spring. That is when school will be wrapping up. How am I supposed to get my work completed with a newborn coming?"

"Mrs. Walters you will have plenty of time because according to my calculation this baby will be born early March. Depending on how well your pregnancy goes you will have more than enough time to focus on your career.

"March?" Bernice questioned.

"How is the baby going to be born in March?"

"You are going on twelve weeks of pregnancy. I am shocked you didn't realize earlier because you are almost out of your first trimester."

Bernice's heart stopped. She started counting and at that moment, realizing James had only been home for three weeks. "Are you sure doctor? Are you sure about the weeks?"

"According to the data you provided you have not had a menstruation cycle since the beginning of June. Therefore, your conception day was probably around June 17-19. Bernice never considered that she had missed her cycle. It happened often when she became stressed. The summer had taken a toll on her with all of the work she had been helping James with as he traveled to and fro.

Bernice realized the week that the doctor had mentioned was the week; James had been out of town. "So that means …Oh my God," Bernice, gasped. "This can't be…," she thought. What am I going to do?"

"Mrs. Walters are you going to be okay?"

"Yes sir I am going to be fine."

"Well I want to give you some vitamins and a prescription for iron." Bernice's mind was racing and she had no idea how this was going to play out. The doctor's calculation did make sense. She knew if it was accurate then the baby could not possibly be her husbands.

Bernice got in the car and placed her head on the steering wheel. This was the time she really needed God to direct her. She knew if she told her husband that she was pregnant that he would be elated in spite of their plans. However, she also knew her husband was not an ignorant man so she had to calculate her dates correctly for it to be a plausible story. She remembered they had a small encounter but her husband was not able to perform adequately. This was two weeks after he had returned home. Bernice felt the weeks were close enough to convince her husband. Then what, Bernice thought. *The baby comes and what. If Will, is the father he can never know, Bernice's heart grew even heavier. If I tell Will, he may tell James, then James will know about my affair, and he will leave me. But I cannot tell Will because I don't know where he is. Oh, God I know I am not worthy. I know I have sinned but I don't know what to do.*

Then a spirit lay heavy on her heart and echoed, *"The Truth will set you free." Free*, she thought to herself. It will be so much easier if I just told the truth. Bernice knew at that very moment what she needed to do. As painful as it was, she knew she had to make the right decisions.

Bernice pulled in her driveway and realized her husband was not home yet. Bernice decided she would take a walk to the park because she needed to clear her head before she had to confess her sins. When Bernice arrived at the park, she just looked at the scenery. She sat on the park and wanted to remember the foolish mistakes she had made but she something in her would not allow her to see the poor decisions. Will was her divinity and she his decadence, and even if this had happened, she accepted everything happens for a reason. How she wished Will would just show up at this very moment so she could just look at his face one more time. All she could see was a vision of his car riding off on a summer afternoon.

Bernice sighed and stood up and began to walk back to her home. Bernice knew her mistakes were foolish but they were memorable. She now needed to focus on what was best for her and her family.

Bernice prepared dinner and made sure the house was spotless. Bernice scurried around the house just to make sure things were just right. She wanted everything to appear perfect. She knew had to forget about her forbidden love.

She heard the car pull up. Then she heard the turn of the front door knob. James walked in the house. James was happy as usual. He greeted his wife with a huge hug and kiss. She embraced her husband letting him know she was overjoyed to see him. Bernice knew her actions were a part of a façade but she was not going to show any other emotion.

"Hey baby, how are you?"

"I am fine honey and kissed her husband on the lips." She took James's coat and directed him to the kitchen.

"Something spells good…!"

Bernice smiled because she knew how happy her husband was when she cooked. She was a nurturing wife in spite of her discrepancies. She knew what it meant to be a good wife.

"I made all of your favorites," said Bernice.

James looked at his wife, he really appreciated her. He loved how she took care of him. He kissed her on the cheek to show his gratitude. He thought there was no special occasion because she always spoiled him with home cooked meals. James was unaware that Bernice had an agenda that came with his meal this time.

"You did all of this for me baby? I don't deserve you. What's the occasion?"

Bernice's heart fluttered for a moment but she knew she had to talk to her husband about her visit to the doctors. *The truth will set you free she thought*. She looked at James and she looked at her stomach that held the unborn child. She knew James would love the baby. She knew James would be an excellent father. She just needed to know if James could be an excellent father to someone else's child. Bernice did not know if she was willing to take the chance of losing the trust of her husband. Bernice felt the truth would cause too much trauma to their happy home. She no longer felt disclosing the information was as important the more she thought about it. She knew she could, but she did not know if she should.

"Oh sweet heart we need to talk. I have something to tell you." Bernice had made her mind up. Her decision was final and she was not able to turn back once she uttered the words she was about to say. Bernice smiled and began to tell her husband...

On Mar 2, 1968 Tracey Jamie Walters was born. James and Bernice were the proud mother and father of a bouncing baby girl.

Generational Dysfunctions
Volume II
Solitary Confinement
Introduction

Part I
Focused

Zariah
"Forgiveness?"

Focused

I understand faith
But embraced anger
Swallowed sin
Dined with loyalty

I understand consequence
But love unconditionally
Breathe hate
Misunderstood my self-esteem

I understand a vision
But hold the word
Shake temptation
Despise untruths

I understand my process
But made bad decisions
Hope for favor
Deny possibilities

But until I understand progress
That there is a purpose
My perspective is entangled with the world
My perception will no longer be tainted

Because submission
Will need to be my next surrender
To Serenity

Zariah

She laid her head on the deflated pillow. Her back hurt from the concrete she laid on day in and day out. It was lined by a mattress but it was made from the same material as her pillow. She wanted to look out of a window and view God but the only sunlight entering in through the cement cove was that of the window pane far up in the ceiling. She grabbed her bible and flipped to her favorite Psalms:

The LORD is my light and my salvation; whom shall I fear? The LORD is the strength of my life; of whom shall I be afraid? When the wicked, [even] mine enemies and my foes, came upon me to eat up my flesh, they stumbled and fell. Though an host should encamp against me, my heart shall not fear: though war should rise against me, in this I be will confident. One [thing] have I desired of the LORD, that will I seek after; that I may dwell in the house of the LORD all the days of my life, to behold the beauty of the LORD, and to inquire in his temple

She read the bible day in and day out because she knew that in this part of her life she would have to hold on to. This was the only thing, which brought patience and peace. Zariah was aware she was being tested and this was the test she could not fail. She was not angry, not going to let rage consume her because of her circumstances. Sure, she slept and ate in a place distant from her husband and children but she knew while on this journey, she would find her purpose. She knew why she was detained, she knew why she felt isolated, but at the end of the day, she knew God did not make mistakes. He would never leave her or forsake her.

Zariah rolled over and looked at the woman who shared a bunk with her. She thought about the stories and horrors she shared when it was time to congregate. She then looked around the dorm and saw the faces of the abused and accused. Each woman had her own plight, of anger and aggressions. Even if the world saw them for what the system deemed them to be, she was not convinced they fully understood the femininity in each of their essences. They reminded her of little pieces of a board game with matching outfits. She knew that each woman was serving a purpose in a divine plan, some knowing, and unknowing. She saw the beauty in the desolate, for her eyes were attuned to what they represented. No one appeared to be different in silence but at daybreak she would witness the host of attitudes, unhappiness, and a mixture of spirits, she would have to rebuke daily.

It was time to close her eyes so she could count another day of her journey but her mind continued to race and sleeping was yet an empty promise that her body resisted. She felt the need to repent but she knew God had already forgiven her. However, she could not understand a void. She believed she had relinquished all of the heaviness to the father, son, and the Holy Ghost. However, had she relinquished herself from all other threats of complacency? She needed to fully forgive herself so she could move forward and allow God to do his perfect work. She closed her eyes and began to pray.

Oh heavenly father,
My heart is heavy but I know you are still working in my favor. I do not know what the plan is. I do now know which direction you are taking me. Nevertheless, I trust you. I trust your word and I know whatever your will is, it will be done.

As Zariah waited for the night to pass she began to ponder on her circumstances. She understood everything was for a reason and there was a lesson to be learned. What was God doing, and how was she going to find her divine purpose while being constricted.

About the author

Anica Lavonne Walston is a native of Petersburg, Virginia. She attended Virginia Episcopal School located in Lynchburg, Virginia from 1989-1992. She returned to Petersburg in 1992 where she completed her senior year at Petersburg High School (1993). She attended Richard Bland College (2004), and Virginia State University (2006), where received her Associates and Bachelor's degrees in Psychology. She is currently seeking her Master's Degree in Counseling Studies, at Capella University.

Anica has been writing for over 15 years. She started writing as a hobby. Immediately some of her family, friends, and teachers recognized her for her creative way to express her thoughts on paper. During her years at Richard Bland's she was published in the school's magazine, Mnemosyne. She continued to write and was later asked to write a few freelance articles for a local magazine, *The Southsider*. Anica has always enjoyed writing poems, short stories, and the art of Spoken word. She recently decided to expand her craft by writing her first novel.

In 2011 she completed her first two poetry books entitled, *To the Little Girl who Loved to Dance & Yes, I am Woman*. Through her life's lessons she decided to create he own brand, "Respect the Gender." Respect the Gender embodies her belief that focuses on women understanding their essence and respecting their roles in the natural order. She hopes to expand her business endeavors by expanding her services. She plans to utilize this *Respect the Gender*, first in her community, by teaching women to become self- motivated, and self – aware of their inner being.

Anica lives according to her faith in God. She believes everyone has a divine purpose, which can only be obtained by being obedient and attending to the God's word. She also believes an individual must remain positive and embrace life, regardless of any circumstance. Through her personal struggles, she has found that the only way for her to succeed, is to trust and believe in the work that God is doing through her.

Anica is the proud mother of two sons, Deltan & Dylan. She currently lives in Petersburg where she is very close to her immediate family. Anica's plans include writing more novels, poetry, and perfecting her craft in Spoken word. She is determined to focus on her purpose and vision, by sharing her talents with everyone.

All of Anica's poetry books and novels are available on Amazom.com as well as her Respect the Gender Website.

http://www.wix.com/anicawalston/rtg

Acknowledgements

I would like to first to give honor to God who is first and foremost in my life. I could not have created a thought without him blessing me with this talent. I give him all the honor and praise. I am grateful for his mercy and grace.

I would also like to thank some people who have always believed in my writings and have supported me throughout the years through this process.

My father and mother, Alvah & Dorothy Walston, sisters, Michelle, Alva, and Brittany, Skylar (niece), Dylan & Deltan.

Friends and Family: Aunts: Doris (deceased), Yvonne, Alva, Arleatha. A host of cousins, and special recognition to Lori Hackett (thank you for helping me with this process, I love you cousin). John & Mary McNeil (I was blessed to have three sets of grandparents. Thank you Mrs. McNeil for the spanking me and teaching me the word of God), Larry & Pat Robinson and family (Thank you Mrs. Pat for always seeing me as professor or doctor), Uncle Muffin (just because I love you), Samuel & Lula Watkins (for loving me and my children and always supporting me), The Muhammad family (Lashawn & Umi for years you all have shown me nothing but love and have always believed and supported me, and I am forever grateful)(Thank you Jameal, for your support during this process), Mark & Elizabeth Jackson and family (Elizabeth you have been wonderful, I thank you for all and everything you have done for me through this last year), Delores Hick's (Delores the phone calls in the morning to get me through, God bless you), Nakisha Hicks (Thank you for suggesting the poem that started this whole process), Sonia Gardner (Sonia love you), Christina & Christopher (for loving me regardless), Shantai and Jamethro Rogers (for giving me the opportunity to write for the magazine), Ms. Lucas (I couldn't have done it without our tears in the morning), Ms. Powell (for your warmth kindness, and encouragement), Facebook Fans (for always reading my post and sharing positive feedback) Tresa (Thank you for taking the time out to critique, much love).

Reginald Conyard you are a true genius. A wonderful friend. I cannot ever repay you for all of the work you have done. You have blessed me so much. You have always been there in my time of need. You never complain, you never ask or require much, you just extend. You are so selfless and I really appreciate you and your support. Your kindness is always appreciated. I will never forget all you have done for me through this entire process. Love you dearly. Stay awesome!

To all that were not mentioned; you know who you are and you know the impact you had on my life. God bless you all!

To my church home, Calvary Temple Church, for providing me with a home to worship and praise.

To my best friends, who never judged me, and always loved me for who I am: Vanessa, Johanna, Jennifer, Phenoris, Yoshiko. Thank you all for your patience throughout the years, your love has always meant so much, and I am happy that I can share this experience with each of you.

Made in the USA
Charleston, SC
18 July 2011